# DOMINANT

'You know the rules, Lana. When we're alone, flirtation is allowed. Touching isn't.'

Her eyes dropped. 'I'm sorry, Cole. I guess I got carried away. The thought of – of – you know, us being free to . . .'

'The first rule of freedom is discipline. You broke my rules, Lana. If you were mine, you'd be punished for that.'

She got off the desk and stood with her head bowed and her hands behind her back. 'I'd accept your punishment, Cole, no matter what.'

He'd never let their games go this far before. When a submissive woman offers herself to a dominant man for discipline, it's the ultimate temptation. If he'd had an ounce of sense, Cole would have backed away, instantly. Perversely, he felt compelled to take the scene just as far as he could without actually violating the rules he'd imposed. It was like being on the brink of an orgasm and holding off for as long as he could, except that in this case, there'd be no climax – no touching.

# DOMINANT

*Felix Baron*

This book is a work of fiction.
In real life, make sure you practise safe, sane and
consensual sex.

First published in 2006 by
Nexus
Thames Wharf Studios
Rainville Road
London W6 9HA

*www.nexus-books.co.uk*

Typeset by TW Typesetting, Plymouth, Devon

ISBN 0 352 34044 4
ISBN 9 780352 340443

Penguin Random House is committed to a sustainable future for
our business, our readers and our planet. This book is made from
Forest Stewardship Council® certified paper.

Printed and bound in Great Britain by Clays Ltd, Elcograf S.p.A.

You'll notice that we have introduced a set of symbols onto our book jackets, so that you can tell at a glance what fetishes each of our brand new novels contains. Here's the key – enjoy!

cp (traditional)

cp (modern)

spanking

restraint/bondage

rope bondage/hojojutsu

latex/rubber/leather/enclosure

fem dom

willing captivity

medical

period setting

uniforms

sex rituals

# One

The beat thumped up through the soles of Cole's shoes. His thighs twitched to its rhythm. He'd been among the first dancers on the floor for every set the Ilford Palais' Big Q Band had played that night, except this one. He was itching to get moving but it was ten past eleven. This set was the important one.

Big Q always played three fast numbers, followed by two slow dances. This'd be the last fast set of the night. If you asked a girl to dance for a fast set it was because you liked her or because she was a good dancer. If you only asked her for slow ones it was because you were after her body. Cole's tactic was to ask her for the fast set and then stay with her for the slow.

He wasn't on the floor yet because he hadn't made up his mind which girl he planned to see home. He'd danced with three. Linda was pretty and sweet and seemed like a 'nice' girl. Darlene was short and plump with a bit of a squint. He'd heard that Darlene gave handjobs to almost anyone and went down on guys she really liked but she didn't fuck. Girls with that sort of reputation struck Cole as sad. They traded sex for a dubious sort of popularity.

His ideal was a girl who was hot to trot for the fun of it. He didn't want to seduce 'good' girls but neither did he want girls who'd put out for the wrong reasons.

1

Maybe Vanessa was what he was looking for. She had big wild eyes and a hard little body. She wasn't a great dancer but when she was on the floor her hips jerked like she was fucking the air.

At 18, Cole had only fucked two girls and one woman – the woman was 35 and married so it hadn't lasted long.

Fucking was his obsession.

He pulled his best mate, Jim, closer and shouted in his ear, 'Come on. We'll cut in on those two.'

Jim nodded. Cole's muscular build, black curly hair and intense dark eyes pulled the birds. Jim always went along with Cole, content to take the second-best girl.

Vanessa and her friend parted to let Cole and Jim in. Cole used his best moves, the ones that made girls sweat to keep up with him. Vanessa's hair became sodden. Her pointy little breasts heaved. The fast set ended. Cole kept hold of Vanessa's damp hand for the pause between sets. She made no move to pull away. When the music started again he pulled her close. He drew her head down into the crook of his neck. His right thigh edged forwards, parting hers a little. She moulded against him. He bent to brush her ear with his lips.

'See you home?'

She nodded and snuggled in tighter. The last number was still playing when he steered her through the crowd to get her coat.

Vanessa lived on Valentine's Road, which was walkable. Her front garden was small but it had a high privet hedge and a deep doorway. Once they were hidden in the shadows he pressed her against the rough brick wall and kissed her. Her lips were already parted for his tongue, which was encouraging. The kisses became harder and deeper. Cole was congratulating himself on having picked a hot one when she slid her arms under his jacket and pinched him, hard.

Cole pulled back and told her, 'Don't do that. It hurts,' before returning to the kiss.

2

She twisted his flesh viciously. He caught her wrists and doubled them behind her. Vanessa went crazy. Her lips spread so wide it seemed she was trying to swallow his face. Her body twisted as if she was struggling to escape but her wrists didn't pull against his grip. Cole forced one leg between hers. Still in constant motion, she sank onto it, rucking her miniskirt high. Her pubes pressed down on his thigh and humped it ferociously.

Cole held her wrists in one fist. He flattened his palm at her waist and worked it up under her fuzzy pink sweater. Vanessa groaned. His fingertips found the thick elastic edge of her bra and forced their way under it. The sturdy fabric popped up, freeing the soft sweet flesh of her teenage breast. Cole found her nipple. Instinctively, he caught it between thumb and finger and squeezed. It had to hurt but she just gyrated faster. Her mouth was so wet her saliva ran down his chin. Cole felt sure she was going to fuck on the first date, which for the time was a rare and wonderful thing.

He pinched her nipple between his nails. If that was the sort of thing she liked, he was up for it. Vanessa lifted both feet from the ground so that all her weight was borne by her pussy against his thigh. Cole's hand dropped to his fly and had it halfway down when Vanessa gave a guttural cry and went limp.

She blinked at him and said, 'Goodnight, Cole. Thanks for seeing me home.'

Her door closed. Cole was left, aching hard, alone.

Three nights later, Vanessa was at the Palais again. Cole politely asked her to dance. She refused. He walked a tall blonde home. Despite the lush promise of her lips, she kissed like a parrot.

By the next time Cole saw Vanessa, he thought he'd figured her out. They announced the last dance. He put his hand firmly on the back of her neck and told her, 'I'm seeing you home.'

She nodded, shivering under his grip.

When they got to her doorway he took hold of the back of her neck again. Her arms snaked under his jacket. Before she could get a grip on his flesh, he yanked her wrists out and behind her back. Last time, he'd held them in the small of her back. This time he pushed them up between her shoulder blades, knowing he was hurting her. Her teeth went for the side of his neck. Before they could close, he had his fist in her hair and her head bent back. Her kisses were just as wet and fierce as before. Cole pinned her to the wall with his body. He had it all worked out. Being held, painfully helpless, turned Vanessa on. If he could stop her from getting off on his leg, she'd fuck.

Her hips bucked. His cock, a rigid vertical bulge, was hammered by her pubes. Cole sucked her squirmy tongue into his mouth and gripped it between his teeth so he didn't have to hold her hair to stop her from biting him. His freed hand popped the buttons of her blouse. Once more, he found her nipple and pinched. Her legs came up high and wrapped around his hips. His hand left her breast and worked down between their bodies. It was under her skirt and fumbling at her pantyhose when she jerked and grunted.

The bitch had got off again.

Cole didn't walk Vanessa home again, but he thought about her, often, over the following years. He hadn't got to fuck her but she'd taught him a valuable lesson. Most girls didn't get off as fast as Vanessa but most girls wanted a guy to take charge. If he used a firm voice and hand, and assumed a girl would fuck, nine out of ten would. He didn't ask girls to dance. He simply told them, in a soft strong voice, that they were going to.

He learnt little 'take charge' tricks, like taking a drink from a girl's hand or her glasses from her face, without asking, then kissing her. When it was time to fuck he simply told them so. Hardly any objected.

4

It seemed that girls were puppets and he knew which strings to pull, and when. After a while it began to bother him. Girls were people. What if his 'power', as he began to think of it, was making them do things they didn't really want to? What if he was ruining their lives?

Cole loved girls. He adored it that they were so different from him; so pliant. The more unlike him a girl was, the more he wanted her. He was strong. Feminine weakness was irresistible. But what if such a girl couldn't say no, even if she wanted to, because his personality was so powerful? Wasn't that some kind of rape?

He joined the army and served for three years in a place where there were no women. By the time he was discharged he'd gained twenty pounds of hard muscle. Cole was a man – a man with a strong thirst for female company.

A week out of the army, he met Janet at a little club on Manor Park Broadway. She'd planned to be a ballerina until her breasts grew too big. Cole found the combination of a slender hard body and enormous breasts irresistible. She let him play with her opulent breasts on their second date and fucked like a minx on their fourth.

Spring came early. Cole drove Janet out to Epping, to the Wheatsheaf. They had a pint of cider each before taking a blanket into the forest. Once the blanket was spread, Janet started to sit on it. He stopped her. Down on one knee, gazing up at her breasts, Cole asked, 'Janet, will you marry me?'

'Of course I will!'

He put an antique marquise ring on her finger. While she admired the ring, he took the hem of her gingham dress in his hands and lifted it. Janet was wearing knee-high socks so there'd be no pantyhose to negotiate. Cole's face was an inch from the cotton of her panties when she stopped him.

'Make love to me, Cole.'

'That's what I was doing.'

'Do it normally, OK? We can do that other stuff to each other once we're married. I want to save something special for our honeymoon. You can understand that, can't you?'

He allowed that he could, and fucked her, hiding his disappointment.

On the second night of their honeymoon at Boscastle, in Cornwall, he nuzzled his way up between her thighs. She stopped him when his mouth was a tongue's length from its succulent goal. Janet wanted to ride him. He tried again on their third night. This time she wanted 'doggy'. On the fourth night, she was just too tired. When he touched her between the cheeks of her bottom, she gave him a flat cold 'no'.

By the time they'd been married six months their sex life had fallen into a pattern. He fingered Janet to a sedate climax and then she let him fuck her, missionary as a rule. Sometimes he didn't bother with the fucking. She didn't mind. All she really wanted was to lie limp in bed and let his fingers get her off before she fell asleep.

Cole took to masturbating. When he did, he fantasised about wild girls who wanted to be restrained and who begged him to take advantage of their helpless condition by doing obscene things to their bodies.

Cole was tempted, often. He didn't stray though. He'd made a commitment to Janet. He felt as guilty as if he was cheating even though he wasn't. He'd stopped loving her, which was a worse betrayal.

Janet wanted to emigrate. She hinted that in a new land, she'd try new things. He doubted she was telling the truth but there was always a chance. They crossed the Atlantic to Canada.

Cole became a real estate agent. He did OK and she made a good salary, but both incomes combined couldn't keep up with Janet's real passion – shopping.

By their fifteenth anniversary they were deep in debt and she was complaining he didn't give her enough affection. Then he met Kate.

# Two

The morning started badly. Janet came into the bathroom while he was shaving and gave him a lecture on the 'right' way to use a razor. Sometimes Cole wondered whether her constant prodding was like Vanessa's pinching – a sign that she wanted to be restrained and ravished. He never put the theory to the test. If he was wrong, the consequences would be awful. If he was right, he'd be committing himself to the role of her 'lord and master'. He couldn't take that responsibility on, not with a woman he barely tolerated. At breakfast, Janet asked him about the deal he'd told her was imminent.

'It fell through.'

'How come?'

'When I went into their finances, the Ritchies couldn't afford to buy that house.'

'They qualified for the mortgage?'

'Yes.'

'Then?'

'They'd have been house-poor. They want to start a family.'

'You told me they were putty in your hands,' she accused. 'You said they'd sign anything you told them to.'

Cole could have explained that it was *because* they'd do anything he said that he'd had to protect them from themselves but Janet had heard that one before. She

8

slapped the pile of unpaid bills on the kitchen table and went to get ready for work.

It was Wednesday, 'caravan day'. Park Realty's agents piled into their cars and toured the Real Estate Board's listings. The third house was an old one by local standards, on Trafalgar Road. Agents try to get vendors out of the way when their homes are shown but the owner of this one hovered in her living room, obviously anxious.

Kate was a redhead, with tumbling curls. Her eyes were molten chocolate. Her thin floral dress was high-waisted and loose from under her bust to her ankles. It was tight over her large soft breasts. Cole was reminded of Janet's figure, as it had been before she gained fifty pounds. Unlike Janet, Kate seemed diffident. She leant against a wall, one foot up behind her, and watched the agents with nervous, needy eyes.

Cole, like all the other agents, left his card. The next day Kate called him.

'I really need to sell.'

'I'll do what I can.'

'I need a man's advice.'

'Rob Smyth is your agent. He's a good man.'

'Please? Can we talk?'

It wasn't ethical for agents to see other agents' clients behind their backs but Cole remembered lush breasts with thimble nipples that pressed through clinging fabric. He suggested, 'Ten? This evening?'

She opened her door wearing a kimono that parted to expose one almost-thin and shockingly pale thigh. Cole followed slender haunches that rippled under satin into her living room. There were two tumblers waiting, each half filled with icy vodka. He decided to sip on his, just to be sociable.

Kate sat opposite him with most of a naked thigh showing. When she leant towards him, her kimono gaped and her breasts swayed. 'My home's been for sale for almost a year and there hasn't been a single offer.'

'Have you thought about the price?'

'I've come down twenty thousand.'

There was no kind way to say it. 'At around fifty thousand, it should sell.'

She frowned. 'That's half what I was told it's worth.'

Cole waited.

'I really need to sell.'

He waited some more.

She slipped the tips of three fingers into the neck of her kimono and let them rest where a breast's swell began. 'Could you get me fifty thousand if I listed with you?'

'I know about the first mortgage. Is there anything else? Liens?'

'Um . . .' The fingers inside her kimono dropped lower, maybe to her nipple.

'I can't help you if I don't know everything. Show me the papers.'

Kate had a first mortgage and a second mortgage and was behind on both. Cole calculated that if she got fifty thousand she could pay them off and have enough left over to pay about half her legal fees. There'd be less than nothing for real estate commissions.

'Walk away. Mail the keys to the mortgage company that holds your first.'

'What about the second mortgage?'

'The mortgage company would dump your home for a quick sale. Whoever holds the second might get about half of what you owe them, if they're lucky.'

'I can't. It's a private mortgage, with family. Can't you help? Please?' Her eyes were big and wet. Her fingers were stroking her own skin inside her kimono. 'I'd put myself in your hands, Cole. I'd do anything you told me to.'

Janet never trusted him in anything, though he'd never failed her. Janet didn't really need him. Kate was willing to put absolute faith in him and was desperate for his help. What could he do?

A tone of voice Cole had avoided using for years returned to him. He said, 'No promises, but I'll see what I can do. Take your home off the market. Get a release from your agent without mentioning me. When you've done that, call me. I'll give you the name of a lawyer who owes me. Use him.'

Her eyes dropped. She whispered, 'Yes, Cole.'

He took a last sip and stood up. She writhed to her feet and came close, too close.

She said, huskily, 'Are you big, Cole?' He didn't understand her question until the backs of her fingers brushed across his fly. 'I see you are.'

Cole left.

Two days later, Kate called to tell him she'd done as he'd told her. He phoned the Ritchies and gave them Kate's number. 'I can't show you the house. This has to be a private deal. If you like it, the price is fifty thousand, not a penny less – and you have to use the lawyer I tell you or it's no deal.'

They liked Kate's house and bought it. Elmore Dunstable, a lawyer Cole sent a lot of business to, did Kate's work at cost. The Ritchies were effusive with their thanks. Cole heard nothing from Kate. Well, he'd done a good deed. Perhaps he'd been taken for a mug. So what?

# Three

Cole had endured living with Janet for six more months before he heard from Kate again. He was in his office when his phone rang. A liquid caramel voice said, 'I need your advice, Cole.'

'Kate?' His voice took on a defensive edge. 'What's the problem now?'

'Can you come and see me?'

'Tell me what your problem is.'

'You have to see it. I promise you, Cole, if you come you'll be glad you did.'

Cole remembered the way satin slid over her bottom and the way her naked thigh showed through the slit in her kimono.

'I'm booked most of the day. I might make it, but not till this evening, if then.'

'I'll be waiting.'

The negotiations Cole had warned Janet might take all day and half the night were completed by three in the afternoon. That left a void in his schedule. He should have done paperwork and then gone home. Instead, he sat at his desk and stewed. Whatever Kate wanted, it wasn't about real estate. It might be that she was in trouble again and he was 'Mr Miracle'. Chances were, she planned to take advantage of him.

Would he let her? Would he solve her problem, just because she was sexy and helpless? He thought about the 'helpless' more than the 'sexy'. Did that bring out the knight-in-shining-armour in him, or the predator? By five he'd decided that Kate was a manipulative little bitch and he'd be an idiot to go. By six, she was a pitiful creature who could only survive by using her sensuality. At seven, he was driving out of the parking lot. Turning right would take him home to Janet, sour faced and nagging. Cole turned left.

Kate buzzed him up and was standing in her apartment door when he got to her floor. She was wearing a tatty old trench coat but had nothing on her feet.

'On your way out?'

'No. Come in.'

He followed her into a small living–dining room.

She posed, looking a bit ridiculous. 'It's about this raincoat. Can I wear it?'

Cole was puzzled. 'If you like.'

'I mean, is it too old?'

Was this a ploy to get him to buy her a new coat? What did she take him for? In a hard voice, he told her, 'It's past wearing. Is that it? Is that what you called me for?'

'Not exactly. Wait here, OK?' She disappeared for a few minutes and returned in a different coat. It was tightly belted, shiny black vinyl and very short, coming no lower than a miniskirt would. There was no sign of a skirt under it. Nothing but skin showed at her cleavage. Cole swallowed, hard.

'It looks good on you.'

'Thank you. My problem is, all my dresses are long. How would it look with a dress showing below it?'

Cole cleared his throat. 'Whatever you're wearing now doesn't show.'

'But I can't go out like this, can I?' She stepped close and lifted his hands to her belt.

Cole needed a minute to think. 'The sale went through OK?' he asked, meaning, 'Why didn't you call me six months ago?'

She said, 'My boyfriend helped me move my things,' answering his unspoken question.

Cole took half a step back, though his hands stayed on her belt buckle. 'Boyfriend?'

'He was very possessive. We've broken up.'

'Oh.' Cole came closer again.

'He abused me, Cole.'

Cole felt a rush of guilt. He'd been blaming her for not contacting him and all the while she'd been in the hands of some brute. Now what? He'd come to fuck Kate – he admitted that to himself now – but she was so vulnerable – helpless – fragile. Was he bastard enough to take advantage of her weakness?

Perhaps Kate thought he was hesitating because he didn't believe her. Perhaps she was impatient for whatever it was she wanted from him. Whichever, she tugged the collar of her raincoat aside, baring her left breast.

It was lush, with a fawn nipple set in a matching areola. Her skin was chalk white, with a smattering of freckles, but it was the bruises that made Cole swallow again. There were dark fresh ones the size of fingertips overlying faded yellow ones. Her breast had been gripped hard, often. There was a curved mark like a healed graze that followed the outer contours of her fleshy orb, as if it had been abraded by a coarse rope. A welt, straight and about two inches long, cut across her halo, just below the jut of her nipple.

Kate thrust her breast forwards, as if proud of its marks. 'You see what he did to me?'

Cole didn't know if it was pity for her that dried his mouth, or envy of the man who'd inflicted these torments on her. His hand rose of its own accord. The tips of his fingers stroked her mottled skin.

She shivered. He snatched his hand away.

'It's OK. It doesn't hurt. You can touch me. Please?' Kate took his hand and returned it to her breast.

He cupped it, unsure. His thumb brushed the horizontal welt. Cole didn't want to think about how it'd been inflicted but it was obvious. Her delicate skin had been struck by something thin and straight, perhaps a cane. He'd fantasised about doing things like that but fantasy women only felt fantasy pain and they disappeared when he climaxed.

Kate was real. She'd endured the sort of treatment he'd dreamt about inflicting. The question was, had she, like the women he'd conjured up, enjoyed the sadistic abuse?

His finger and thumb closed on her nipple, firmly but not viciously. It was resilient, with the texture of a berry. His fingers tightened.

Kate gasped and came in close, face tilted up, lips parted, with just the tip of her tongue protruding. Cole's lips closed gently on her lower one, the preliminary to a deeper kiss but her mouth squirmed and pressed and sucked. His tongue lay on hers for a moment, savouring. Hers retreated and stabbed forwards, slithering into his mouth, wet and voracious.

Cole observed himself. Something strange was happening to him. As Kate's mouth demanded that his ravish it, he began to feel stronger. He was aware that his feet were set apart, on heavily muscled legs. His shoulders felt broader. His arms seemed thicker and more toned. Cole was filled with a sense of his own physical power. His cock wasn't fully erect but it had lengthened and felt heavy.

Dark desire filled him. He knew that it was his right to use her for his pleasure. Further, he was absolutely certain that his using her would fulfil her. She needed to serve him. That's what she was – an aching void. Only he could complete her.

Cole realised that his fingers were crushing her nipple. His other hand was knotted in her hair. Held between those grips, she was writhing. Her hips twisted from side to side, rubbing her mound on the shaft of his cock. Her left leg wrapped around his right one. Kate humped, abrading her exposed sex on the fabric of his trousers.

Cole pushed her back, his hands still on her breast and in her hair. Her raincoat hung loose. Below those opulent breasts she was thin. He could see the sculptured lines of her ribs. Her tummy was hollowed. Her hip bones were sharp under their skin. Her mound was a slight thickening over her pubic bone. Its pelt was sparse and pale. Below it, narrow lips protruded, parted enough to betray a sliver of glistening pink.

'Do I please you, Cole?' she asked.

'You please me,' he told her in a voice so steady and firm that it surprised him.

'May I? Your cock? I've been thinking about it, ever since . . .'

He released her. Kate dropped to her knees and stared at his trousers as if they held a birthday present she hoped was the one thing she really wanted but didn't dare unwrap in case she were disappointed. He put his hand to the tab of his fly. She brushed his fingers aside and drew it down slowly, prolonging her expectation. Hesitant fingers reached inside. He felt them touch him, just below the head of his cock, through his briefs. Kate leant closer. She found the elastic waistband and tenderly lifted it away from him, and down. His cock, fully rampant now, sprang free.

'Oh!' she said, looking up into his eyes. 'Thank you.' Her mouth worked. Cool fingers wrapped his stem. She directed it down so that it jutted at 45 degrees. With her lips a half-inch from its wet purple plum, she asked, 'May I taste?'

During all his years of marriage, this was a moment Cole had dreamt of. He'd been lucky if Janet had so much as touched him there, and never with her mouth. On the rare occasions she'd caressed his cock, he'd felt it had been with distaste, as a special favour. Now he

16

was being begged for it. He said, 'You may,' and held his breath.

Kate rose up a little. Her mouth worked again. Her lips pursed above his knob and dribbled saliva. Drool descended on a silvery string. A bubbly blob of spit landed directly into the eye of Cole's cock and overflowed it. The sensation was so delicate that he could hardly feel it, but the knowledge that a woman's warm saliva was coating his cock's dome drew his balls up and tightened his sphincter.

Kate moved his foreskin up, then down again. She seemed enraptured. Her lips formed an 'O'. With shocking speed, she swooped. Her lips didn't touch his cock until it impacted the back of her throat and they closed, gently and lovingly, encircling his shaft halfway down its length. Her eyes turned up to meet his. Her hands gripped his thighs. She pulled, forcing him deeper. Her face moved from side to side, working down. At last, her lips were pressed to his tight curls. She looked up at him as her throat worked, almost gagging.

Concerned she might gag, he pulled her off by her hair and told her, 'Good girl.'

She grinned and strained forwards again but only to take half his cock into her slavering mouth. Cole found that he preferred mumbling lips and slithering tongue to the feeling of being half swallowed but didn't say so. It was obvious that Kate prided herself on her ability to deep-throat.

She began to bob, with her hand working in unison.

Cole pulled her off again. 'If you keep that up, I'll come.'

'Please, Cole? Please? I want it so much.' She went back to pumping, with an open-mouthed slurp at the top of each stroke. Between licks, she babbled, 'I want your come, Cole. Give it to me. Come lots. Fill my mouth. Give it to me on my tongue. Please, Cole.'

17

Whether it was her words or the exquisite sensations, Cole's balls tightened and his thighs stiffened. He thrust, slapping his cockhead on her flattened and extended tongue.

She squealed, 'Yes!' and opened wide.

He watched as his cock jerked in her hands and spat a stream of hot jism directly between her lips. Kate poked her tongue out to show him the great creamy gob that sat in its hollow, then took his second and third jet, the last splattering her lips.

She swallowed and licked and swallowed again, grinning up at him. 'You don't make much noise when you come.'

Cole excused himself with, 'You took my breath away.'

He tried to find the words to explain that he might be incapacitated for a while.

She said, 'Now you should rest, please. Should I wake you in an hour?'

Feeling guilty that he'd climaxed and she hadn't, he nodded. She stood, leaving her raincoat on the floor, and undressed him. When he was naked, she led him to her bedroom and pulled the covers of her brass bed down for him. 'I'll just watch you while you sleep, if I may?'

He was asleep within minutes, totally content.

He woke with Kate on her side in his lap, lean haunches moving subtly from side to side. The bed-clothes had been thrown back. Both of her hands were between her thighs. One was toying with his cock, slapping it up against her flaccid lips. The other was playing with her pussy. When she felt him stir she guided his cockhead up into her wet heat.

'Is this OK, Cole?'

He pushed her head lower and surged towards her. The full length of his engorged cock slid all the way in. She was fevered and wet. When he adjusted his angle, he felt different textures, tight slickness, a spongy resistance, a pulpy mass that his cock crushed against the hardness of her pubic bone.

'Thank you, Cole.' Her fingers played, frotting her clit, jiggling his balls, stroking his shaft as it emerged. 'May I come, please?'

That feeling of power emerged again. He told her, 'Not till I tell you,' and drove deeper.

A bent finger worked in beside his shaft. The increased tightness was delightfully erotic but it was the thought that she wanted to fondle his cock even as he fucked her that excited him the most. Kate, unlike Janet, seemed to love his cock.

'You need to come?' he asked.

'Please?'

'When I say.' It was ridiculous for him to think he could order her to climax but he counted down, 'Five, four, three, two, now!'

Kate convulsed. He thought she had to be faking it but her vagina clenched on his shaft and gushed hot and wet. She blurted, 'Fuck, fuck, fuck,' and juddered back against him.

Cole kept fucking, though she was mushy from her climax now and each stroke made wet sucking sounds. Minutes later, she must have recovered because she tightened inside and jerked back at him. Kate doubled down until she could grasp her ankles. Cole arched back. Their only contact was inside her. They'd been reduced to their sexual parts, in violent lubricated friction. Cole became completely focused. The sensations in the head of his cock were all that existed. With her bent like that, the head of his cock was rubbing hard against the slippery rear wall of her vagina.

He felt the pressure build, and paused. After a deep breath, he pushed again, twice, slowly, before pausing again. His need to come was exquisitely unbearable. His cock was desperate. He shifted his hips an inch to change the angle, withdrew slowly, then pounded deep and fast.

Kate gasped, 'Give it to me, Cole.'

He pressed, gaining an inch more penetration, and pressed again, straining, flattening her lean buttocks with his belly.

How long could he keep this up, balancing on the edge, teasing himself?

'I need your come, Cole. I need to feel you come inside me. Please?'

Her words provided his excuse. He pistoned and released. Kate jerked on him, each spasm drawing an after-climax spurt from his depths. She twisted onto her back, his cock clamped inside her, to throw one leg across his waist. Kate's hand went to her slit, where ivory foam drooled. Two fingers squirmed inside and emerged coated. She lifted them to her mouth and sucked them avidly.

The obscenity of what she was doing inspired one last dribble from his spent cock.

# Four

Cole called Kate from his office the next morning. The line was busy. He called again, from a pay phone, that afternoon. It was still busy. After nine calls, he began to worry but he couldn't call her from home. He tried again at nine in the morning of the following day, with the same result.

An old lady with her arms full of shopping thanked him for holding the building's door. Cole followed her in. He knocked on Kate's door for ten full minutes before he turned away.

'Oh, it's you!'

He spun. Her door was open. Kate's tousled head peered round it.

'I called you all day yesterday. I was worried.'

'I was sick. I took the phone off the hook.'

'Are you better?'

'Yes. Did you want to come in?' She must have assumed he did because she disappeared, leaving the door ajar.

Cole closed the door behind himself just in time to see her naked bottom as she turned into her bedroom. He followed to find her in bed with the clothes drawn up to her chin but one long thin leg was exposed all the way up to the delicate hollow at her groin. He sat on the edge of the bed and took her ankle in his hand.

'I was worried about you,' he repeated.

'I wasn't well.' She blinked and dropped her eyes. 'Am I a bad girl?'

'No, it's just . . .'

'You didn't tell me you were going to call.'

His hand tightened on her ankle. 'After my last visit? How would you not expect me to call?'

'Some men wouldn't. Are you angry with me?'

'Why would you think that?'

'The way you're crushing my ankle.'

'Oh.' He let his fist relax but some instinct prompted him to tighten it again.

'What are you going to do to me?'

'What do you think you deserve?'

'You aren't going to hit me, are you?'

'Of course not. What do you take me for?'

'Dave would have.' She was pouting, which puzzled Cole.

'Dave? Your old boyfriend? Do you want to talk about him?' Perhaps if she did, he'd be able to understand her better. Submissive masochism he could grasp but her ambivalence puzzled him.

'You saw my bruises.' Her face lightened. She pushed her bedclothes down to her narrow waist. 'They're faded now, see?'

Cole could see. He could see two lush breasts, too large and heavy to support themselves, white as talc except for their freckles and with translucent skin that showed a faint tracery of delicate blue veins. Her nipples stared back at him, not yet engorged but proud. He cleared his throat. 'We were talking about how worried you made me and how you should be punished.'

She threw her bedclothes aside and rolled over. Backing towards him, for he still held her ankle, she knelt with her bottom high and her face pressed down on the crumpled sheet. Every time Cole had tried to inspect Janet's sex in detail, she'd shied away as if ashamed of her own private parts. Now he was offered a pussy to look at, at his leisure. He'd never had one presented blatantly for his inspection. He bent down.

Her legs were too close together. Cole pulled firmly on her ankle and pushed her other leg. Kate spread. His flattened hand pushed down on the small of her back. Kate thrust her sex back at him. There it was, displayed, framed between pale thin thighs. He licked his lips. Her outer lips weren't as plump as he'd expected but her inner ones were thick fleshy petals that protruded by about an inch. They were wrinkled, reminding him of a pulpy pink clam shell.

He squatted to bring his face closer, and inhaled. Her aroma was that of fresh-baked bread but with acid undertones, like canned pineapple. He exhaled. A few stray tiny light-brown hairs quivered. As he watched, her petals uncrinkled.

Cole rested his fingertips on the base of Kate's spine. Unlike Janet, she wasn't padded there. He could feel the ridges of her coccyx. His hands drifted down, over the lean ovals of her buttocks, with the balls of his thumbs smoothing the cleft between them.

Kate mewed.

So, she liked to be touched in that intimate crease, did she? His eyes lifted. The core of her bottom showed a pinprick hole, haloed by striated fawn skin.

He was looking, with her acquiescence, directly at her anus. It was the most intimate experience he'd ever enjoyed. One finger brushed the pucker. It twitched, but not to clamp tighter. She was spreading, inviting him in.

Cole was tempted to stand up, unzip and bugger her. He resisted the urge, even though he'd never fucked a girl there and he *really* wanted to. Her bum was his to plunder, he was sure. Cole could wait. He'd *make* himself wait. His attention returned to her pussy. With his fingers dancing across the taut skin of her bottom, he extended his tongue. Its tip touched one flaccid lip and lightly pushed it aside. When he backed off a few inches, that lip stayed in place. Between it and its mate, there was a thin parting, just wide enough to show a pale and glistening slit. His head went down again. His tongue entered. There was the source of that pineapple flavour. He gripped her thighs and dragged her pussy onto his tongue, pushing it into her as deeply as he could strain it.

Kate made a sound deep in her throat.

Cole nuzzled, opening her wider. Her lips spread across his mouth. He was kissing her, inside. He sucked and nibbled. He twisted his face to the side and drew the inner surface of one lip into his mouth.

Kate whimpered and pushed back.

Remembering the hickeys he'd given and got in his teens, Cole sucked hard. He'd be leaving his mark – inside her – where no one but he would ever see it. The most intimate love bite he'd ever given a girl was the one he'd left on Mavis Adams's breast, just below her right nipple. He'd been proud at the time. If only his teenage self could see him now!

Something stirred inside Cole. He'd indulged in sadistic fantasies for as long as he could remember. They'd been strictly that – fantasies. He'd never given serious consideration to acting them out in real life, with a real woman feeling real pain. Now he was with a woman who whimpered and moaned when he hurt her and who showed no signs of objecting. He dismissed his doubts about her stability. She wanted to take what he wanted to give. Why question that?

But did he dare release the sadistic beast inside him? If he did, could he control it or would it take over and turn him into a monster? Somehow, he found, he was certain that he could keep that side of himself under tight control. Kate made him feel incredibly powerful. That new-found strength, he was sure, included the power to control his own cruelty.

He decided to test his conviction.

Holding the lip of Kate's sex between his teeth, Cole worked two fingers inside her and slid his thumb up the smooth slickness between her folds until it felt the engorged protrusion of her clit. His grip tightened, his thumb crushing her hard clit against one side of her pubic bone and his fingers mashing her pulpy G-spot against the other.

Kate gave a strangled yelp. It was followed by a deep sigh. He had her bone, her actual bone, in an iron grip, and it seemed that his taking ownership of her body thrilled her.

His teeth compressed the yielding flesh they held. If he'd read her correctly, Kate needed to feel threatened. Fear turned her on. It wasn't in him to inflict real harm but he could indulge her by faking menace.

Kate sobbed, 'Cole, Cole, Cole.'

He knew he was bruising her: her clit, her G-spot, the lip of her sex. He felt the urge to bite harder, to penetrate her skin, but held it in check.

Cole was Master – of himself, first, and of Kate. It was exhilarating.

Her body was his toy. Was her mind?

He released her and drew back. Her sex was swollen and discoloured. If he fucked her, it'd hurt her, but he already knew he could fuck her and he wanted to explore her limits. He told her, 'Stay.'

Cole stripped naked and drew his belt from its loops. She looked back and licked her lips. Did she think he planned to beat her with his belt? Did the thought excite her? He wasn't sure he was ready for that, yet, but he made a mental note.

Kate looked deliciously vulnerable, bent over, bum high, but that position pressed her breasts to the bed.

'Further up the bed. Hold the top rail.' He looped his belt around one thin wrist, then the other, over the rail, back around both wrists and round the rail again. He had to pull hard to get the pin of the buckle through the last hole. Leather bit into her wrists.

His left hand went under her, roughly. He squeezed a pendant breast, distorting it. Kate looked at him with imploring, adoring eyes. The look in them told him that this was exactly what she wanted. He gripped her nipple and pulled, drawing it out to its limits. Pain filled her eyes but her mouth was slack and wet.

Still twisting her nipple, he knelt up on the bed beside her. She craned round, neck extended, mouth reaching for his cock.

'You want to suck me?'

'Please.'

'If you're brave, maybe later, as a reward.'

'I promise I'll be brave, Cole.'

His right hand stroked up her flank to the curve of her bottom's left cheek. Cole knew his own strength. One full blow from his palm would bruise her to the bone. She'd be limping for a week. The trick would be to slap hard enough to sting while pulling his blow so as not to drive the force deep.

He raised his hand. 'I'm going to spank you, Kate.'

'Yes, Cole. Have I been bad?'

'I'm going to spank you because I choose to, not to punish you. Do you understand?'

'Yes.'

His hand came down, clipping her flesh. 'Did that hurt?'

'Some,' she admitted, sounding almost disappointed.

'Tell me when the pain becomes too much for you to bear.'

She nodded, biting her lip. His hand descended again, harder, on the same cheek, then the other, alternating as he mentally counted his slaps. Each clap of his hand seemed to pump his cock harder. Exercising this sort of power was incredibly exhilarating. By the twentieth slap, her entire rump was glowing except for a thin contrasting white strip between her cheeks. His cock was so rigid it ached. By forty, she was writhing against her bonds and her eyes were wet.

Cole moved back down the bed a little. Her vulva was still an engorged flower. He let his hand drop down until the backs of his fingers touched the sheet. Cupped, it slapped upwards. His fingers impacted the squishy wetness of her bruised sex with enough force to lift her knees an inch off the bed.

'Oh, God! Oh, fuck! Oh, Cole!'

His hand fell and rose, fell and rose, each blow pulled but hard enough to bruise her most sensitive parts. The sounds changed from 'cracks' to 'splats' as she seeped liquid lust. Surely she'd beg for mercy soon? She didn't, and Cole's cock was desperate to penetrate her. She'd endured sixty slaps, forty on her bottom and twenty directly on her pussy, when Cole decided she'd had enough.

He moved back to kneel behind her. It was her ass he wanted. He'd never buggered a girl. He couldn't ram into her dry, though, even if his cock wanted him to. His thumb forced his cock down to her sex. He slid in, fast, and swayed his hips to work his cockhead against her inner walls before pulling out, lubricated with her juices.

There was her anus, a tiny hole in the centre of a muscular ring. He spat and hit her tailbone, and spat again. His spittle was a bubbly blob in her crease but above its target. His thumb rubbed it down, over her pucker. Cole took himself in his fist and aimed his cockhead. It didn't seem possible that so small a hole could stretch to accommodate the rampant cudgel that was about to dilate it. When he pressed his plum to her skin, it totally obscured the ring of her anus. He leant. Her flesh indented. Cole pushed harder. In his mind, he saw that minute sphincter give, grow larger, open up to him. He shifted his knees closer and gripped her hips. As he pushed, he pulled her back. For a second it seemed that his steely cock must bend. There was a 'plopping' sensation. He looked down, savouring the moment. Her anus was a tightly stretched ring around his cock, just behind its head.

He was in. For the first time in his entire life, his cock was in a woman's ass.

One hand left Kate's hip and stretched forwards to grip her hair. Pulling her by that painful hold, he eased forwards. Her rectum was strangling tight. It dragged on the skin over his dome, stimulating every single nerve-ending.

Kate was panting. Her body was taut and stiff. Her hands, wrapping the bar of her bed's head, were gripping so hard that her knuckles were white.

Was she enduring the pain he was inflicting just to please him or was the pain a pleasure for her? He couldn't ask her. Cole was almost sure that for Kate, humiliation, being *used,* was part of what she craved. He compromised.

'Half my cock's up your ass.' He paused to give her time to speak. 'You can take it all, right?'

She nodded as best she could with his hand holding her hair.

That was all the assent Cole needed. He surged. Her flesh yielded to him. His thighs hit hers. His cock was buried in Kate as far as it could reach. He held it there, rotating his hips slightly, soaking in both the sensations and the thrill of at last having committed the delicious obscenity.

He pulled back an inch, then eased forwards. His own sphincter contracted. His thighs were trembling. Cole's body was fighting his will. It demanded release. He wanted to extend his pleasure. Holding perfectly still, he hissed, 'Do it!'

Kate took a deep breath. To Cole's delight, the muscles in her rectum clamped, then relaxed, squeezing his shaft in a steady rhythm. She tucked her tail down a little, then jerked it up. Kate, Cole realised, had been buggered before, often enough that she'd learnt skills he'd never guessed a woman might possess. Her hips made small tight circles, spiralling closer to him, then drawing away until his cock almost emerged before she thrust back, impaling herself. Cole was impressed. Kate could massage him internally and, at the same time, bump and grind like a stripper.

He'd thought he was debauching her but it was obvious there was nothing he'd done to her that hadn't been done before. In a way, he was disappointed. Still, it was early days. He had fifteen years of lonely fantasies to draw on. Sooner or later, he'd find something to do to her that'd pop her pretty eyes.

Her gyrations became urgent. She was grunting now, sounding almost angry. Cole gave her rump a slap and took over, plunging into her. Their movements conflicted at first but she surrendered to his rhythm, thrusting back to meet him, pulling forwards off his retreats. Her grunts melded into a low growl. It was like sodomising a tiger. He released her hair and dug his fingers into her hips. His belly and thighs slapped at her bum, faster and faster. His balls swung against her wetness. Every thrust seemed to take him deeper.

Kate shuddered all over, let out a howl, and collapsed under him. The little bitch had climaxed from being buggered. Cole hadn't known that was possible.

He writhed on top of her limp body, giving his cock permission to let go. It did. He let the big one flood out of him, grabbed his cock's root, yanked out and scurried forwards over her, desperately holding back. Her face turned. He flopped sideways with his cock next to her sweaty face and pulled her head by its hair. Her lips parted. Cole released his second, third and fourth spurt: two in her mouth and two, more trickles than jets, onto her cheek and chin.

'Thank you, Cole.'

He grunted. Forming words would take too much effort.

'My hands, please?' She looked up to where her wrists were secured.

29

Wearily, Cole reached up to release her. When she was unstrapped, he toppled backwards onto the bed, landing to face her mottled sex. A breath stirred the hairs on his balls. Fuck! Falling back, he'd landed so that they were face to sex and, for now, all his cock wanted was to be left alone.

A gently inquisitive hand cupped his scrotum. Did she expect him to go again?

'Tell me about yourself, Kate,' he said, quickly. 'Tell me everything.'

She rolled off the bed and returned with two tumblers, each half filled with frigid vodka. Cole began to sit up but she climbed on the bed and resumed the same position, but with her thigh serving as his pillow and her pubes a few inches from his eyes.

She began, 'I was born in Australia but my folks came here when I was five.' She'd had an uncle who'd come with them and shared their home. He'd tried to teach her some games that frightened her. She didn't give Cole the details, which was a relief. She'd lost her virginity in her teens, forced into it by a neighbour. As soon as she was old enough, she'd left home and done some modelling, mainly lingerie. Unfortunately, her breasts had kept growing while the rest of her stayed slim. She'd done some hosiery work but that petered out. Pretty well destitute, she'd taken up with an older man who was a darling until he had a few drinks. Drunk, he beat her. Kate'd run away from him and . . .

Her story went on, and on. Man after man had used and abused her. Cole couldn't understand why she still liked men after all her terrible experiences but that wasn't a thought he wanted to put in her mind. She was into her tenth or twelfth tale of woe when Cole felt a finger wriggle between his thighs to tickle behind his balls.

His glazed eyes focused on the purple and swollen lips he faced. He wouldn't have thought his cock'd had time to recover but, resting on Kate's forearm, it twitched.

30

'My bum's leaking your come,' Kate told him, and giggled. 'It can't swallow like my mouth can. You've come in my bum and my mouth today. Now what does that leave? My poor pussy is feeling neglected.'

'Your "poor neglected pussy" got plenty of attention. It looks pretty tender, to me – too tender for . . .'

'If you wanted it, you'd take it.' She lifted her upper leg to point her toes at the ceiling. 'You wouldn't let it being a bit bruised stop you.'

Cole touched her discoloured lips with a tentative finger. Kate's response was to plant a kiss on the head of his limp cock. His finger parted her gently. Between her lips, she was moist. He everted one. Its inner side was dappled with bruises. An arc of tiny indentations showed where he'd nibbled her. Cole felt a pang. After her tale of being used so cruelly, he felt guilty about what he'd done to her, even though she'd shown every sign of liking it. He wondered if one day she might tell some new man about the terrible things *he*'d done to her, with him cast as an abusive brute. Cole dismissed the uncomfortable thought.

'Is it pretty?' As she spoke, her lips brushed his foreskin. 'Does it look good, bruised?'

Cole's foreskin began to retract. Her tongue's tip danced on his cockhead. 'Mm, tastes good,' she purred. 'Come to Kate.'

His cock was growing, pushing at her mumbling lips. He worked his finger deeper into her yielding flesh and hooked it up behind her pubic bone. The swelling he felt was textured with tiny bumps but slick with her seepage. As delicately as he could, he rotated the pad of his finger on it.

Kate hissed, 'Yes. That makes me so wet, Cole.' She finished her sentence by drawing his cockhead into her mouth and closing her lips on his shaft. Kate suckled like a baby, gently drawing on his sensitive glans.

It would have been churlish of him to not return the favour. Cole withdrew his finger and snuggled his face

31

into her. His tongue extended and explored. It lanced into her, then wandered between her lips, moving upwards over the smooth hardness above her opening, parting her folds as it travelled. When it found a tiny protuberance, it flickered. Kate's clit emerged from its sheath to meet his tongue. His lips closed on it, trapping it. It was about the size of a split pea. He'd read that a clit has as many nerve-endings as a cockhead. How exquisite! He put a hand up to her raised leg, just below her knee, to hold it in place. His tongue made spirals, settled on her clithead, and flickered.

Cole had known he'd like the taste, scent and texture of a woman. He hadn't anticipated how exciting it was to know that each movement of his tongue was thrilling her.

Kate's suction drew the head of his cock in and out. Her head shifted back. Cole's shaft had reached its fullest length and all her attentions were focused on its dome. She began to make little throat sounds. Cole wasn't sure if it was his licking that inspired them or her glee that his cock had been restored.

She took her lips off him and murmured, 'Please, Cole?'

'What do you want?'

'Fuck me?' She pulled her leg from his grasp and rolled onto her back.

He sat up and covered her, supported on his arms. Looking down into her eyes, he told her, 'It might take me a long time to come again so soon.'

She nodded. Her arm snaked down between them. A cool hand guided his cock until its head was lodged between her lips. 'Long and slow or short and fast. It's up to you, Cole. It's always up to you.' She put both hands above her head on the pillow, wrists crossed.

Cole knew what she wanted. He gripped her wrists in one hand, looming over her. A convulsion of his abdomen drove him up into her. His free hand wrapped

32

one lolling breast and squeezed. Humping in slow strong surges, he dipped his head to suck on her nipple. She arched, pressing more breast flesh into his mouth. Her shoulders shook from side to side. He almost lost his grip on her hard peak but bit down to keep it captive.

Kate grunted and arched more. 'You're so strong, Cole. You have hands of iron. I'm helpless. I'm a slave, bound for my master's pleasure. No matter how you use me, I can't escape.'

Her legs spread under him and lifted. Cole rose high to give her room to move. Kate's knees came up, all the way to her breasts, and straightened. She curled up under him until all her weight was on her shoulders and her toes touched the wall above the bed.

Cole reared up, caught her crossed ankles in his free hand and trapped them. She was held, rump tilted, sex pointing straight up. He pushed forwards on his toes and went straight down into her like a pneumatic drill.

Cole remembered that the flesh he was grinding into was bruised and tender. However, that realisation inspired no mercy. Instead, it made him thrust harder and deeper, battering down into her.

Kate screwed her eyes shut, jerked up to meet his pistoning, and moaned, 'I'm gonna come, Cole. Don't stop! It's better if you keep fucking me. I can come again. I can. I can!' She convulsed under him.

His cock was bathed in hot fluids. Cole kept thrusting.

'Yes! Here comes another one!' She gyrated at him. Her head pressed back onto her pillow.

Cole chewed Kate's nipple and kept pumping. He'd made her climax three times, so far. He was a *man*. Sweat dripped from his face and chest onto her, coating her torso. Kate made a face as if she were concentrating. The inside of her vagina rippled, milking him.

She stared up at him fiercely. 'Come in me, and on me, Cole.'

The pressure in his balls built. He let it go, the first squirt in her depths, then pulling out to splatter her lolling tits.

'You came four times,' he gloated.

'Did I? I've come more.'

# Five

Instead of driving past the FOR SALE BY OWNER sign, as he'd done twice a day for six months, Cole turned into the driveway. He told the owner, gently but firmly, exactly why he hadn't managed to sell in so long. An hour and a half later, he walked out with a listing.

He waited till noon to call Kate.

'My bum,' she said.

'What about it?'

'There's not a mark on it.'

Cole pondered her meaning. 'I'll see you at four tomorrow,' he told her. 'I'll bring supper.'

That afternoon he presented an offer on a house he'd been trying to sell for ten weeks. It was accepted with no negotiations. Was Kate a good-luck charm? He worked at his desk until five and surprised Janet by taking her out to wine and dine. It wasn't out of guilt. Making sure she was stuffed and a little squiffy ensured him a good night's sleep and would make her more tolerant when he got home late from Kate's tomorrow. It was strange that Janet hadn't noticed the change in him. Perhaps it took a womanly woman to notice how manly a man was.

Cole had used his office PC to surf 'S/M'. He knew a lot, in theory. It was time for him to put theory into practice.

In the morning he went to a tack shop. The riding crops were only eight bucks. He bought three. They had a sale on leather straps that were thick and heavy and would look much better against Kate's pale skin than they would around a horse. From there, he went to a butcher's and picked up ten T-bone steaks. At a liquor store, he chose a magnum of Californian champagne, a bottle of vodka for Kate and a bottle of Scotch for himself. Then he went to the supermarket.

Cole thought about flowers, but flowers smacked of 'courtship' and that wasn't their relationship. There was a sex-shop a few doors along. He'd never seen any underwear on Kate, not of any kind, so he skipped that and spent his money on vibrators and 'love oils'.

Kate had come more than four times with other men, had she? She was disappointed that her bottom's marks had faded by the next day, was she? He'd show her.

She was wearing jeans and a sweater when she opened the door. The jeans were so tight they cut up between the lips of her sex, showing a split bulge. Cole followed her wildly rotating bottom into the living room. She took the bottles and set them aside.

'Shall we open the champagne?' she asked.

'I'll open it when I'm ready. Take your clothes off, Kate.'

Kate gave him a quizzical look, but she obeyed, jeans first. Cole grinned when she had to pluck the crotch seam of her jeans out of her body's moist clutches. Kate took her time getting her sweater over her head. He suspected she knew how the position lengthened her torso and lifted her ribs, emphasising the contrast between her heavy breasts and her slender body. Perhaps she expected him to be overcome by lust and grab her. He was hard as Brighton rock but totally controlled.

She turned and posed as if waiting for applause.

Coldly, he told her, 'Kneel up on the armchair, facing the back.'

She climbed up, wagging her rump at him. His coolness seemed to be getting to her. Cole left her there and went to the kitchen. He unpacked his groceries, put eight steaks in her almost empty freezer and left two on the counter.

When he got back to her she was fidgeting. He let her wriggle while he opened the rest of his packages. A long strap, around her waist and the back of the chair, clamped her tightly against the battered leather. The back was the perfect height for her breasts to rest on. A shorter strap secured her arms folded across her back.

'What?' she asked.

'You'll see.' He found glasses, not flutes but quite good wine glasses, popped the champagne and poured. When he held a glass to her lips she drank but some spilled onto her breasts. He told her, 'Clumsy. You'll be punished.'

Kate dropped her eyes. 'Yes, Cole.'

His fist in her hair dragged her mouth to his. There was no tenderness in his kiss. It was an assault, crushing her lips against her teeth, exploring her mouth, sucking her tongue.

He showed her the longest crop he'd bought. 'This one is for your ass. This one –' showing her the shortest crop '– you will hold.' He put it between her teeth, sideways. 'When you can't stand the pain any more, drop the crop. You understand?'

She nodded, with apprehension in her eyes.

Cole arranged her legs on the seat of the chair to his satisfaction and, without a further word, began. His blows were clipped, never full force, but each one left a livid welt. He'd never done this before, outside his fantasies, so he followed the guidelines he'd read on the internet. Starting with the crease where her thighs met her bottom, he laid his strokes carefully, aiming to make parallel marks an inch apart. It wasn't easy. The fourth crossed the third and the fifth was at an angle. He'd get better with practice. The sixth was across the fullest part of her rump. He decided that she was too lean for him to go higher so he put the seventh below the first, high on her thighs. She was wriggling by then, twisting at her waist to look back at him. There were tears on her cheeks but she gripped the crop in her mouth desperately.

'There'll be marks, tomorrow,' he told her.

She nodded.

'Tender?'

Another nod.

'Good.' He set the crop aside. 'You'll feel this the more, then.' He slapped, hand open, hard across her bum's left cheek.

Kate jerked and whimpered.

Right cheek, left cheek, right again. He gave her twenty, slow and steady, before checking her pussy. It was swollen and drooling. A vein in its left lip pulsed. 'You get off on this, you little bitch, don't you?'

She nodded.

'How much pain does it take to make you come?'

She shrugged.

'We'll just have to find out.' He picked up his crop and rounded the chair.

When she saw where he intended to beat her she shook her head but she didn't drop the crop.

His first slash came down two inches above her nipples. The second landed on the upper edge of her areolae. Cole didn't have it in him to damage those ample mounds but he was determined she'd give up before he did. He stood directly in front of her, pointed his crop at her, and tapped the loop at its tip on her left nipple. Kate strained back, sobbing, but holding onto the crop. He tapped again to be sure he had his aim and distance right before bringing the crop whistling down. It was the loop, not the shaft, that hit her nipple, but it must have been agonising. Before he could relent, he

38

struck again, on her other nipple. She jerked so hard that the chair moved on its feet, but she still kept her grip on the crop.

Both nipples were bruised dark and as hard as nuts. His fingers tested them. Kate writhed. He walked around the chair again. Her knees had come together so he fetched more straps. One looped each ankle, then down to the chair's legs. Stooping, he put his face close to her bum cheeks. The welts he'd left were white ridges edged with purple. When he ran the flat of his tongue over them, she winced.

With the loop of the crop touching up between her thighs, he asked her, 'You know what comes next, don't you?'

She nodded.

'Do you want to drop the crop?'

Her head shook.

'Very well.' The crop slapped up. At first he made sure it was the loop that hit her pouting lips but when that failed to dislodge the crop in her mouth he extended his arm a couple of inches and moved it to the side. The crop's shaft was too cruel an instrument for him to use directly on her slit but the bulges to either side were puffy and less delicate. He alternated, short strokes, left and right. He'd hit Kate ten times when she suddenly bucked, gasping, and let out a curdled yelp. The crop she'd held clattered to the floor. Cole put a hand beneath her, gripped her entire sex and squeezed. She bucked again and again. Dewy fluid flowed into his palm. He held her, working her bruised flesh between his fingers until she subsided, gasping.

'So pain does make you come. So does being buggered. What else?'

Kate mumbled, 'My tits. If someone plays with them for a long time, I can come.'

'Want me to play with them now?'

'Too tender. Please don't.'

'Perhaps I'll be lenient with you. Perhaps I won't.'

He washed her tear-streaked face and unstrapped her, before helping her down with one hand in her hair and one steadying her shoulder. She sat, gingerly, on a kitchen chair while he broiled steaks and sautéed mushrooms. He set one place, for himself, and fed her from his overladen plate. Kate guzzled her glass of champagne so he rationed her. He wanted her mind to be clear.

'Come,' he said, when they had finished eating. Cole arranged her on her bed, face up, across the width, with one pillow under her bottom and another under her shoulders, close to the edge, so that her head hung down. 'You're going to get yourself off for my entertainment.'

'Yes, Cole.' Her hands went to her pubes.

'No.' He showed her two vibrators: one a jelly-textured imitation cock and the other small and blunt, with a flat ridged head. 'Use these.'

Kate licked her lips. 'How do I . . .?'

'I'll show you.' He put one into each of her hands. Being gentle, he parted her lips for her. His hand, over hers, guided the jelly up into her, angled to press against her G-spot. He dabbed lube – 'guaranteed to grow warm on contact' – onto her clit. A turn of each vibrator's base started them humming.

Kate said, 'Oh' and spread her thighs further.

Cole stripped and sat so that he was looking up between her legs. Kate manoeuvred the jelly a fraction and pressed harder on the clit-vibe. After a few minutes she was pumping the jelly in and out and grinding the other toy down. Her belly tensed. The long muscles in her thighs writhed.

'You like me to watch you, don't you, Kate?'

She mumbled, 'Yes.'

'You're a depraved little slut, aren't you?'

'Yes.'

'Sluts just want to come, Kate. Come for me. Show me what a nasty little bitch you are.'

She stabbed herself with the jelly much more viciously than Cole would have. Flecks of white froth appeared on her pussy lips. When she pushed in, they inverted. When she pulled out, they elongated, clinging to the plastic. After she'd jerked and shuddered through three climaxes she seemed to have trouble reaching her fourth. Cole knelt up on the bed, holding his cock where she could see it. He wet a finger in the foam she'd exuded and reached under her to put it to her anus. The damned thing actually worked on at his fingertip, trying to draw it in.

'You want my come?'

'Yes,' she moaned, tossing her sodden curls from side to side.

'You want it in your mouth?'

'Please!'

Cole chose his words for their crudeness. 'You want me to fuck your slutty face and fill your nasty mouth with my hot come?'

She humped violently. 'Please! Please!'

He rotated his finger, pressing the first joint into her anus. 'Tell me, Kate. Tell me what you want.'

'I want your big hard cock in my mouth, fucking it. I want to drink your come, every last drop.'

'Then come when I tell you. Three, two, one . . .' He rammed his finger into her rectum. Her belly rippled. She half sat up, grunting, and shuddered before flopping back. She was saturated in sweat. The clit-vibe fell from her hand. An after-convulsion ejected the foam-coated jelly.

Cole picked it up. 'Good slut. Now clean this.' He held the imitation cock to her lips. She licked and sucked voraciously, looking at him over it with wicked gleeful eyes. 'You do know how to treat a girl, after all, Cole.'

'I'm not done with you yet.'

He went to the side of the bed her head dangled over. One hand lifted her head by her hair while the other adjusted the pillow under her neck. He arranged her with care, so that her mouth and throat were in line, horizontal. Cole had to bend at the knees to get his cock down to the right height. Still holding her hair, he told her, 'Open.'

Her lips parted. He put his cockhead to them. Her tongue stretched out and lapped. A fraction of an inch at a time, he advanced. Her lips parted as his cock entered her mouth. Cole rubbed the head of his cock on the flat of her tongue before leaning closer. The sensation, glans sliding over tongue, was exquisite. For his own sake, he'd have been content to enjoy that until he climaxed but Kate needed to feel violated.

'Ready?'

She nodded.

He thrust, past the root of her tongue, urging into her mouth until he felt the tight constriction of her throat. His entire cock was in her. His pubic hair was touching her chin. Her nose divided his scrotum so that one ball hung to either side. Each breath she exhaled tickled his anus.

Cole was ready to pull back at the first sign that she was choking but when her throat worked, it wasn't because she was gagging. She was massaging his cock with it.

He released her hair. Her head wasn't going to move. He wet two fingertips in his mouth and put them to the bruised raspberries of her nipples. He rotated them gently. Kate winced but worked her throat harder and she tried to push back on the bed to take more of him into her mouth – except there was no more for her to take.

He rocked, slow-fucking her mouth, until the frenzy came over him and he thrust wildly, slapping her face with his balls. When he came, he doubted she tasted it. His jet squirted directly down her throat.

# Six

Cole was duty agent the next day, which meant staying in the office unless another agent volunteered to relieve him. It was a good time to get through paperwork or make phone calls. He made four, reaching two of his clients, then pulled the 'for sale' listings up onto his screen. In another window, he surfed the net for BDSM sites, specifically, those run by submissive women.

The things he'd done to Kate had fulfilled most of his wildest fantasies. The rest of his erotic dreams involved two or three women. Even if Kate was willing, where would he find them?

Cole's problem was that yesterday had been the most intense sexual experience of his life, but he was sure it wasn't the same for Kate. He was equally certain that to keep Kate happy, he'd have to do even kinkier things to her. How far did she want him to go? What more could a submissive masochist want that he'd be willing to do?

Some of the things his surfing revealed were obviously sick fantasies, concocted by illiterates. There were others, though, described and even pictured, that he hadn't considered a woman, no matter how much she loved to be hurt and humiliated, would enjoy. The authors of some of the sites seemed sane and intelligent.

He came across the phrase, 'safe, sane and consensual' again and again. That appealed to him. The 'rules' were explicit and made sense.

That was, provided the people involved were sane about their kinky desires. He knew he was. Was Kate?

She called him at two. 'I've got marks on my thighs and all over my bum.' Her voice was sulky but satisfied.

'You would have.'

'Cole?'

'Yes, Kate?'

'Tomorrow, maybe around four?'

He flipped open his daybook. 'Five-thirty,' he said, even though the entire afternoon was free.

'Yes, Cole. Cole?'

'Yes?'

'What will you do to me?'

He couldn't ask her what she'd like. That was forbidden by the dynamic of their relationship. He hedged with 'Something new.'

'What?'

His mind raced. 'You'll be restrained.'

'Yes.' Was there a hint of impatience in her voice?

'Your breasts need attention.'

'Yes, Cole. Will it be painful?'

'Yes.'

Breathless, she asked, 'Will there be marks?'

'Yes.'

'Oh. Cole, may I use those vibrators?'

'Now?'

'Please?'

His sweet perplexing slut, who'd complained – or had she? – about the bruises her old lover had left on the delicate skin of her breasts, was so excited by the idea that he was going to do the same that she needed to masturbate. Bitch!

In a frigid voice, he told her, 'No.'

'Just fingers?'

'No. No climaxes, none at all, until I'm with you.'

'You want me to be desperately horny, don't you?'

He didn't reply.

'You're cruel, Cole.' There was admiration in her voice. Cole liked that, but it put him under obligation to fulfil her expectations.

'Goodbye, Kate,' he said.

Debbie, the receptionist, brought him two envelopes, two commission cheques. On his way home, he deposited one in the joint account and opened a new account with the other. He avoided thinking about why.

That night, Janet told him she was up for a promotion so she'd need some new clothes. There was no use his pointing out that they needed all the money they had to pay bills. He'd tried that before. It just lead to open hostilities. It was better to live under the threat of war than with open conflict. What bothered Cole the most about their battles was the fear that one day he'd lose his temper, *his* way. He knew he'd never lay a hand on Janet but if he attacked her verbally, he could destroy her utterly with the power of his words. It was strange. With a woman he had affection for, who craved pain, he was a sadist. But it hurt him to say a harsh word to the woman he detested.

Kate greeted him with a bath towel wrapped so low around her spare hips that it barely covered her pubes.

'I haven't come, Cole,' she whispered. 'I used a new lotion.' Her fingers touched one breast to tell him where she'd used it. 'My skin is very soft.'

'And unmarked,' he observed. 'Good.'

'Thank you.'

He turned her, knotted a fist in her hair and propelled her into the dining area. Cole pulled a straight chair into the middle of the room and sat her on it. As she sat, the towel came loose, covering the seat, baring her. Kate put both hands in her lap.

'It's silly, but it embarrasses me a bit if I'm naked and you've still got your clothes on.'

45

'I know,' Cole said, though the thought had never occurred to him. 'Put your hands at your sides.'

He put his briefcase on the table and took his new purchases from it. She eyed them with apprehension but didn't ask any questions.

His hand on the back of her neck pushed her face down to her knees. 'Arms behind your back.' A strip of silk pulled her upper arms together until her elbows almost touched. From there, it went around her wrists and down, to be tied to the chair's legs, pulling her upright. With a hank of coarse hairy twine in one hand and a coil of soft white cord in the other, Cole asked, 'Which do you prefer?'

She frowned. 'It's up to you.'

It was the answer he'd expected but he watched her eyes as she looked from one to the other. He'd trained himself, when showing homes, to watch clients' eyes. Kate's told him she'd rather be bound by the crude twine. Of course. It was abrasive. It'd be more uncomfortable and would leave marks. He cut about ten feet off, using a pair of tailor's shears. When she saw those wicked blades, she swallowed and licked her lips.

Cole had read about 'edge-play'. That hadn't been in his mind, but . . .

He ran twine around her in the crease under her breasts, crossed it behind her and round her again, tight on her ample mounds' upper slopes. That tilted them up and projected them forwards. The long end came down beside her left breast from the upper strand, under the lower, below her breast, up over the top, down again, under her right breast and back to the top strand again. He pulled the loose end. The two encircling strands were drawn together. As he tugged, hairy twine slowly strangled her flesh. It sank in until most of it was invisible. Her voluptuous mounds became narrow-necked globes.

He went behind her with the twine held between his teeth. Cole's hands descended over her shoulders. He kneaded her breasts so deeply that he could feel the glandular structures compress and move between his fingers. He crushed, perfectly controlled. The pressure he exerted was enough to threaten damage but not so extreme as to do any. His hands urged blood towards her nipples. Kate crossed her legs and squeezed her thighs together. Her head lolled back with her eyes closed and her lips parted.

Cole pulled his twine hard and tied it off. He'd expected her skin to grow glossy from the pressure but instead, as her breasts turned pale purple, her skin turned matte, almost like velvet. Her veins stood out, pulsating ridges. 'Watch,' he told her.

Kate's head lifted. She gazed down at the engorged obscenities he'd turned her breasts into. He spread the blades of his shears and rested them on her breast, bracketing her nipple with sharp steel.

Her head flopped from side to side. 'Cole, Cole, please, no!' She was drooling.

Cole had no intention of cutting her. Kate got off on fear. He was indulging her. He lifted the scissors and closed them with a loud 'snip'. Turning them to hold the blades, he pushed the handles down between her thighs. 'Hold these.'

With deft speed, Cole pulled a nipple so that it was elongated. He wrapped its base with a twist-tie – stiff wire covered in plastic. Hurrying, he did the same to her other darkened spike. With the ties cutting off their circulation, her nipples turned into dark cherries, tight spheres perched on garrotted stems.

He had to move swiftly. Tourniquets shouldn't be left on for long. His fingernails 'pinged' both of her nipples at once. Kate jerked in her bonds. He kept pinging in a steady rhythm, watching her face. Her eyelids fluttered. A muscle in her cheek twitched. Her mouth was slack. She drew a rattling breath each time his nails flicked her.

Cole checked the clock. The ties had been on for over three minutes and he'd set himself a limit of four.

He pinched, twisting and crushing. Kate made a noise like an explosive cough, arched against her bonds, shuddered and relaxed.

Cole untwisted the ties from her nipples, snatched the shears from between her thighs and snipped through the twine.

She fell forwards into his arms. He held her tenderly until her juddering subsided and her eyes focused, looking up into his.

'I haven't finished with your tits yet.'

Kate frowned. 'I don't know if I . . .'

'I'm not going to hurt them.' Cole stood astride her thighs, unzipped and pulled his cock out.

Kate leant forwards, lips parted. He pulled her head up by her hair. Holding her there, he began to stroke his shaft, slowly. Her eyes followed. Cole divided his attention between watching the grooves he'd left in her breasts fill in, her nipples slowly regain their natural shape, and the longing in her eyes.

She was a remarkable woman. It was just minutes since she'd been wracked by an explosive orgasm but she seemed to be in a fever of lust again. She tugged against his restraining hand, mouth wide, tongue extended. Cole manoeuvred so that his cock touched the tip of her tongue, then bent it down to lightly brush a nipple.

'You want it, Kate?' he taunted.

'Yes!'

'Tell me, then.'

'I want your come, Cole. I need it. Give it to me.'

'You're drooling, Kate. What sort of a woman salivates at the sight of a cock?'

She looked up into his eyes. 'A slut, Cole. A horny slut. A bitch in heat. I'm bad, Cole. I'm a whore, *your* whore. Do me, Cole. Do anything you like to me. I deserve it. I *want* it. Treat me like the fucking bitch I am.'

Words have power. His words could control and they could destroy. Kate's words had a different strength. They could suck the come from his balls as surely as her mouth could.

Cole forced his cock down as he climaxed. His jism splattered Kate's left breast. He felt pressure in his chest, like a mighty shout demanding to erupt. He suppressed it. If he'd released it, he'd have betrayed the full extent of his glee. That would have given her power over him.

When his vision cleared, Kate was straining down to get her tongue to her breast. Cole lifted it gently on one palm and pressed down on the back of her head with his other hand. Her tongue slavered over her own bruised flesh, lapping his come into her greedy mouth. She couldn't quite reach the gobbet that drooled from the tip of her nipple. Cole contorted her breast in his hand so she could suck it off.

'Thanks!' She grinned at him. 'Are you going to release my hands?'

'No.'

'More?'

'Are you ready for more?'

'When I come that hard, I get a kind of high. The least little thing can set me off again. I really want more, please? Pretty please?'

He put his hand down between her thighs. The towel she'd been sitting on was saturated and aromatic. 'Just a minute.' Cole went to the bathroom and called Janet on his cell phone. His call was forwarded to her cell phone. She was at the mall, shopping. He lied that he was in the middle of a deal that could take hours and hung up. One of his women was happy doing what she liked best. That left him free to take care of his other one's needs. He stripped in the bathroom. That way, he wouldn't have to pause in whatever he was going to do to Kate. Now, how was he going to top what he'd just done? Foolishly, he'd thought that if the tit torture worked the way he hoped, she'd be sated. Luckily, he'd already made his plans for their next tryst.

Cole moved furniture with Kate watching, anticipation on her face. With a small table and a chair shifted, he had room to lug her sofa away from the wall. It had a deep seat and a low back. He'd been thinking about ways to use it since he'd first seen it.

Cole untied Kate and helped rub the circulation back into her arms.

'No more on my tits, please, Cole. I don't think they could take it.'

'Talking about "limits", do you know what a "safeword" is?'

Surprisingly, considering what an ardent masochist she was, he had to explain the concept to her. When he had, he told her that she had three words to remember: 'green' meant she was fine and he should continue at will; 'amber' meant she was on the brink and proceed with caution, please; 'red' signalled she was in too much pain or fear and please stop immediately.

'Are you going to try to make me say "red"?' she asked with relish.

'We'll see.'

'I won't say it.'

'If you need to, you must.'

'Yes, Cole.'

'Promise?'

'I promise.'

He stood her with her back to the back of the sofa. Her bottom was six inches higher than the seam in the leather. 'Hold on tight.'

She reached out to both sides and gripped the back of the sofa. Cole knelt and spread her feet wide. He ran his soft cord from a loop around her left ankle, behind the sofa's bun foot, around the other foot, and back to her right ankle. He pulled the cord. Her feet were tugged apart. When she was spread until her legs were a little over ninety degrees apart, he tied off the slack. Her bottom was perched on the sofa's edge.

'I can't stay balanced like this for long,' she told him.

'You won't have to.' He walked around to the front of the sofa and reached across the seat to grip her hair. 'Come back.' Cole lowered her by her hair until the back of her neck rested on the edge of the seat.

'I don't know . . .' she started.

'What colour?'

Kate shimmied to adjust her position before replying, 'Um, green, very green.'

'Good girl.'

Cole secured her arms to the front feet of the sofa, spread like her legs, and took a moment to contemplate his work. From head to hips she looked comfortable enough, despite sloping upwards. From where he was standing her legs were invisible. The skin on her lower belly and over her pubes was taut. Pale though she was, she was even whiter where her skin was stretched over the jut of her hip bones. When he returned to the back of the sofa, he saw that her weight had stretched the cord but, even so, her thighs were bent back from her body at an angle he'd have thought only a contortionist could have achieved.

'You're very limber,' he said.

'Thank you, Cole. I took acrobatics when I was young but I dropped out when my instructor –'

'Tell me another time.'

'Sorry.'

Cole laid the toys he intended to use on a side table. The lubricating lotion came in a squirt bottle with a phallic nozzle. He tested the lips of Kate's sex. They were sticky with her oozings. When he parted them and pressed them against her puffy pubes, they stuck there.

51

Cole admired the effect. She was pallid pink inside. Her glistening slot was bracketed by petals that shaded from pale rose at their deepest to purple along their edges. Her sex was a kite-shaped exotic flower.

Almost by reflex, he slapped up between her thighs.

'Are you going to beat me there?' she whispered.

'No.'

'Oh.' There was curiosity in her breathy voice.

'You'll see.' He squirted lubricant over the exposed inner surfaces until it ran down the crease of her bottom. Squatting to get on eye level, Cole inserted the plastic bottle between her inner lips until he felt the first obstruction, and squeezed it, varying his angle to coat as much of her insides as he could.

'Remember your words.' His forefinger slid into her as his thumb's ball rubbed up over the nub of her clit. He retracted, and probed with two fingers. Out again, then three, then four. She was elastic enough that four fingers of his flattened hand met no resistance until they were in to their last joints, when the width of his hand pressed up on her pubic bone. He pulled back and folded his thumb into his palm.

'Ready?' Without waiting for a reply, he pressed, slowly. When his knuckles met her outer lips, there was a resilient resistance. Cole leant in. His knuckles slid past the tightness. His fingers had room to wiggle. The tunnel of tight flesh opened out a little. More pressure put the tips of his fingers against the walls of a warm wet sac. Those walls felt slick but corrugated. The joint of his wrist lodged between Kate's lips.

Her belly was heaving. She was panting. Cole pressed on. Her labia were invisible, forced to invert. Her clit had been dragged down. It looked as if another straight push would take it inside her, out of reach. Cole rotated his wrist a little, slowly screwing his hand into her so that it didn't take her clit with it. The inside of Kate's sex was a clinging, muscular, rubber blanket. He wouldn't get deeper without risking damaging her. His fingers folded into a fist. His hand was a solid, knobbly lump, buried so deep that if he'd worn anything on his wrist, it would be scratching her.

'Light?'

'Green. Amber.'

Cole turned his wrist left, then right. Her flesh clung to his fingers. The base of his thumb must have been grinding on her G-spot. His hand was bathed in hot fluids that weren't the lubricant.

Kate mumbled, 'Amber.'

'Good girl.' He stretched sideways for the stubby vibrator. Her clit was pressing down on his wrist. Cole sandwiched it between his hard bone and the textured head of the vibe.

'Amber. Green. Amb –'

Cole's wrist rocked from side to side. A vein in Kate's groin pulsated. When he looked up, her tummy was rippling. She shook, wobbling her bruised breasts. Her gasps were open mouthed.

She convulsed inside. Cole was surprised by the strength of those inner muscles. They were clamping down on his hand with crushing force.

Kate let out one of those coughing barks that signalled her climax. She contracted as if trying to eject his fist. His hand cramped agonisingly. Cole's reflex was to snatch it back but, if he did, he'd likely damage her. With an enormous effort of will, he forced his hand to relax and drew it back slowly, unfolding his fingers when he could. It came out of her with an obscene slurp, followed by a gush of hot liquid.

On his drive back to the hell he called home, Cole decided that Kate probably wasn't any more insatiable than he was. He was seeing her every few days, not living with her. Both of them were coming out of periods of celibacy – though his was much longer than hers. It was only natural that they'd both be ravenous when they got together. Chances were, two or three intense sessions a week were all she needed. Kate needed recovery time more than he did. She had to heal.

Allowing himself to feel smug, it seemed to Cole that he was Kate's saviour. If she didn't have him to give her what she craved, she wouldn't be able to stop herself seeking another man – one who might be a brute who'd do real harm to her. That was the story of her life, wasn't it?

Which meant what? If he broke up with Kate one day, would that condemn her to dangerous abuse, as opposed to his safe sane sadism? Was he now as committed to her as he was to Janet?

# Seven

Over the following two months, Cole lived two lives. He visited Kate twice a week, sometimes three times. He always took her something, groceries and booze as a rule. As far as he knew, she lived on welfare cheques but offering her money would be crass, even if he did slip a few bills into her purse from time to time.

Kate never asked him to come again. He only saw her once that wasn't by his instigation. He'd been busy and was forced to neglect her for a week. That day, when he got into his car to go to lunch, she was waiting in it, wearing her shiny black raincoat.

'I've got an appointment in an hour,' he explained. His eyes roamed from her neckline to her hemline, seeking confirmation that she was naked beneath it.

'Can you make time to run me back to my apartment?'

'No problem.'

As soon as he was out of the parking lot, Kate turned to him and ducked down. Her fingers fumbled for the tab on his fly.

'I can't . . . There won't be time for . . .' he started.

'Yes, there will,' she stated, more assertive than he'd ever known her be.

Cole moved his seat back and drove with arms and legs stretched. Her head snuggled down between his lap and the steering wheel. He glanced down at the back of her head. 'I really don't think I'll be able to come under these circumstances, Kate.'

She didn't answer. Her hot wet mouth was busy, her head bobbing urgently.

Cole took a route that avoided trucks even though it was a longer way round. Kate proved her point. They were still a couple of miles from her apartment building when he flooded her mouth.

As she zipped him, she asked, 'Is it OK for me to take care of myself when I get home?'

'Yes. I'll come as soon as I can, Kate.'

'I know you have another life, Cole.' Nothing could have made him feel guiltier than her understanding words.

'What – what if I didn't?'

'I'd make you happy, I promise.'

As she got out of his car, she flashed her coat open long enough to show him one of the shorter straps he'd bought, buckled tightly high around one bare thigh. His heart melted.


At breakfast, Janet told him she'd got that promotion, with a nice raise in pay. She said that now she'd need a new car, to keep up with her elevated position. Cole asked her to wait until they'd paid their credit cards down a bit.

'I can afford a new car all by myself, now. I've worked out a budget. I can pay the mortgage, and a car lease, *and* all the bills. I don't need you, financially. You never make love to me any more. What bloody use are you?'

'You don't need me?'

She hesitated before saying, 'No.'

'Are you sure?'

'Yes.'

'Then I might as well move out.'

She barked a laugh. 'You need me, Cole. You can't survive without me.'

'I could try.'

'In your dreams.'

'Take the Buick today, if you're ashamed of the Horizon.'

'Trying to butter me up?'

When she'd gone, Cole called Kate. He spent most of the day sorting his books from Janet's and packing his clothes. It took four trips to transfer what he was taking to Kate's apartment. On the last, he tied his home office chair to the roof of the little old car. He turned out of his street as Janet turned in, driving the bigger and newer Buick. She didn't notice him.

By the time he finished unloading his last carton, Kate was made up, wearing her kimono.

'I've run you a bath,' she said.

'I take showers.'

'You're stiff from all that hard work and you're uptight from what you've done. A bath will relax you. *I'll* relax you.'

The water was hot and aromatic. He'd just sunk into it when Kate came into the bathroom, naked. She was carrying an enormous Scotch and an equally generous vodka.

'Lean back, close your eyes and rest.'

Cole let his head fall onto a plastic pillow. The glass touched his lips. He took a sip. Kate set the glasses aside and made lather between her palms.

'Leave everything to Kate.' One soapy hand found his cock. Leaning over him, Kate kissed him, her tongue stabbing between his lips in rhythm with her hand's pumping. She was right. She did relax him.

# Eight

When word that Cole'd left his wife got out, the other agents in his office started treating him differently. Doug, dour and rumoured to be henpecked, sought his company, mainly to bore Cole by going on endlessly about his 'big one'. Cole knew of several agents who were working on incredibly lucrative deals, some of them for years, that never materialised. Their dreams of 'big scores' kept some agents poor. They didn't have time to work on lesser sales.

Anthea was an older agent but stringily preserved, who boasted that if she met a man she fancied she tripped him and beat him to the floor. She started asking his advice about the technicalities of writing offers. She didn't need it. Anthea had been a successful agent for over twenty years. Now she thought he was available, she figured she'd 'trip' him.

When Debbie, the cute young receptionist, brought him paperwork, her soft breast inevitably brushed his shoulder. He was flattered but even if he hadn't had Kate, he wouldn't have taken her up on her unspoken offer. The girl was naïve. If she knew the sort of things he did to Kate, she'd likely flee in terror. He flirted with her, though. Real estate receptionists hand out office leads.

A year before, the thought of any kind of sex, with almost any woman but Janet, had excited him. Now, vanilla sex, even with a lovely young girl, didn't interest him one bit. Once a man has sampled exotic forbidden fruit he loses his appetite for bland dishes.

Life was good, except for Janet. Guilt towards her curdled in his gut. She helped him feel better by accosting him in the mall, dropping to her knees, promising him regular oral sex, but not buggery – she wasn't prepared to do that, even to get him back – if only he'd return to her. A week later she drove straight at him in a parking lot and dinged a Corvette. That confirmed his wisdom in leaving her. Janet filed for divorce. Cole agreed to what he wryly called a 50/50 split: she took the assets; he assumed the liabilities.

For almost a month, Kate was the perfect mate. She sashayed around the apartment, bubbling with glee that she was his. He had a woman whom he made happy, which, combined with copious kinky sex, made him feel complete. If he'd told her when to expect him, she had a hot meal waiting. If he couldn't predict his homecoming, she'd fry or grill something quick. Sexually, she was at his command but never demanding. When he came home in the wee smalls, exhausted but horny, a crook of his finger brought her mouth to his cock, following which she seemed content to take care of herself with one of the growing stock of vibrators he'd picked up for her.

From time to time, he found part-full vodka bottles hidden – under towels in the linen cupboard, in the toilet tank. He shrugged that off. She'd been through a lot. Now she had him, he was confident she wouldn't rely on booze so much.

The first time she asked for attention was at the end of a week of him working fourteen-hour days, making money but neglecting her. He stepped out of the shower to find Kate waiting, naked, with a tub of butter in her hand.

'I have to leave by nine,' he explained.

'I know. It won't take a minute.'

She slathered butter over his cock, turned, knelt up on the toilet seat and made an obscene display of working two greasy fingers in and out of her bottom hole. Head on the tank, she reached back and spread her cheeks. Cole entered her and pounded, hard and fast. It took him under five minutes to climax.

'I hate to leave you like . . .' he started.

'I can take care of myself. Go sell a house.'

He left the apartment glowing with love, or a good imitation of it.

Cole got back early that day. He could have worked later – real estate agents always can – but he wanted to make it up to her for leaving her hanging that morning. Kate had anticipated his wish. No sooner had they eaten than she asked him, 'Do you really love me, Cole?'

His stomach turned over. When a woman asks that question, it usually means trouble. He told her, 'More than ever.'

'You don't show it, lately.'

'I don't?'

'Not *real* love. Show me now?'

'Of course.' He stood up, meaning to take her in his arms and whisper romantic words into her ear, but she flounced from the room. Cole followed her to the bedroom. What she meant by 'show me that you love me' was immediately obvious. The leather straps were laid in a neat row across the foot of the bed. She'd spread a cloth on the side table and arranged all her vibrators, lotions and his three crops on it. To Kate, you showed her your love by restraining her and beating her.

It had been a while. Cole was beginning to miss it. 'Strip.'

'Yes, Cole.' Her robe – all she wore – fell to the floor.

He laid a strap across the middle of the bed. She was light and she loved to be manhandled. Cole scooped her up and dumped her unceremoniously so that the strap was beneath her waist. A second strap secured her ankles together. He took her feet in one fist and doubled her up until her knees touched her shoulders, with her heavy breasts compressed between them. One handed, he pulled the strap that was under her up, over the undersides of her thighs, just below her knees, slotted the end through the buckle and pulled it tight. Kate was trapped, folded, bum tilted up off the bed. A third strap, threaded through the one around her ankles and tethered to the head of the bed, held her in place.

'You've wanted this for a long time,' he said. His fingers unbuckled the belt around his waist and pulled it from its loops.

'Your belt,' she gasped.

'Whenever I wear it, from now on, I'll remember what I'm about to do to you.' He reached between her thighs to massage her sex, squeezing it between his fingers, palpitating it so that the lips of her sex projected up between her thighs. 'This will be extremely painful,' he warned her.

'Yes, Cole.'

He put his belt buckle in the palm of his hand and wrapped the strap around his fist until only a foot was loose. 'Remember your words.'

She nodded.

Cole let the end of his belt dangle. It tickled the wet slot that bulged up between her thighs, trailed between her legs over her folded tummy and tapped lightly on each nipple. He raised it high above her. Her thighs tensed. His arm went back. When the belt's end came down, it didn't land where she'd been prepared for it, on her sex. It slapped across her right breast, precisely on her nipple.

Her bottom jerked up. The belt descended again, left nipple. Kate bit her lower lip. Cole stepped back. The belt came down across the backs of her legs, with more force than he'd intended. When he inspected her puffy sex, the red line that extended across both thighs had left an indentation across her malleable lips.

She was panting. Her eyes were glazed and her mouth was slack. Kate was in some sort of masochistic nirvana where only the pleasure of pain could reach her. Elated by his power, Cole brought the belt down again and again, criss-crossing her thighs, flicking the soft mounds of her breasts, finally concentrating on the pulpy fruit of her sex. When she was striped bright pink from behind her knees to her bum, with barely a streak of pale skin showing between the welts, he tossed the belt aside.

Kate humped her sex up. The bitch hadn't had enough.

Cole dared not use the belt any more. He squirted lube on his left thumb and plunged it into her bumhole. Gripping her like that, his thumb buried in her rectum and his fingers spread over her tailbone, he cupped his right hand and slapped a rapid tattoo on her wet sex.

Kate moaned and writhed. Her legs fought the strap that bound them to her torso. Their muscles strained. Strong leather bit into the backs of her legs. Cole was inexorable. Only two things could stop him – her using 'red light' or her orgasm.

After an age, she coughed out the strange barking cry that signalled her climax. Cole's palm was soaked. Her lips twitched.

Cole checked the bedside clock. Kate had been restrained for forty minutes. No one should stay bound in one position beyond an hour. Swiftly, he released her ankles from the bed's head and flipped her bodily. Cole stripped and climbed onto the bed. Kneeling, as she was forced to do, her bottom was too high. He pressed it down, presented his cock to her pucker and plunged into her.

'Relax,' he said.

Using her knees as a fulcrum, Cole rocked Kate up and down, masturbating himself with her bottom. His cock was steely and his lust was overwhelming but he was racing the clock. Somehow he couldn't quite get there. With just a couple of minutes to go till the hour was up, he gave in. Flipping her again, he released her legs and flopped back.

'You didn't come,' she complained.

'You can take care of that.' He dragged her face to his cock by her sodden hair and relaxed with his hands behind his head. What her bum had failed to do, her mouth accomplished.

# Nine

In the following weeks, Cole discovered that although Kate liked pain, being restrained was at least as important to her, perhaps more so. That was a relief, in one way. He'd worried about escalating the sadomasochism without harming her. On the other hand, she recovered from bondage faster. Now she expected sex of some sort every day. Even if he'd caned her or used his belt on her, the next day she still wanted to be bound and fucked.

Cole left her in bed every morning. He knew what time she got up because that's when she called him to ask what he had planned for her that night. It was never before three in the afternoon. He kept her drinking under some sort of control in the evenings but he discovered that often, after he'd fallen into a sated sleep, she hit the vodka hard.

It was ironic. He'd gone from a woman whose sexual demands were boring and infrequent to one he could barely keep up with. Cole searched the internet, and his imagination, for new ways to confine his lover. Her being so flexible helped him vary their scenes. Kate could be tied in positions that most women couldn't have endured.

Cole found the 'worry balls' in Chinatown. They were two-and-a-half inches in diameter, stainless steel, without visible seams, with ball-bearings inside. The theory was that you rolled them in your hands and were soothed by the action and the way they chimed. Cole had other ideas for them.

They'd had supper. He'd showered and Kate went to bathe. She returned naked, her way of telling him she expected to be fucked.

'Sit on the ottoman,' he told her.

She sat, expectant. He took her hair and lowered her backwards to rest her head on the cushion he'd set in place on the floor. His hands spread her thighs wide. Cole started with the squeezy bottle. It'd long run out of the original lubricant but he'd refilled it with a mixture of baby oil and peppermint essence. That worked better and was cheaper than the contents it'd come with. He squirted it onto and into her. It was something he'd done a dozen times before but it never failed to excite him. There was something about her glistening slippery folds that thickened his cock and tightened his balls. Her pussy was *his*, to use at will. The warm wet mushiness of it called to his cock, his mouth and his hands. Heaven, to Cole, would be to fuck one woman while eating another, with his fingers working inside two more.

He put his palms on each side of her vulva and pressed to spread its lips. Kate opened, from the little fleshy cup at the bottom, where her juices pooled when she was excited, all the way up to the shy nubbin of her clitoris. Its tiny pink head emerged from its sheath. Cole rubbed the ball of his thumb over it, marvelling at how it elongated to meet his touch. A woman had to feel much the same sense of power when her caresses coaxed a cock to grow. It was an 'I-did-that' thrill. How could a man not want to play with pussies? They were intricate living toys that he knew he could never tire of, except immediately after coming. Even then, Cole could enjoy fondling Kate's because she was always up for more, unlike Janet, who'd wanted nothing after one of her tight little orgasms but to be left alone. Giving pleasure was as much, or perhaps more, fun than being pleased.

Tonight he had plans that he was sure would please them both. She didn't know what he had in mind, so she'd have the added thrill of surprise. He knew and had been thinking about it all day, so he had the fun of anticipation. That was fair.

Cole retrieved the balls from where he'd hidden them under a cushion. When he touched the cold metal of one of the balls to her humid opening, Kate twitched.

'What's that?' she asked.

He made the ball chime, to deepen her puzzlement. His fingers revolved the ball as he pushed. Kate opened for him. When it popped past the restriction of her lips, she gave a little jerk as if to explore what it was he'd inserted.

'It's heavy.'

'Yes, they are.'

'They?'

He began to work the second ball in after the first.

'How many?'

'Just two.'

'Oh. I think two will fill me.'

'Perhaps, unless I decide to buy more.'

'Of course. Sorry.'

The second ball clinked against the first. Cole pressed. There was some resistance but he knew how much Kate could take. He persevered until her lips closed around the second metal sphere.

'Hold them inside you and stand up. Don't drop them.'

Normally, Kate would writhe to her feet off the ottoman. With the bulky masses inside her, she rolled over and clambered up gingerly.

'Is it hard to hold them?'

'Yes, Cole.'

'We'll see. I'll be disappointed if they fall. You wouldn't want that, would you?'

'No, Cole.' There was concentration on her face. Her belly was taut.

'Rotate your hips for me.'

Kate made a little hula movement. Cole strained to hear a chime but he didn't. 'Can you feel them move?'

'I think so.'

'Gyrate.'

Kate did a tentative bump and grind until she became sure that she could hold the heavy mobile load, gradually becoming wilder. Then, 'Oops!' She folded at her narrow waist. Her forehead creased, and then cleared.

'You almost dropped one,' Cole accused, grinning.

'Almost. Not quite.' There were beads of sweat at her temples.

'If you do, this game's over.'

'Please, Cole?'

'Fetch the box of straps.'

He watched her bottom as she left the room. It was clenched tight. Cole congratulated himself on devising this game. Kate was having to work for her thrills.

When she returned with the box, he sorted the straps by length. A long one went around her waist, looped around both her arms, then had to be strained to buckle in the small of her back. He turned her a couple of times, admiring the way leather bit into her, creasing her skin and cinching her middle. He put the next strap around her thighs, high up, just inches below her sex.

'That'll help you hold them.'

'Thank you.'

Another strip of leather held her legs together just above her knees, with the last, with brass studs – it'd been made to collar a large dog – snug around her fine-boned ankles.

Cole scooped Kate up, set her knees on the ottoman and lowered her head until her face rested on the cushion on the floor. Her bum was high. Her back sloped down at forty-five degrees. Kate's perch was unsteady. He held her in place with one hand gripping the strap around her waist. Cole raised the other.

'This'll be interesting,' he told her. His hand slapped down on her left buttock. 'Did that move my little balls?'

'Yes.' The way she hissed told him it was true.

His hand rose and fell. With each slap, the balls clinked together and chimed. He couldn't hear them. He could imagine them, though. He visualised them rolling about inside that muscular sac. Their vibrations wouldn't do a lot to her. Their movements would. It would feel unnatural, heavy objects moving inside her, bumping and distorting her insides. She was likely clamping on them, trying to hold them still. He made his slaps irregular to frustrate that.

Kate blurted, 'I have to come.'

'Then come.'

'I might push them out.'

'You won't. Come. Do it now!' He moved back, still holding her so he could watch.

Her lips fluttered. They made an obscene noise as they squirted thick froth.

Cole reached for the peppermint lube, steadying Kate between his knees. It was cold on his cock. As he rubbed it in, his glans started to tingle. His cock grew even more rigid. Cole needed it to. It was going to have to overcome more resistance than it had ever met before.

He put its head to Kate's pucker.

'Amber!'

'What is it?'

'It's going to be very tight.'

'I know.'

'Please, slowly?'

'I'll be careful. Give me a "green" when you're ready.'
Cole was elated. She rarely called 'amber' and had never before done so in anticipation.

Kate's shoulders rose and fell. She was taking deep breaths, preparing herself. After a while, she squeezed out a 'green'.

Cole pressed forwards. She opened easily for him until his cock was three inches up her rectum. There, the narrow tube was compressed flat by the upwards pressure of the lowest ball.

'Colour?'

'Green. I can take it, Cole. Do me hard. Make me take it.'

He gripped her hips and pushed. Kate made little 'oh, oh, oh', noises. Perhaps what he was trying to do was impossible. The resistance seemed impassable. She was slippery but incredibly tight. He pulled back an inch. His fingers dug into her flesh. His muscles tensed. With a surge, Cole pushed with his hips and pulled with both hands. The obstruction moved, forced down by the power of his cock's thrust. It had to be doing devastating things to her but Cole was committed. It seemed he felt the ball roll as the head of his cock shoved past it.

He took a deep breath. 'Colour?'

'Um – give me a minute.'

He waited while she panted.

'Green, Cole. If I scream, take no notice.'

He rocked, rolling the ball that was pressed to the underside of his shaft, butting the head of his cock against the constriction of the second.

'Now, Cole. Now.'

His fingers felt the bones of her hips. They'd show bruises later. His thighs braced. Looking down between their bodies, he saw that only three inches of his stem protruded from the dilated indentation of her anus. Three inches. He could do that.

He heaved. His pubes smacked the base of Kate's spine. The second ball hadn't depressed downwards like the first. It'd moved to one side. Guilt stabbed into him. In his lust, he'd likely shifted her internal organs. Cole tried to remember which ones flanked a woman's vagina and rectum but nothing came to mind.

The little bitch moved! Slowly and gingerly, her hips rotated. The slut was savouring her terrible impalement. So be it. Moving no more than a couple of inches with each thrust, he worked his cock to and fro inside her. Surely, even if she wasn't in agony, the obscenity he was committing had to devastate her? It seemed not. Apparently gaining confidence, she bucked back at him. Two-inch thrusts weren't enough for her. She lunged forwards and plunged back.

'Oh fuck,' she gasped. 'I've never ... This is so ... Oh, Cole!' She convulsed.

Almost relieved that Kate's ordeal had achieved its desired effect, Cole tugged his cock from her anus. She toppled and rolled onto her back, gasping for air. He watched in fascination as a sliver of silver showed between her lips, grew, and rolled out. Kate turned over again and heaved herself to her hands and knees, facing away from him.

'Watch this,' she said.

The second ball emerged and plopped to the floor, ejected by the powerful muscles of her vagina. 'You need a handjob,' she told him.

Later, when they lay in the warm cocoon of mutual satisfaction, Kate whispered, 'I need the pain, Cole.'

'I know.'

'I need to be protected.'

'What scares you, Kate? What do you want me to protect you from?'

'Me, Cole. Protect me from myself.'

# Ten

Cole set his signs out and opened up 1207 Pinetree Court. It was the show house for a new, small sub-division, an 'office' listing. For agents, the value of open houses isn't from selling them. People rarely buy the open houses they visit. The pay-off comes from picking up potential buyers.

Willy and Bill came through at about eleven. They were both in working clothes, dusty and paint-spattered. They didn't look like potential buyers of high-end homes but Cole treated them like they were.

'I like the way it's decorated,' Willy said.

'Thanks.'

'What do you think of cream walls with chocolate trim?'

'Nice, but not how I'd decorate a home for sale.'

Willy gave Bill a meaningful look. To Cole, he asked, 'How would you do up a house that you wanted to sell?'

'Champagne or beige carpet, everything else off-white. Keep it bright and neutral. Maybe some mirrors if it was a small place.'

'Why?' Bill asked.

'Place 'em right, you can make the rooms look bigger.'

Willy pulled out a tattered spiral-bound notebook and scribbled in it with the chewed stub of a pencil.

'You're renovators, aren't you?' Cole asked. 'Buy junk homes, fix 'em up and sell 'em?'

Both men shrugged.

'How's business?'

Willy's face twisted. 'The last two, I reckon we lost money.'

'Who's your agent, helping you buy?'

'Whoever has the "for sale" listing.'

'No wonder you lose money.'

'What do you mean?' Bill demanded.

'You're buying through agents who are working for the vendors, against you. You should find a friendly agent who'd work for *you,* and stick with him.'

Willy squinted at Cole, sizing him up. 'If it was you, how'd you work it?'

'Me? The new listings are released at seven in the morning. By half past, I'd have gone through 'em. If any looked promising, I'd go take a look right away. Any I liked, I'd work out what I could sell them for if they were done up right. I'd deduct the legals and commissions from that, then the cost of fixing them up, including a fair wage for whoever did the work. Then I'd take off what the profit should be. I'd offer what was left, no negotiating, take it or leave it. Half the time there'd be no deal. The other half, my renovators would make money.'

Bill snorted. 'A real estate man who'd work for his commissions? I don't believe it.'

'Try me.'

Willy mused, 'Maybe we will. Take my number. If you see anything that looks likely, call me.'

Cole did. His plan worked. The commissions were small but regular. The only problem was that he had to be at the office by seven every morning, no matter if he'd worked till gone midnight the night before and staggered home, to spend hours taking care of Kate's urgent needs.

He became adept at that. He learnt that she was more masochistic than submissive. She was less interested in having a man to worship than she was in being restrained and forced to endure pain. The restraint was her priority. If Cole devised a new way to contort her, she was hissing with lust by the time he'd tied the last knot or done up the final buckle. If it hadn't been dangerous, he thought he might have got away with binding her and going for a nap while she worked herself into a climax.

He got close to that, one night.

The dining-room chairs had vertical rungs at their backs. Cole set two of them a little apart, backs to each other at ninety degrees. He laid out his toys on the table.

'What are you going to do to me, Cole?' Kate asked.

'This.' He wrapped an arm around her thin waist and heaved her off her feet. 'Legs up, and spread.'

Her legs made a horizontal 'V'. He plonked her down, each thigh on the seat of a chair, bum and pussy suspended between them. A strap around her body and threaded through the backs of the chairs made sure she couldn't fall. Cole secured her arms behind her with another strap. She'd feel precarious but it'd be safe. He showed her a fistful of spring-loaded clothes pegs. 'You know what these are for?'

She shook her head.

'One, here.' A peg closed on her left nipple. The pressure squeezed its base almost flat. 'Painful?'

She nodded.

'The next one, here.' Wooden jaws crushed her left nipple. 'I've five left. Do you know where I'm going to put them?'

'My . . . my pussy?'

'Clever girl.' He squatted and rubbed an inner lip between his fingers until it engorged. 'Colour?'

'Green. Uh!' Her grunt came as the peg nipped her tender flesh. Each time he added a peg, she gasped and humped but she didn't evoke 'amber'. With four pegs decorating her lips, Cole went lower and nuzzled into her. Kate's clit was already proud, waiting for him. He sucked and licked, then masturbated it between finger and thumb as if it had been a tiny cock. When he felt it was as exposed as he could make it, he pressed the last clothes peg to the base of its shaft and slowly let the jaws close.

Kate yelped. 'Amber, amber!'

'That's the last peg. Enjoy.'

He sat at the table behind her, where she couldn't see that he was watching her closely, and timed five full minutes. When he returned to her and knelt to inspect her tortured flesh, there was a drooling string of her cream from it to the floor.

He snatched all five pegs away at once. Kate screamed. His hand came up, slapping hard and fast between her legs, again and again, until she coughed out a climax.

Her compressed nipples were deep-crimson balls. His hands massaged her breasts, urging blood towards her nipples. She writhed in her bonds. The pain had to be lancing into her flesh. Her contorted face turned up, eyes begging. Cole made crushing fists. The grip of the clothes pegs couldn't withstand the pressure. They popped off. As the blood rushed into her breasts' peaks, Kate came again.

When she'd recovered, Kate asked, 'How do you want to fuck me?'

He shook his head and unbuckled her. 'Maybe tomorrow.'

Kate started dropping hints about him taking her out. The first evening he had free, he let her choose where they'd go.

'A drive-in? I used to love drive-in movies, when I was young. My first time was in the back seat of a Ford Woody, at a drive-in.'

That contradicted both of the other tales she'd told him about how she'd lost her virginity but he let it pass.

She packed snacks so they wouldn't have to buy triple-fried translucent fries and oiled-leather burgers at the concession.

The show was a creature-feature marathon, which suited Cole's guilty taste for the macabre. Kate didn't care what was showing. It was the act of going she wanted. She wore her short black raincoat so Cole knew what to expect.

As soon as the floodlights went off, she produced a vacuum flask. Cole tried the paper cup she handed him. He'd expected it to be alcoholic but, by the taste, she'd brought a quart of vodka diluted with an ounce of orange juice. He'd sip through the first movie and abstain after that. Kate'd likely be stewed by the time the third came on. He'd be able to go home and to bed.

The first movie was one of the *Dr Phibes* movies. He was a fan of Vincent Price. Phibes's mysterious assistant made it even more watchable. Vulnavia, dressed in all white, was playing a white violin, when he felt Kate's hand in his lap. Well, the idea was for Kate to relive drive-ins past, so her groping wasn't unexpected. Her long thin fingers plucked his cock from his pants. Cole checked out the windows. No one was around to see in and he'd parked well away from the path to the concession. When Kate took his hand and tucked it under her raincoat, on her pubes, he didn't object.

Her fingertips tickled up his length. 'Slow and easy, please, Cole? Let's not come till the very end.'

Cole dabbled two fingers in Kate's wetness. Kate withdrew her hand, peppermint-lubed her palm and took hold of him again. His hand squeezed her mound. Hers slithered up and down his shaft. It was very pleasant: watching Phibes's elaborate death traps work with impossible precision; sipping vodka; enjoying the buzzing tingle as Kate massaged peppermint into his

75

cock. She was right. They should enjoy the gentle pleasures for as long as they could.

He glanced sideways. Kate's head was thrown back. The flask was tilted at her lips. By its angle, she'd drunk about half, minus the cup he still had. Cole turned his attention to the screen.

Vulnavia was posed with one long shapely leg bent through the slit in her dramatic costume.

Kate's hand applied more pressure and moved faster. 'She turn you on, Cole?'

'She's very attractive.' He paused as a happy suspicion grew. 'How about you, Kate? Would you bed her?'

'If I was drunk,' she admitted.

Cole grinned. That was as close to a 'yes' as a foreskin is to a cock. 'Did you ever, with another woman?'

'Once.' Her words were mushy. 'Maybe twice.'

His cock twitched in Kate's hand. Since Kate, he'd done everything he'd ever dreamt of doing, with one woman. Was it possible that one day, eventually, there might be two female forms for him to play with at once, if just for one night?

He half watched the movie, half fantasised about Vulvania and Kate, together, with him master of ceremonies. As he dreamt his erotic dream, his fingertips found Kate's clit. They closed on its shaft and worked it with the same rhythm as she was stroking him.

She shook the last drops from the flask into her mouth. 'Damn!'

He handed her his cup.

'Y'good to me, Cole.' She bent, almost toppling, to set the cup on the floor. 'I be good to you.' Kate put her head into his lap and took his cock into her mouth. 'Cock,' she mumbled. 'Cole's cock.'

He started the engine and pulled away slowly. The cup on the floor fell over, spilling vodka onto the mat. Kate slurped and bobbed on him all the way out of the drive-in and for a mile beyond before she passed out.

Cole reached down and extracted his cock. Sometimes, in her sleep, Kate ground her teeth.

The second time Cole tried to take Kate out was when Anthea gave him two invitations to a preview of a new wine bar, which she'd arranged the lease for. For a full week, he debated taking Kate before finally deciding that she deserved a treat. Unfortunately, there was an unlimited supply of free wine. After an hour Kate was dishevelled: blouse gaping and skirt hiked high. Cole had to go to the men's room. He got back to find her sprawled across an embarrassed man's lap. Cole half carried her outside, held her head while she vomited into some bushes, slung her over his shoulder and dumped her, snoring, onto the back seat of his car. Somehow he got her up to the apartment.

The next day he had two small deals on the go, both for Willy and Bill. The first went quickly but the second dragged on till two in the morning. When he got home, Kate, naked, was reeling drunk again, or still.

'Do me, Cole,' she demanded, a bottle of his Scotch, half empty, dangling from her fingers.

'You're drunk.'

The bottle fell. Cole retrieved it before too much gurgled out.

'If you was a man, you'd do me, drunk or not. You're not much of a man, are you, Cole? Last night, when that man tried to rape me, you let him get away with it.'

Cole could have devastated Kate with a scalpel-precise analysis of all her conflicting tales of rape and abuse. He wasn't that cruel.

Kate spread unsteady legs, pubes thrust forwards, and jerked two fingers up inside herself. 'You're a soft man with a limp dick, Cole. Can you get it up for this? Fuck me or take your belt to me. Beat the crap out of me if you like, but be a *man* for once.' She advanced on him, masturbating with one hand, the other fumbling for his belt.

He put three fingertips between her breasts and gave her a gentle push. She staggered back and toppled over the ottoman. Sprawled, she glared up at him. 'A man'd teach me a lesson. You're not a man, are you. Safewords! Who the fuck wants to fuck a fucking wimp what doesn't *make* me do what he wants. You don't like it that I take a little drink? Why the fuck haven't you beat it out of me? You got fists, Cole? Why the fuck haven't I ever seen you make one?'

If she could have seen through his trousers, she'd have seen his fists. They were clenched deep in his pockets. The rage in him wanted to beat some sense into her. She'd never had it so good. Now she was throwing his protection away.

Cole went to the bedroom. His suitcases were under the bed. An hour later, Kate was snoring on the floor and he was lugging his possessions out of the door.

# Eleven

Cole found a motel with a neon sign that fizzed. The furniture was finished in cigarette-marked Formica. For three days he tried to get drunk and failed. Each glass of Scotch only served to chill him deeper. It seemed to him that something deep inside had died. He'd done his best, first with Janet and then with Kate. He'd tried to give them what they needed from him. Neither had reciprocated. Yes, he wanted sex, kinky sex. He'd also wanted to protect his women and make them happy. They'd seen that as weakness.

It wasn't just women. Just a month before, there'd been his experience with Aaron Kobolski. The grizzled old man had decided, after forty years in Canada, to return to his roots in Poland. His house was almost impossible to value. It was the only one on the street that wasn't 2,000 feet and typically suburban. Aaron loved wood. He'd panelled his 1,200 foot home with pine: walls, floors and ceilings. His oversized lot was bare concrete, without as much as a shrub. In the back, he had a workshop/garage, two-floors high: an asbestos-sheathed eyesore. Cole had listed it at the highest price possible. A week later, there'd been an offer, full price. The purchaser was in the aluminium siding business. He wanted parking and storage space. As for the asbestos, whatever he bought he'd planned to cover with his own product. Every house has an ideal purchaser, who'll overpay. By the wildest luck, he'd come along. Cole was sure that if he hadn't, the house would have stuck on the market for months and sold for ten thousand less.

A week after the deal closed, Aaron filed a complaint against Cole. He claimed that Cole had underpriced his property to make a quick commission.

No matter what you did for people, by luck or by sweat, they didn't appreciate it. So be it. Cole returned to work with an icy void where his conscience had been.

When Cole had first arrived in Canada he'd done a favour for the friend of an acquaintance. Del Barker had a restaurant to get ready for opening and a deadline to meet. There'd been delays. Cole, and a few others, donated a week of grunt-work. The place had been ready on time. For sixteen years, Cole had sent Del Barker Christmas cards, just in case the old favour might be rewarded, someday. The day arrived.

Del told him, 'I'm looking for a location, somewhere nice, maybe a historic building I can renovate.'

'How much?'

'Up to eight-hundred thousand, including renovations.'

'Let me look around. I'll get back to you.'

There was a Victorian brick building, on Lakeshore, that had started out as a coach works. At some point, someone had divided it into ten offices. Nine of the offices were vacant but weren't being advertised. Cole called on the owner. Yes, he'd like to sell – and would – once the last tenant's lease expired. Cole got a listing, conditional on the tenant moving out within three months. An hour on the net informed Cole that the tenant was a registered nurse who couldn't be making any money. She did grief counselling for free and charged couples for her relationship advice, based on her studies in psychology, though she hadn't taken her doctorate.

Cole's view was that women who run small businesses that can't make money do so because they are in bad

80

marriages. They're looking for fulfilment. Their husbands subsidise them to keep them out of their hair.

Cole dropped by Nurse Margaret Furley's office. She was in her fifties, with a plain but pleasant face, no make-up. Her uniform was the kind nurses don't wear any more – starched cap and collar, narrow blue and white stripes, broad elastic belt. She was the type you wouldn't look at twice but if you did you might notice that beneath the severe uniform she was solidly plump but quite shapely.

Cole announced, 'I don't need counselling. I'm here with an ulterior motive.'

Her eyes widened.

Cole continued, 'I can sell this building if you move out.'

'I have a lease.'

'With eight months to run. I want you to break it. There's an office vacant about a block south of where I work, on Brand Street. It's the same size but a hundred a month cheaper. It doesn't have the exposure this one does. You don't need exposure for your work.'

'You're very direct.'

'I'll manipulate you with my words but I won't lie to you.' Saying that, Cole realised it was true. Lying was a strain and it'd got him nowhere. He'd faked loving Janet. He'd exaggerated his affection for Kate, even to himself. From now on, he'd use everything he had to get people to do as he wanted, except lie to them. It felt as if a load had been lifted. He said, 'Tell me about your work.'

'You're a strange man, Mr –?' he handed her his card '– Cole.' As if floodgates had opened, she told him what she did to help people through grief. Cole listened with growing respect. He didn't have a lot of time for do-gooders. Most of them had hidden agendas. Margaret seemed to be an exception. Subconsciously, she might be filling a void in her own life but she genuinely wanted to help people.

81

'How about the marriage counselling?'

She was less sure about that.

Cole let her stumble on for a while before interrupting. 'Isn't sexual incompatibility a major source of problems in marriages?'

She nodded, biting her lower lip.

'Do you have qualifications in that area?'

Her head shook as she told him, 'I've read a lot.'

'But practical experience?'

'I was chaste when I married my husband, thirty years ago.'

'And you've been faithful. Has your sex life been fulfilling?'

Margaret looked defiant as she told him, 'My husband has a heart condition.'

'Does that mean you aren't getting any?'

She squared her shoulders and gave him a scolding 'Cole!' in a voice she might have used to reprimand a naughty child.

He got to his feet. 'Come here, Margaret.'

Looking nervous and puzzled, she stood up and rounded her desk. Cole put one arm around her and tilted her face with his other hand. 'I'm going to kiss you, Margaret.'

'But . . .'

Her lips compressed as his brushed them. He ignored that rejection and nibbled at her lower lip.

'Please . . .' she started.

His tongue slid into her mouth. She stiffened but almost instantly relaxed. After a few moments of submitting to his exploration of her mouth, she kissed him back, almost sobbing. Cole felt a sense of satisfaction. Margaret had a healthy appetite but she'd been starved for years, maybe decades. All she'd needed was a little push.

He held her back a little and looked into her hungry eyes. 'I want to see your body. Don't move.' He went to her door, turned her sign to CLOSED and locked it. She was in the exact spot he'd left her, shivering, with her arms folded across her bosom, when he returned. Without a word, he moved her arms to her sides and began unbuttoning her uniform.

'What are you going to do to me, Cole?' she whispered.

'I'm going to give you orgasms.' His fingers unclipped her belt.

'Orgasms?'

'Yes, plural.'

'I've never ...' She paused. 'So that I'll give up my lease?'

'Partly. Partly because I'll enjoy it. Partly because you deserve to be fucked.'

Her eyes opened even wider.

'You don't like that word, "fucked"? I only use it in context. It's a perfectly good word, used correctly.'

'Yes, Cole.' She repeated 'fucked', rolling it around her mouth like a delicious candy.

He knelt to undo her last button. Margaret was wearing pantyhose, which he detested. It wasn't the right time to instruct her. She needed her confidence boosted, not undermined. His fingers rolled the ugly garment, with her plain cotton panties, down to her ankles, then off, along with her sensible shoes. Her skin was dilute beige, totally uniform, no lighter at her intimate parts, no darker where it was exposed more frequently. Margaret's legs tapered from sturdy thighs to trim ankles.

She had both hands over her sex.

'Modesty isn't allowed,' he told her, and moved her hands away. The vertical crease was very straight, very neat and closed, almost virginal. It was partly veiled by fine brown silky hair that looked freshly brushed. Her belly was a gentle curve, punctuated by a navel that would have held a robin's egg.

'It's embarrassing,' she said.

83

'What is?'

'Me being naked when you're not.'

Cole rose. 'You aren't naked, yet.' He took her uniform from her shoulders, turned her, undid her unattractive bra and tossed it onto the desk before turning her to face him again. 'Now you are.'

She trembled. As Cole shed his own clothes, Margaret asked, 'Am I really doing this?'

'*We're* doing it,' he corrected. 'What I'm doing to you I can do because you allow me to.'

Her breasts were plump but hadn't sagged when he'd taken the bra away. Her areolae were dark and large, covering half her breasts. Her nipples were chocolate-dipped strawberries. Once she was naked, he cupped her breasts. They had a delightful heft, as if Margaret's flesh was denser than other women's. He smoothed the balls of his thumbs over her peaks.

Margaret looked down between their bodies. 'You're . . .'

'Erect?'

'Yes. Why?'

'Because you are a lovely, sexy woman, and I'm going to fuck you.'

'Am I bad, Cole?'

'Allowing a man you met an hour ago to strip you naked? That's "naughty". "Bad" is what I am going to teach you to be.'

'Oh!'

He led her to an old psychiatrist-style couch and sat her down, while he remained standing. Her face was six inches from his rampant cock. 'Look at it, Margaret. Touch it. Get to know it.'

She looked up at him with enormous eyes. 'Do I dare?'

'Yes.'

Her fingers, tentative and trembling, reached out. They stroked his skin delicately. One hand cupped his balls.

'You have a nice touch,' he said.

'Do I?' She stroked him with more confidence.

'Use your other hand on yourself.'

'On myself? How?'

'You've never masturbated?'

'No.'

'Poor thing.' Cole squatted and pushed her back to lie on the couch. His hand eased her knees to each side. She was almost vibrating with tension. 'Play with your breasts while I take care of you down here.'

She cupped her voluminous flesh, two fingers of each hand plucking her nipples. Cole made spider-fingers up the insides of her thighs. He caressed the creases of her groin, eyes intent on her plump pussy. If it was reacting to his touches, it was internally. He wet a finger and traced Margaret's crease. Little by little, it eased apart. Cole leant in to get his lips to the glistening slit.

'Oh! Do men really do that?'

'This man does.' His tongue wormed into her. To Cole's surprise, Margaret's feet came up off the floor and spread apart. She reached out to grip both ankles and rolled back, spread like a frog, heels as high as her hips.

'You're supple.'

'Yoga.'

'I promise you, I'll take full advantage of your flexibility.' His mouth returned to its feast. He paid her little compliments from time to time, to reassure her. A woman who's never been eaten always has doubts about her flavour and aroma. His fingers parted her wider as he searched for her clit. It wasn't as high up her pubic bone as Kate's and was deeper between her plump folds.

When his tongue found the shy polyp, Margaret went stiff and shivered. 'Oh God! Oh, oh dear. Oh! I never dreamt . . .'

Her appreciation spurred Cole's efforts. His tongue flickered, fast and furious, whipping Margaret into a squealing climax. As she juddered, he rubbed the pulpy mass behind her pubic bone, drawing out her pleasure.

'No more! I can't take any more!'

'Yes, you can.'

Cole heaved her bodily to her feet and threw himself full length down on the couch, on his back.

'What?' Margaret asked.

'You're going to ride me.'

'Oh. I think I'd like that.'

'Then try it.'

Margaret threw a leg over Cole, leaving the other foot on the floor. His cock lay on his belly. She looked at it as if waiting for it to change angle.

'You have to steer it,' he said.

'Oh.' She took a firm grip and directed it straight up. 'Will I be able to take it?'

'Let's see, shall we?'

Her hips lifted and descended. Margaret had no problem accommodating his full length. Cole found it very pleasant, having his cock in a fresh pussy. In many ways, most are alike once you're in them, but there are subtleties that a discerning cock enjoys exploring. Cole lay back and let Margaret's movements reveal the differences between her sex and Kate's. He hardly remembered what Janet's had felt like.

It was refreshing, having a woman gyrate on him, expecting nothing and appreciating everything. Margaret's starched cap was lopsided on her hair now and looked likely to fall. Her breasts hardly jiggled, though she was getting frantic. He put his hands up to remind himself of their resilience. Margaret's looks were deceptive. She appeared to be softly plump but her flesh had the firmness of rubber. He squeezed one breast, its nipple pinched between his knuckles. Her torso undulated. That deep navel disappeared between two folds and then emerged, almost protruding at him. She was

86

working, hard. It seemed that every muscle in her abdomen was contracting and expanding.

The poor woman was getting desperate. Cole understood. Her clit, high and deep, wasn't getting the friction it needed. He put a hand down to where he entered her. Two fingers insinuated up along the underside of his cock. Margaret hadn't flooded with lubrication but she was moist inside. He withdrew damp fingers and sucked one.

'Delicious.'

Her eyes grew wide with delighted shock. They grew even wider when he put the second finger to her mouth. Her lips closed on it and pursed as she sucked.

'Tasty?' he asked.

She nodded.

'Do you want to come?'

'I don't seem . . .'

'You will.' He put his hand down again. His thumb, ball up, worked between them. 'Grind on that, Margaret.'

Her eyes closed. Her head fell back, shedding her cap. Her hips, pressing down as hard as they could, rotated twice then bumped. Margaret babbled, 'Oh, Cole, oh, Cole,' over and over. Beads of sweat appeared between her breasts. The tendons in her neck became tight cords. She was on the edge, straining to fall over it.

Cole decided to be merciful. The fingers of his free hand gripped the solid resilience of a dark-brown nipple and crushed it.

Margaret flopped forwards at him. Her hands slapped the couch to either side of his head. She glared down at him, mouth working but wordless.

Cole twisted and pinched. Her thin high scream shocked his ears. Margaret collapsed on him, sobbing, 'Thank you! Thank you!'

He let her rest but his cock, twitching inside her, reminded her. 'You haven't?' she asked.

'Not yet.'

'But you must.'

'I will. Would you like to watch?'

'Watch?'

'Watch me come.'

'Please.'

'Then you'll have to get off me.' He rolled her aside to tumble to the floor. She sat up and stared at his stiff glistening cock, fascinated. He said, 'Another time, I'll teach you how to fellate me.'

She nodded, looking thoughtful. 'Now?'

'You wouldn't be able to watch if my cock was in your mouth. This'll be "fellatio 101". Rest your head here.' He patted his thigh.

Margaret nestled her cheek on his leg, watching his cock intently. Cole stroked himself, long gentle strokes at first, becoming shorter and harder and faster until the muscles in his thighs clenched and he released a long squirt that flopped down, spattering his skin from his belly to his shoulder.

'There's a lot of it, isn't there,' she mused.

'My tribute to you, Margaret.' He scooped a tiny droplet up on one fingertip and presented it to her lips.

After she'd sucked it clean, she said, 'I thought it'd taste bad, but it doesn't.'

'You like the flavour?'

'I'm not sure. I'd have to try more.'

'Maybe next time.' He eased her head off his leg and swung off the couch.

'Cole? I'm ready to do as you ask. I'll move.'

'Don't tell me that yet. On Thursday, I'll show you that new office. If you like it and still want to, tell me then.'

She grinned. 'Before or after you fuck me, Cole?'

'How about between?'

# Twelve

Cole met the Carters at an open house. They knew exactly what they wanted in a home. That can be a blessing or a curse. If buyers have no idea what they want, an agent doesn't know what to show them. If they have too many rigid demands, what they're determined to find might not exist. In those cases, some poor schmuck shows them twenty or thirty homes before they finally realise they'll have to compromise. When they do, they don't want to admit it, so they buy through another agent. The first agent has wasted a month of ten-hour days.

Mrs Carter was crazy about her two toddlers. She wanted a bungalow close to a school and within walking distance of a nice safe park. Mr Carter wanted to buy near the city's eastern border, close to the highway, to keep his commuting time down. Cole's problem was that there was only one park in that area and it was surrounded by two-storey homes.

He picked them up at nine and showed them three houses that were overpriced. That was so that the house he intended them to buy would look like a bargain. He took them to it by a circuitous route so that they had no idea where they were. It was a sprawling ranch. The back garden shared a fence with a school. Toddlers could be lifted right into the schoolyard. The park was less than a block away. Mrs Carter loved it.

Cole bowed his head. 'I'm sorry. I showed you this one to be sure I understood what you wanted. You can't buy this one.'

'It's ideal,' she said. 'Why can't we buy it?'

'Location. We're central here, not east. I've timed it, just in case. It's a full eight minutes further west than your husband would like to be.' Cole shook his head sorrowfully. 'It's a shame, Mrs Carter, but you really can't expect the poor man to drive an extra sixteen minutes a day, five days a week, just so you and your lovely children can enjoy all the amenities you want in safety.'

Mrs Carter looked at Mr Carter. Mr Carter sighed and said, 'Draw up the offer.'

Before his conscience froze, Cole would never have played husband against wife. He'd neglected a powerful tool.

Mr O'Hara chain-smoked. Mrs O'Hara detested the filthy habit. She nagged her husband about it through the first four showings. Mr O'Hara tried to change the subject to his favourite topic – growing vegetables – but to no avail.

Her eyes lit up when she saw the kitchen of the fifth home.

Cole said, 'Why don't you wander around and see where you think your furniture would fit? I'll take your husband into the back garden so he can enjoy a cigarette.'

Both of them gave Cole grateful looks.

In the garden, as the husband lit up, Cole stooped to a plot of freshly turned earth against the house's back wall. He picked up a clump of dirt and crumbled it.

'What're you doing?' Mr O'Hara asked.

'I was wondering what would grow here, so close to the house.'

'There? Ideal for tomatoes. South-east exposure, you

see. No wind, lots of sun. Dig in some peat moss and a bit of cow manure, perfect.'

'You think?' Cole asked, putting doubt into his voice.

'Big Boys, alternate with Red Rockets. Two crops. I tell you, come back in six months and I'll show you tomatoes as big as basketballs.'

'Then we'd better hope your wife likes the inside, right?'

Cole thought he was on a roll with the O'Haras but the man was one of those unreasonable bastards who insist on low-balling. Cole had known vendors flatly refuse to sell at any price after what they considered insulting offers. Cole tried to talk him up but the man was adamant. Luckily, Cole'd had the foresight to warn the vendors this could happen.

He told them, 'We'll mark it back at your very best price. If they don't accept it, I'll tell them you refuse to look at another offer.'

He walked in on the O'Haras looking doleful and shaking his head. 'Sorry, but you've lost it.'

'What do you mean?' she demanded. 'We've just started negotiating, haven't we?'

Mr O'Hara said, 'I'm not paying a penny more.'

'Exactly what I told them,' Cole said. He looked at Mrs O'Hara. 'It's a pity you don't smoke.'

'What?' she screeched. 'It's a filthy –'

'You see,' Cole interrupted, 'I've worked it out. The difference between their lowest figure and your highest, added to the mortgage, comes to the price of a pack of cigarettes a day. If you smoked three packs a day, Mrs O'Hara, like your husband, you could cut back by a pack a day and it'd buy you your home.'

She turned on her husband.

He said, 'Where do we sign?'

# Thirteen

Cole helped Margaret into his car. She wore no pantyhose. Her shoes were new, with little heels. She learnt fast. As he drove, he moved her skirt up a little and put his hand on her bare knee. She started at his touch but moved her thighs apart. He didn't take advantage. Imagining his fingers slithering over her skin would have more effect on her than real caresses.

The office was almost finished being redecorated. The walls were off-white. The windows were large. There was new broadloom on the floor. The place was empty except for a stepladder that was anchored to a radiator. It was sturdy. Cole had checked that earlier, when he'd left his briefcase there.

'What's not to like?' Margaret asked. 'Show me the lease.'

'Don't rush. I told you what we'd be doing, other than business.'

She blushed. 'I wasn't sure . . .'

'I keep my promises.' His fingers worked down her buttons and belt.

'Where? I mean, there's no couch or anything. The floor?'

'The last time I tried that I had raw knees for a week.'

Her bra was pale blue, with lace trim. Her panties matched. They weren't the sexiest undies he'd seen but she was trying.

'What then?'

'We have these steps.'

'How do we . . . I mean . . .'

Cole kept kissing her as he freed her breasts and eased her panties down to her knees. Stepping back, he told her, 'Undress me.'

It was cute the way she did it. As his shoulders were bared, she planted chaste little kisses on them. She did the same for his chest, all the way down to his belt, but as she eased his pants down, she kept her lips and eyes above his waist.

'You've seen my cock before,' he said. 'Look at it.'

Her eyes dropped. 'Oh! It's so nice. It's even nicer than I remembered.'

'You may kiss it.'

She pursed her lips and pecked her way along its rising length without opening her mouth.

'Shy?' he asked. Cole dropped a hand to her mouth and parted her lips with an insistent thumb. 'Tongue,' he commanded.

She poked it out, hesitant. He wagged his cock, slapping the flat of her tongue.

'Should I suck you?'

'Later. Turn around. Climb up two steps.'

Margaret peered down at him over her shoulder. 'I don't see how . . .?'

'You will.' Cole adjusted her position with firm hands. He wanted her to hold onto the steps, upper body parallel to them, bottom pushed out and down. 'Hold that pose, exactly.'

Posing her was a minor exercise of domination, but he enjoyed it. With her lush body contorted to suit his fancy, Cole ran his hands up her legs from her ankles to the generous curves of her bottom.

'The way you've put me,' she protested. 'It's embarrassing. It's . . .'

'Obscene?' he finished for her. 'Yes, it is. Margaret, you are many women.' He hefted her breasts on his palms. 'You're a kind nurturer. I'm sure that you're a dutiful wife and mother. Right now, though, you are a bitch in heat.' He alternated plucking and strumming her nipples. 'I'm releasing the hot little slut in you.'

Her head dropped, as if in shame, but she whispered, 'Thank you, Cole.'

'I'm going to do some things to you that you might consider perverted. "Perverted" is fine, so long as it's fun. Let yourself be a horny bitch, Margaret, but if I do anything, anything at all, that troubles you deep down, ask me and I'll stop. Do you understand?'

She nodded.

Cole crouched behind her and parted her buttocks with his palms.

'Oh!'

'What is it?'

'You're looking at me *there*.'

'Yes, I am, and I like what I see.' He pressed his face between her cheeks and stretched his tongue to the crinkle of her anus.

Margaret gasped, 'Oh' several times, but she pushed back, impaling herself on his wet squirmy tongue. His fingers moved beneath her. One hand's fingers explored her insides. The other's burrowed between her fleshy lips, searching for her shy little clit.

'This is so bad,' she said with wicked glee in her voice.

'Bad is fun, isn't it?' Cole resumed his triple assault, intensifying, strumming her clit, stretching her sex, stabbing her bottom with his tongue.

Margaret tensed, made a strangled cry, and relaxed. Cole's fingers, inside her, dabbled. She wasn't saturated in there but she was wetter than last time.

She lowered one foot to the first step.

'No. I haven't finished with you in that position yet.'

He fetched lube from his case. When he squirted it into her bottom, she jerked. 'What are you doing?'

'Making you slippery.'

'Are you going to put it in there?'

'Yes.'

'Will it hurt?'

'It might, at first. If you fight it, it will, so relax.'

'Will I like it?'

'Some women can't stand it. Some like it OK, once in a while. Some women, once they've tried it, can't get enough.'

'What kind am I?'

'That's what we are going to find out.'

He steered her bottom lower, spread his feet, hunched down and humped up.

'That's not my . . . That's my . . .'

'Your pussy, not your ass? I know. Pussy first, Margaret.' He ground and thrust a dozen times. The more excited she was, the easier she'd take being buggered. When Margaret was quivering between his hands, he withdrew and lubed his cock.

'Ready?'

'I don't know.'

'I think you are.' His thumbs spread her bum cheeks. Cole's hips swayed, wagging his cock to line it up. He leant in, butting his plum against her tight pucker. Gentle pressure lodged his cock in place without penetrating her.

'It's up to you, Margaret. When you're ready, push down on me.'

'You do it.'

'Don't argue. On three – one, two, three.' He cheated a little, pulling down on her hips, but without enough force to compel her.

Margaret's bum bobbed down, hard. The head of his cock sank in deep enough that the muscular ring closed behind it. That sight, a distended anus, impaled on his shaft, was one he'd never tire of.

Margaret bobbed again, squirming, driving his cock in deep.

'You horny little bitch!' Cole exclaimed.

'It hurt a bit, going in, but I'm getting used to it.'

'In that case . . .' He began slow pumping, driving to his hilt, pulling back until her anus was a tight ring around his cockhead. 'Play with your clit, Margaret.'

One hand dropped from the steps to cup herself. Delicate fingertips toyed with his swaying sac. 'Hold me steady, Cole.'

A second hand joined the first. He had her weight in his hands under her bottom and on his cock. Margaret frotted her clit as their combined efforts raised and lowered her. Cole began to sweat. It wasn't an easy position to fuck in. Fortunately, before his back gave out, she screamed her climax.

They both fell to the floor, panting.

'Can I sign the papers now?' she asked.

'Yeah.' He crawled to his briefcase.

'And then you promised to teach me how to fellate you.'

'Just so I don't have to stand up.'

# Fourteen

The sale of the building that Margaret's office had been in closed. Cole banked the biggest commission cheque of his life. Smaller deals were closing once or twice a week. He used the Horizon as part of the deposit on a 'previously enjoyed' Lexus with tinted windows. He didn't enjoy living in a tatty motel but when he moved, he wanted it to be to something he couldn't afford yet, like a condo apartment in the Tiara Towers.

Debbie, the receptionist, plonked the obituary section of the paper on his desk and stayed there, leaning over, hands flat, arms slightly pressed in to deepen her cleavage. Cole admired it. She usually wore that blouse with just the top two buttons undone. Today it was three. He was sure she'd undone the third for his benefit. When he reached for the paper, the back of his hand brushed the peak of one pretty breast.

'Sorry.'

'That's OK, Cole. Cole, if you ever miss home-cooked meals . . .'

'Thanks. Maybe I'll take you up on that someday.' Cole allowed himself social lies. He'd never get involved with the girl but a flat 'no' would hurt her feelings. While she had hope, she'd continue to give him preference on the leads. He hoped he wouldn't have to go further than 'accidentally' brushing her breast to keep her expectations alive.

One obituary caught his eye. It was in larger print, with a picture of the deceased. Daniel Silvetti was survived by Olivia Silvetti and her sister, Portia. The wording was peculiar. If Olivia had been his wife, why hadn't it said so straight out instead of by implication? The way the obituary was phrased, someone wasn't being forthcoming.

Cole Googled 'Daniel Silvetti'. He'd been a successful investment broker. His address was given as Tiara Towers, with no number. Cole tingled. Tiara Towers! It was like an omen, or something.

He went to Debbie's desk and stood behind her, where she'd know he was looking down her blouse.

'Yes, Cole.'

'Um, sorry, I was distracted for a moment. I need a phone number. It's probably unlisted.'

'Give me the name and address and I'll see what I can do.'

Cole laid a fingertip on her nape. Debbie shivered. 'I'd appreciate it, Debbie.'

The Silvettis' number was on his desk the next morning.

'Hello?' a subdued contralto answered.

'Olivia Silvetti?'

'No, it's Portia. Who is this?'

'I'd like to offer my condolences.'

'Thank you. Were you a friend of Daniel's?'

'No. Everyone in the business community knew and admired him, of course, but I can't claim to have been his friend.'

'So what can I do for you?'

'I'd like to do business with you and your sister, someday. Right now, I'm offering my services, no obligation, in the hope that when the time comes that you need someone in real estate, you'll remember me.'

'That's refreshing. We've had dozens of calls offering us help since Daniel passed, all with hidden agendas.'

'My "agenda" is on the table.'

'That's why I haven't hung up. Exactly what "services" are you offering, "free of obligation"?'

'You'll need an evaluation of your apartment to settle the estate. If I give you one, it'll be lower than the one the tax department arrives at. That could save you money.'

'We might be willing to talk about it. Tonight?'

'No. I need to prepare if I'm to talk sense. I need your full address, for a start.'

'Penthouse one, the Tiara Towers. Is that enough?'

Cole swallowed. The Tiara Towers were twin highrises. Each building had one penthouse that covered an entire floor. The Silvetti home had to be worth millions.

'That's enough. Seven, tomorrow evening? Do I need an access code?'

'The concierge will send you up. *Au revoir.*'

Cole looked up the registered title to penthouse number one. Strangely, only Daniel's name was on it. If he'd lived in it with his spouse, she'd be included automatically. That made for some interesting speculation.

Cole spent the afternoon shopping for new clothes, from the skin out. He already had one pair of really good shoes. New ones would betray his finery as fresh bought.

The concierge showed him to a scented elevator that was lined with moiré silk and pink mirrors. The muzak was Chopin. There was only one button. Cole pressed it and was whisked up to the fortieth floor. When the doors opened he stepped directly into the suite. Two diminutive ballerinas greeted him. Their perfectly oval olive-skinned faces were discreetly made up. Olivia's midnight hair cascaded to her waist. Portia's was short, in a quirky geometric cut that had likely cost more than his new suit. They wore identical little black dresses that brushed their nyloned knees and V'd at their throats to deeper than the pert nipples that poked at clinging knitted silk jersey. Either they'd dressed up for him or this was how they lounged about. He suspected the former.

Cole glanced about the room, absorbing its impressive dimensions so he'd feel more confident in it. He said, 'I'd like to look around, first.' He deliberately omitted a 'please'.

Olivia drawled, 'Help yourself.' Both women walked elegantly, on teetering-high heels, to a couch that could have seated eight.

Cole found four full bathrooms, in onyx marble and what he suspected was gold plate. The baths were sunken. There were separate showers in each. Two had bidets. In the en suite to the master bedroom he found a shaving mug and soap, an old-fashioned cut-throat razor and a well-used strop. Daniel must have been very macho.

There were four bedrooms in all. Three were large. The master was enormous. One was obviously a guest room, luxurious but impersonal. Two were feminine but when Cole checked the walk-in closets, all the clothes he saw were for winter, and it was July.

The master bed was one-and-a-half times king sized. There were two couches and three club chairs, all heavy and dark-brown leather, very masculine. One walk-in was full of men's suits. The other was the size of his motel room. Three walls were lined with racks of feminine garb, mostly frivolous and sexy. The fourth was mirrored. It was the twin shoe racks that interested him the most. They weren't divided by style. The one on the left had as many heels and as many flats as the one on the right. Cole picked up two identical pumps, one from each rack. There was a one-size difference.

He returned to the drawing room. The top of a baby grand was covered with silver-framed photos. He picked one up. 'You three made a handsome trio,' he remarked. 'You were very close, weren't you, *all three of you.*'

Portia looked at the floor between her toes. 'He knows.'

Olivia's eyes met Cole's, defiantly. 'Do you?'

'Yes.'

'Are you offended?'

'No.' Cole shrugged, mentally. So what if Daniel had married one sister and slept with both? Lucky him!

'It was better, socially, if people assumed I was his wife, not his sister.'

'I understand.' And now he did. Not only had Daniel slept with both sisters, but he was their brother. The trio was kinkier than he'd suspected. It *had* to work in his favour.

'Let me explain,' Olivia started.

'There's no need.' He stared pointedly at the coffee table. 'I see you ladies are drinking.'

Portia looked up. 'Sorry. Would you like a sherry?'

'I prefer Scotch.'

'Of course. That's what Daniel always drank. Very masculine. Is Johnnie Walker acceptable?'

Cole nodded. As Portia poured his drink, he said, 'You girls have lost the man in your lives. You must feel that, greatly. It's hard to lose someone you love, especially your lord and master.' He braced, ready for a rebuff for using that loaded phrase.

Olivia's eyes narrowed. 'You're very understanding.'

Portia handed him a crystal tumbler with two amber inches and added, 'He would be, Olivia. Can't you tell?'

'Yes. He shares some of Daniel's *special* qualities, I believe.'

Using his most portentous voice, Cole said, 'I'll protect your interests to the very best of my abilities, for as long as you need me. I pledge that, on my honour.'

They nodded solemnly.

'You will be guided by me. I can't fill the void that Daniel has left but I can make your transition to a new life easier. Now tell me what your immediate plans are.'

Olivia explained that they intended to sell up and move to the West Coast, where they had a cousin who was *'sympatico'*. Cole could imagine what that meant. Now they couldn't fuck their brother, they were headed to another relative's bed. Maybe he'd have to modify his plans. He was dark, like them and their dead brother, but he wasn't a relative.

He talked, authoritatively, about real estate and death duties. He told them that he'd list the apartment, exclusively, so he'd have full control. Whatever the offer, he'd tell the right buyer that it had to be one price officially but part unofficial, in cash. That'd reduce the taxes.

'Isn't that illegal?' Portia asked.

'Yes, but I'd risk it, for you and to cheat the taxman.'

'But . . .' Olivia started.

'Just do as I tell you, *exactly* as I tell you, and I'll look after everything.'

Both murmured, 'Yes, Cole.'

'Portia, you will clear your clothes and shoes from the master bedroom. I don't want anyone to suspect the true relationship you three shared. We don't want gossip.'

'Yes, Cole.'

'Now, about your happiness. Daniel would expect you to grieve but he wouldn't deny you the comfort of affection.'

Olivia looked at him. 'Meaning, Cole?'

'Hug your sister. Give her a kiss.'

The women moved together and put their arms around each other. Their lips brushed.

'Properly,' he told them.

Their lips meshed. Cole caught glimpses of their tongues as they savoured each other's mouths. He strode to them, lifted Olivia's hand and placed it on the almost imperceptible swell of her sister's breast. Their lips parted. Both turned to look at him with hooded, speculative eyes.

102

'Will you be staying a while, Cole?' Olivia asked.

'No,' he said reluctantly. 'I have work to do, on your behalf. Instruct the concierge that I'm to have free access to the building. Meanwhile, comfort each other in every way you can.'

Portia gave a timid little grin. 'It won't be the same without Daniel.'

'He'll be with you in spirit. I'll be back.' He did the best he could to hide his raging erection as he made for the elevator. Riding down, he punched the air and allowed himself an exultant 'Yes!'

Bedding sisters had been his fantasy since puberty. The ones he'd dreamt up were oriental bisexual contortionist twins but the Silvetti sisters were close enough. It'd been obvious he could have stayed the night; but he'd left. Cole wondered why. Perhaps he wasn't confident he could handle the situation? Perhaps he felt he should do something *for* them, before he did things *to* them. Whatever, when the time was ripe, it'd be an amazing experience.

He spent the next morning researching and drawing up a listing contract that gave him as much control as was legal. In the afternoon he bought a pair of grey flannel slacks, a blue serge blazer and an Irish tweed sports jacket. He'd have to look very successful, considering the clientele he'd be working with.

At six he called on the sisters. They were still in black – diaphanous peignoir sets. With a dry mouth and an aching-hard cock, he had them sign his documents and made his escape. Perhaps tomorrow?

Cole's hundred-dollar bill made sure the concierge would remember him. Back in his dismal motel room, he cursed himself. He could have been romping between satin sheets with two eager playmates but there he was, alone and horny. It was too late to see Margaret. She wasn't in the same class as the sisters but she'd developed a voracious mouth, under his tutelage.

He thought about ordering a pizza but he'd gained five pounds from living on fast food. He needed more exercise. Thinking that reminded him that the Tiara Towers had a spa and recreation area. He had access. It'd be exercise and research at once.

An hour later he marched past the front desk in shorts and a T-shirt, carrying his gym bag. 'Evening, John,' he said to the uniformed man behind it.

The spa was enormous and empty. He did fifty lengths of the Olympic-sized pool. It was a good start. Wandering through the maze of exercise machines, his-and-hers saunas and fully equipped free-weight rooms, he came to an area with four pool tables and three table-tennis tables. He bounced a ball on a beautifully balanced paddle while he debated the merits of playing snooker solo.

'Hello, stranger!'

He turned, feeling guilty. The woman looked about forty but her body was twenty years younger. The indentation that ran down her lithe torso from beneath a cropped top to the waistband of a brief pleated skirt spoke of thousands of 'crunches'.

'Just moved in?' she asked. Her hazel eyes were directed at his bare legs, or a little higher.

'I'm not a tenant,' he confessed. Cole fished a card case from his hip pocket.

'Real estate? Peddling one of the apartments?'

'The penthouse,' he announced.

Her eyebrows rose. 'The twisted sisters' place? How interesting.'

'You know the Silvetti family?'

'Know *of* them. They're recluses – well, they would be, wouldn't they?'

'They would?'

'Very close, those three. I've never known siblings so close, so *loving*.'

Cole grinned. 'You know, then.'

'Everyone here does. Everyone's curious, especially me. Daniel was a handsome man. His sisters are dolls, like Dresden or something.' She licked her lips.

'My relationship with them is professional.'

'But you're tempted, I'm sure. Who wouldn't be?'

Cole bounced the ping-pong ball on the table.

'Looking for a game?' the woman asked. 'I'm Melinda, by the way, Melinda Southern.'

'I wouldn't mind a game, Mrs Southern.'

'Not "Mrs". There's no Mr Southern. Call me Melinda. So, what shall we play for?'

'I don't make bets with women, Melinda. I couldn't take their money.'

'Not even bets for forfeits?'

'What did you have in mind?'

'If I beat you, you dish me all the dirt on the Silvettis.'

'And if I win?'

Her hips moved, subtly. 'What do you suggest?'

Cole took his time looking her over, from her designer running shoes to her bubbly blonde head, letting his eyes dwell on small, high, hard and un-restrained breasts, thinly covered by her top. If she'd flinched under his suggestive scrutiny, he'd have backed out, but she sucked her tummy in and set a manicured hand on one hip.

He held the paddle up. 'I suspect that you're a bad woman, Melinda.'

'So?'

'If I win, ten strokes with this, on your pretty bottom.'

She laughed. 'Are you serious?'

'Very.'

Melinda shrugged, moving her nipples against the cotton. 'I'm good,' she warned.

Cole encouraged her with, 'And I haven't played in years.'

'Then you're on.'

Cole really hadn't played in years but in the army he'd played a lot, against young soldiers who were fit, fast and strong.

Melinda served, low enough that the ball barely cleared the net and fast enough that Cole had to dance back to get a swing at it after it just clipped the edge of the table. She was eight points ahead of him before Cole's eye and arm came back to him. He'd have liked to excuse himself by claiming that her jiggling breasts were a distraction but Cole never made excuses.

His paddle sliced down, putting vicious backspin on the ball. Melinda was ready for where she thought it'd go but it died as soon as it hit the surface. She swung at nothing.

From then on, Cole was merciless. The ball became *his*. It hit the table where he aimed it, to within an inch. If her return was high, he was across the table, slamming it down, impossible to reach. His paddle flashed, imparting top or bottom spin at will. One of his smashes hit her left breast. Melinda rubbed the spot ruefully and for an unnecessarily long time, holding his eyes with hers.

'Sorry if I hurt you,' he apologised.

'I can take a little pain.'

Cole's cock twitched. Her invitation couldn't have been clearer if she'd been naked and kneeling, presenting him with a crop.

'I need three points,' he observed. He got them with three rocketing serves that left her standing, flat footed.

'I think I've been hustled,' Melinda complained, pouting prettily.

'Double or nothing?'

'Oh no! I know when I've met a master.' She paused. 'At table tennis.'

Cole rounded the table, paddle wagging in his hand.

'You aren't joking?' she asked.

'No.'

'Here? Now?'

'It's dead down here. We won't be interrupted unless you squeal too loudly.'

'No one makes me squeal.'

'Is that a challenge? Another bet?'

She looked at his paddle and whispered, 'No.'

'Then bend over the table, or must I bend you?'

Melinda pressed her thighs to the edge, leant over till her breasts were squished on the surface, and gripped both sides. Cole lifted her skirt at the back.

'What?'

'The wager was ten on your bottom, not on your skirt.' Her rump was two streamlined ovals that kissed. If it hadn't been for the thin strip of pale-green satin that disappeared between them, he'd have thought she was naked under her skirt. He grinned. 'I like thongs. We won't need to remove yours.' He rested the paddle's rubber surface on her right cheek. Her bum tensed. Cole waited until it relaxed and lifted the paddle. She clenched again. He continued to wait. As soon as her taut muscles softened again, he clipped her, as if to impart topspin. His blow was designed to deliver maximum sting but without deep impact.

Melinda's fingers tightened on the edges of the table but she didn't make a sound.

'You've been paddled before.'

'Um, maybe.'

He snapped the paddle across her left cheek. ' "Maybe" isn't an answer.'

'OK – yes.'

'Then you know to count.'

'That's two.'

'Too late. Haven't you been taught that smacks you don't count, don't count?'

'No.'

'Then you're learning now. We'll start again, with you counting.'

'You're so cruel,' she said, savouring the words.

'Yes. Lucky you.' He struck up from below, impacting both cheeks at once.

'Three, I mean one. What do you mean, "Lucky me"?'

'You know exactly what I mean. Melinda, if you try to deceive me, we'll start over.'

'No, please. Yes, OK, I know what you mean. Do you have to rub it in?'

'Like this?' His hand compressed a burning cheek, working its firm flesh. 'You know what you are, Melinda, and you know what I am. We must be honest.' His blow descended from above, glancing across her right cheek.

'Two. What am I, Cole?'

'A delicious little pain-slut.'

'And what are you?'

'I'm the man who is going to give you what you need. Admit you need it, Melinda.'

'Fuck you!'

'That's an extra six.'

'Sorry. All right, I get off on it. Is that what you wanted to hear?'

'What *I* want to hear is –' he clapped the paddle down with a resounding crack '– this.'

She jerked. 'Three.'

'Lucky thirteen to go.'

'Cole?'

'Yes?'

'You swing a mean paddle. I'm not sure if I can take that many.'

'I'll stop if you yelp.'

'I don't yelp, on principle.'

'Your choice.' The paddle smacked down again.

'Four.'

She'd endured another eight before she gritted out, 'OK, I yelp.' Her cheeks were glowing and mottled.

'I should make you yelp for real but, as this is our first time, I'll allow that.'

She straightened up, rubbing her bottom.

'I wasn't easy on you, Melinda,' he said. 'You're very brave.'

Demurely, she said, 'Thank you, Cole. Cole?'

'Yes?'

'Are you going to leave me like this?'

'Like what?'

She lifted the front of her skirt and pointed to the wet patch that stained the tiny triangle of her pale thong.

'Horny?' he asked.

She nodded, pouting.

He pointed to his bulge. 'Is this what you need?'

Melinda came closer, bent a little and ran a hand up inside the leg of his shorts to where his cock fought the restriction of his bikini briefs. 'Oh yes! This is *exactly* what Melinda needs.'

Cole knew from the internet that some submissives like to be referred to in the third person when they're involved in a 'scene' but there was a deeper level of humility he could impose on her that she'd likely enjoy.

Affecting a bored but imperious tone, he told her, 'Then Melinda may show me the way to her apartment. She will call herself "this girl" until I give her leave to use her name.'

Melinda's eyes lit up for a second before she dropped them. 'This girl thanks her Sir for his understanding.' When she looked up again, her eyes betrayed glee. For her, submission was a game, it seemed. That was a relief. Cole wanted to play but not to assume the responsibility of a 24/7 clinging slave.

# Fifteen

Melinda's apartment was pink, white and girlish. It was saved from being saccharine by a number of elegant bronze statuettes, all nudes, mainly female. The pictures were Aubrey Beardsley prints for the most part, plus a few erotic subjects by an artist Cole didn't recognise. One was of the lower half of a woman's face, with voluptuous lips sucking on a stiletto heel. Another was of just a breast, bound with barbed wire. Melinda didn't hide her sexual predilections from her guests, it seemed.

'May this girl pour Sir a drink?'

'Scotch. You may join me, anything you like.'

'This girl has champagne chilled.'

'Then you may have some.'

He sat in an armchair that looked too fragile to fuck on and was upholstered in a fabric that bodily fluids would ruin. The broadloom was white, with pale-pink scatter rugs. When he fucked her, it'd better be in another room.

She knelt to give him his drink. Her bottle was a split. Kate would have drained a magnum.

'Lose the running shoes and thong and sit there,' he said, pointing to a matching couch.

'This girl apologises for her unseemly attire.'

'You were dressed appropriately for what you were doing. You didn't know you'd meet me.'

'Sir is too kind.' She peeled the runners and her socks from delicate high-arched feet.

Cole got the subtle hint. 'This girl' craved humiliation. Excusing her spoilt the mood.

She posed as she reached under her skirt to tug her thong down. Cole affected disinterest. 'Sit on the edge,' he said. 'Lean back and spread your legs. Lift your skirt high. Give me a good view of your pussy.'

'This girl obeys.'

Her pubes were bald. Cole detected a glint of metal where the ridge of her prominent clitoris divided her lips. 'You're pierced,' he observed.

'Does that please Sir?'

'Do you have any more?'

She started to tug her waistband down.

'You might as well strip. Keep your legs apart.'

Her top came off easily. Working her skirt down over legs that were spread was awkward. Naked, she lolled back, pubes pushed forwards and thighs spread, looking incredibly obscene.

Cole knew she was tempting him to show excitement at her impalements. If he'd done so, it would have shown weakness on his part and empowered her. The last thing submissives want is power but they feel compelled to test those whom they choose to allow mastery over them.

Cole sipped Scotch with his face carefully blank. She'd been pierced three times: left nipple, navel and clitoral ridge. Much as he would have liked to inspect her punctures and their adornments, he said, 'Flat on your belly, face pressed to the carpet. Don't forget to keep those legs apart.' He toed the floor to show her where her head should come.

She had to wriggle across the floor to get to him. He wondered what the carpet's nap felt like as she dragged her skin over it. Did it catch on the metal she wore?

Looking down on the back of her head, he told her, 'Bare my feet.'

Without lifting her eyes from the carpet, she fumbled with his laces, removed his runners and socks and set them neatly aside. Cole set the sole of his bare right foot on the back of her neck. Melinda shivered. He waited for a minute, letting her humiliation sink in. His left foot prodded her cheek, turning her face to the side. His big toe brushed her lips.

'Open.'

He hadn't thought of his feet as erogenous zones before but her pumping little sucks and the sensation of her wet tongue slithering between his toes excited him in special ways. Not only did it feel good but it was elevating, psychologically. Melinda's submission was very different from Kate's. For Kate, it was all physical. With Melinda, what went on in her mind was as important as what was done to her body. She enjoyed both. The red and blue blotches on her bottom testified to her lust for spanking. Her bum cheeks were clenching and relaxing. The subtle movements likely abraded her clitoris.

Cole enjoyed five minutes of her oral worship before saying, 'Perhaps you'd like to show me your piercings.'

'This girl would enjoy that, Sir,' she mumbled around his baby toe.

'Then stand.'

His hand around her thigh hooked her to stand beside him, to his left. Cole massaged the inside of her thigh as he took a closer look at her intimate jewellery. She had a barbell through her left nipple. A bright metal bead on each side kept it in place. Pendant from that cruel rod, was a U big enough to accommodate a finger. Cole tried it between his fingers. The metal was springy. He could compress the arms of the U, pinching her flesh. Melinda trembled when he did.

Idly, he asked, 'What's your safe word?'

'This girl thanks Sir for asking. It's *ça suffit.*'

The decoration at her navel matched. The barbell pierced the soft lip on either side of her indentation. Cole toyed with her navel's U for a while, as if he wasn't eager to get to the lowest, most intimate, perforation. His massaging fingers pinched, lightly, at the delicate flesh in the hollow of her groin.

The third piercing was similar but with an embellishment. The rod penetrated her clit's sheath but passed beneath its shaft. The U was exactly long enough so that when her clit was in its aroused state, as it was then, its pink arrowhead butted against a small golden bead. Cole tried it with a delicate fingertip. It rotated, rolling easily at his touch. When Melinda walked, if she was the least bit aroused, it would caress her where she was most sensitive.

And she'd played a vigorous game of table tennis. No wonder she'd been ready for sex after.

Cole was fascinated. He tried rolling the ball this way, then that. His fingers closed on her clit's sheath and worked it up and down. The ball bounced on her clit's head.

'May this girl speak, Sir?'

'Yes.'

'When this girl climaxes, she makes a lot of wet.'

'You lubricate copiously?'

'This girl, she humbly confesses, squirts.'

'Ah. You, er, actually ejaculate?'

'To this girl's shame, yes.'

Cole thought about that, and about delicate fabrics. 'Where's your bedroom?'

She pointed.

'Bring the drinks.' He strode to the door she'd indicated. After the brightness and wedding cake décor of the other room, it took his eyes a moment to adjust. The floor was covered in imitation black leather, so padded it was like walking on a firm mattress. The walls and ceiling were crimson, with an enormous pink mirror over the bed and on one wall. The light was from two floor lamps, each six feet tall and comprised of four pink vertical neon tubes. The bed was king sized, made of wrought iron, a four-poster with crossbars for a canopy but without drapes. A pair of manacles dangled six feet above pillows the colour of blood. The coverlet was more imitation black leather. The bedside cabinets were ebony, each with a gooseneck lamp. There were stools and padded benches scattered about the room. One was about five-feet long, with thicker padding where a head might rest and with buckled straps attached to the foot of each leg.

The only discordant note was the way Cole was dressed. Bare, but for chaps, would have been appropriate. He didn't have chaps so he compromised by stripping naked.

Melinda set her flute, his refilled glass and her split on a cabinet and turned to him, legs still spread, hands clasped behind her back, head bowed.

'That bench,' he said, 'bring it here.'

Her finely toned body rippled as she moved the bench.

'Kneel on it, facing me.'

He sat down on the bed. Her kneeling up raised her mound to the level of his eyes. Cole turned a lamp on and adjusted its strong beam to spotlight her sex. Her knees were about a foot apart. Cole moved one, to spread them by eighteen inches. The fingers of his right hand tickled up the inside of her right thigh. 'Hold onto my shoulders.' His attention returned to the ingenious jewel that both desecrated and adorned the natural beauty of her sex.

Once more, he manipulated the metal U. Melinda's clitoral shaft was as long as, but more slender than, two joints of his little finger. Its sheath had withdrawn to leave its head completely exposed. Cole spat on it.

'So, you're a squirter. Let's see.' His right thumb and index finger took a delicate grip on her sheath, above her clit's head. A slight pressure moved it up, exposing about an eighth of an inch of its pink neck – like skinning back a man's foreskin. He pulled down, then pushed up, masturbating her. He bunched three fingers of his free hand together, touched their tips to her smooth lips, spread to part them, then probed up into her humid depths. Cupping that hand towards himself, Cole rubbed behind her pubic bone until he found the bumpy sponginess of her G-spot. Two fingers of his left hand rotated on that with increasing pressure. Two fingers of his right manipulated her clit's sheath.

With her leaning on his shoulders, her breasts were inches from his face. Cole craned forwards and closed his mouth around her left nipple. His tongue hooked into the U and curled back to tug on it.

Four fingers and one tongue worked in unison, sliding her sheath, massaging her G-spot, plucking at her nipple. His pace was measured and constant. Cole's one regret was that he had nothing to assail her anus with.

Melinda began to pant. The long muscles in her thighs flexed, keeping time with Cole's attentions. Her lean belly rippled.

'This girl,' she moaned. 'This girl . . .'

Her entire body undulated. Melinda's abdomen bulged and then sucked in. 'I'm . . .' She shivered, as if in the grip of a fever.

Cole's fingers, inside her, felt a powerful contraction. He plucked his hand from her clinging flesh and cupped it beneath her.

Melinda squirted, long and hard, filling his palm with her aromatic nectar.

Cole was ready. A shrug toppled her. She sprawled face down on the bed from her waist up. He lifted her head by her hair and shoved a palm that was pooled with her juices under her face.

115

'Lap that up!'

Two fingers of his free hand thrust into the crease between her buttocks. They opened her anus and drove inside, merciless, forcing two joints into her rectum.

Melinda yelped, slobbered and lapped. Cole finger-fucked her anus, burrowing deeper with each sadistic thrust, until she'd licked the last drop of her own spending from his hand.

She glanced at him, grinning wickedly.

'Did I say you could look at me?' he demanded.

Her eyes dropped. 'This girl humbly begs Sir's pardon.'

'On the floor. I want you sitting, back against the bed, legs under the bench.'

Melinda slithered off the bed. Her eyes were fixed on the rampant length of cock that wagged a foot from her face. The drinks were within easy reach. Cole knelt on the bench with one hand on the bed. His body formed a bridge over Melinda's head with his cock pointing down at an angle. 'Open wide.' He rested the head of his cock on her lower lip. The champagne struck cold on his burning flesh. He tilted the bottle carefully, so that wine ran down his shaft to her mouth. 'Suck.'

As he poured and she slurped, Cole contemplated his next move. He hadn't fucked her or buggered her. Both tempted him but Melinda craved degradation and giving a woman what she wanted came first, always. He pulled his cock back and poured champagne into her mouth. 'Hold it. Don't swallow.'

Her head tilted back, lips parted.

His finger depressed his cock and steered it between her lips. 'Close.'

Her mouth closed around his shaft. Rocking gently, penetrating no more than an inch or two, Cole fucked a mouth that was full of champagne. It was cold on his burning flesh at first. He was disappointed that he couldn't feel the wine's sparkle but the novelty made up

116

for that. Cole reduced a lovely, elegant woman to nothing more than a receptacle. She had to love that. He couldn't see her eyes but her little gargling sounds confirmed her pleasure.

Pressure built in his balls. Cole accelerated, shallower, fucking the head of his cock between her lips. When he was sure his flow was imminent, he twitched his hips, plucking his cock from her lips' soft grip, snatched up her flute and aimed.

By the time he'd finished discharging, the glass held over an inch of frothy cream.

He set it aside, climbed off the bench and sat on the bed. 'You may sit here.' He patted the bench.

She got up and sat, glancing from the flute to Cole and back again. He topped the flute up with champagne and handed her the jism-and-wine cocktail. 'Drain it.'

It wasn't like he'd come in her mouth and she'd swallowed in the heat of passion. This was Cole degrading her, almost impersonally, cold. It was the coldness of the act that made it so hot.

Melinda put the glass to her lips, tilted her head back, poured the cold mixture into her mouth and swallowed. Cole watched her throat work, once, twice, three times, before she set the empty flute aside and licked her lips. She gave herself a little shake, as if waking from deep sleep.

Cole flopped back on the bed.

Melinda threw herself down beside him, chuckling. 'That was fun, Cole. You're good.' 'This girl' was gone. Melinda was back.

Cole was flattered by her compliment. She was sophisticated and experienced in playing these games. He was a novice by comparison. The success of a D/s scene depends on the skills of the dominant. Melinda had likely been degraded and humiliated by the best.

'Are you going to spill the dirt on the Silvetti ménage?' she asked.

He shrugged. 'You know it was an incestuous three-way. That's as much as me.'

'But you're going to fuck the sisters, right?'

'Could be.'

'What I'd give to be a fly on the wall when you do, or better, a slut in the same bed.' She toyed with his nipple. 'By the way, "this girl" really enjoys being called "slut", or "bitch" – that sort of thing.'

'I'll remember, for next time.'

'There'll be a "next time" won't there, Cole?'

'I'm going to be pretty busy selling the penthouse, but for "this girl" I'll make time.'

'I might be able to help you with that. We might help each other.'

Cole turned to face her. 'How?'

'I have a situation, Cole. A girlfriend of mine is married to a pig – a rich pig.'

'I don't do murder.'

'No, silly! Let me explain. The Pig is away a lot, overseas. He has to check on his sweatshops, I think. When he's away, Willow – that's her name – and I get to play. We're worried though. Her coming here, me going to her place, people might notice.'

'What's wrong with friends visiting each other?'

'Pig doesn't know I exist, and mustn't. It'd make things too complicated.'

'So?'

'Pig's thinking of moving. Willow has a lot of influence over him. What if we three worked it so they bought the penthouse? It'd be very handy, having her an elevator ride away.'

'She's your domme?' Cole asked.

'No. She's sub, like I am most of the time, but different. She's not into all sorts of scenes like I am. Willow likes . . . Well, maybe you'll find out, someday.' Her fingers drifted over his belly. 'Cole, I really like you. I don't often offer on a first session, but would you like a regular fuck, Melinda and Cole, not Sir and "this girl"?'

His cock twitched. 'I might be persuaded.'

'I'll see what I can do.' She reached under a pillow and pulled out an oversized vibrator. 'Let's see if this can revive that handsome cock of yours.'

# Sixteen

It was eleven in the morning. The Silvetti sisters greeted Cole fully made-up but wearing identical black lace negligees. The swirling patterns were dense over their breasts and pubic areas, but skin tones showed through at their tiny waists. From the tops of their slender thighs to their fine-boned ankles, the fabric was unembroidered sheer voile. He could see they were wearing hose and wondered if they had anything else on beneath their flimsy robes. The black velvet chokers that circled their pretty throats hinted they were ready to submit, not that Cole needed hints.

When he'd first met them, they'd worn demure little dresses. On his second visit, they'd been in peignoir sets. It was an interesting progression. He wondered whether, if he didn't make a move on them today, next time he'd find them stark naked.

Portia tightened her sash and looked up from the couch at Cole, expectantly.

'I've found you a potential buyer,' he said. 'That's nothing to get excited about, yet.'

Portia clutched Olivia's hand.

'You two don't go out much,' he continued. 'On Thursday, you are going to have to.'

Two perfect little full-lipped mouths formed 'O's .

'It's better if your place is empty, for a number of reasons,' he explained.

'But where will we go?' Olivia asked with a little shiver.

'You won't have to leave the building. There's a charming woman who lives ten floors down. She's looking forward to having you as her guests on Thursday, from ten till two, at least. Longer if you like. She'll have an errand to run while you're there but it won't take her long.'

'That's very kind of her,' Olivia said. 'Should we have our girl come in early Thursday to clean up and make the bed?'

Cole hadn't thought of that. Of course, the sisters couldn't possibly tidy up or load a dishwasher. He nodded. 'Did you move Portia's things as I told you?'

'We had it taken care of.'

'Show me.'

He followed their mobile haunches into the master bedroom, trying to detect panty lines and failing.

One wall and one shoe rack were bare. The rest of the closet was still crowded with Olivia's things. 'No,' he said. 'Like this.' He moved clothes and shoes at random, spreading them over the vacant spaces. 'Now,' he said. 'What else needs to be moved, to be discrete?'

They gave him blank looks.

'Daniel had toys. Where did he keep them?'

'Toys?' they asked in unison.

'When you three made love, he used things on you – things that vibrated, things that restrained you, things that ...' He gestured, not sure if he'd jumped to conclusions.

They both looked at the floor, blushing.

Portia murmured, 'How did you know, Cole?'

Olivia nudged her sister. 'Cole's like Daniel, silly. He just "knows" things.'

Cole asked, 'Where are they?'

Olivia turned to the mirrored wall. Her finger dug at a mirror's edge and tugged. The mirror opened. The closet behind it was six inches deep and three feet wide,

121

floor to ceiling. It was divided into compartments. There were shelves for slender vibrators that Cole took to be anal probes; a compartment for sets of tiny ben-wa balls that looked to be handcrafted; a large vertical rack of percussion toys – short whips, crops, canes, paddles, tawses and slappers in various designs, and shelf after shelf of restraints – single-sleeves, leather cuffs, steel cuffs, straps, collars and piles of thin chains that were fitted with rings.

Cole wondered what he might find if he searched every apartment in the Tiara Towers. He'd only been in two and both were equipped for exploring SM fantasies.

Portia opened a second mirror door. It revealed a similar assortment.

'What's behind the last mirror?' Cole asked.

'That one's just a mirror,' Olivia told him, smiling.

'All this has to go,' he said.

Both looked crestfallen.

'Where?' Olivia asked. 'How?'

Portia frowned. 'When will we get them back?'

'You may pick six favourite items each. We'll find a suitcase or something that they can be locked in. As for the rest, I'll be back tomorrow with a trunk. We'll pack everything else in it and I'll take them down to my friend below to keep for you until your place is sold.'

'What if your friend looks in the trunk?'

'She won't have to. I'll show her. She won't be shocked and she can keep a secret. Melinda will be amused, I promise.'

Olivia swayed and looked at the floor. 'Is Melinda a bad girl, like us?'

Cole grinned. 'Melinda is very naughty. Whether she's naughtier than you two, I can't say. I don't know you well enough, yet, do I?'

Olivia chuckled. ' "Yet", Cole?'

'Why do you think I want you to pick out your favourites?'

The sisters exchanged sly glances. Olivia mouthed, 'I told you so.' Aloud, she asked Cole, 'You won't be upset if we're shy, will you? We've only . . . Daniel has been our only . . .'

'You've never made love with anyone but your brother?'

'No.'

'Then it'll be a learning experience for you both. Now, is there a robe of Daniel's for me to borrow?'

'Cole?'

'I'm going to take a shower while you two pick out your favourite toys.'

'There's one hanging behind the master bathroom door.'

'I'll be back, ready, in ten minutes.'

Cole hadn't thought to bring a razor but after he stepped out of the shower he stole some of Daniel's aftershave anyway. It might make the sisters more comfortable if he smelt like their brother. The robe was crimson satin with black trim. Cole admired himself in it, braced his shoulders and returned to the sisters.

They were seated side by side on the edge of the enormous bed. The little minxes had shed their negligees. Cole grinned to himself. He'd been concerned about making them feel comfortable? Their black, lacy-topped stockings came halfway up their gleaming thighs. Their legs were crossed at identical angles. A stiletto-heeled pump dangled, swaying, from each sister's right foot. The shoes were in motion because the sisters were subtly rubbing their legs together. In the quiet of the bedroom, Cole could hear the soft hiss of nylon on nylon. The svelte little sluts had posed carefully, for his enjoyment. Daniel had trained his sisters well.

A selection of toys was laid out on the chest at the bed's foot. There were cuffs and chains, two crops, two whippy canes and four of the anal probes. Something was missing. Cole went over them again. No full-sized dildos or vibrators.

123

He picked up a short slender flexible rod with a little ball at the end. 'None bigger than this?'

'How do you mean, Cole?'

'Life sized or bigger?'

'Isn't that life sized?' Olivia asked.

Cole kept a straight face. No wonder Daniel had kept his sisters to himself and himself to his sisters. He must have had a minute cock. If they'd never seen a normal one, they wouldn't have realised they were being short changed.

'Ladies,' he announced, 'this is going to be interesting.' He threw himself onto the bed, on his back. 'You'd better take a look at what's going to be getting into you.'

Olivia crawled onto the bed from his right, Portia from his left. Olivia pulled Cole's robe aside. Both sisters gasped. Cole wasn't erect yet but his cock was rising.

'Oh!' Olivia exclaimed. 'Can it? Does it?'

'Fit? Why not?' He pulled Portia up to sprawl beside him. Although she was slender she wasn't buff, like Melinda. She looked soft, malleable. Her breasts were virginal swellings, like a girl entering puberty. Their nipples were tiny buttons, as pale as her skin. For a moment he thought her prominent pubes were bald but when he looked closer he saw they were coated with fine fuzz. He'd heard the expression, 'like a split peach' but he'd never seen a pussy that fitted the description so aptly before.

'Do you like her body?' Olivia whispered into his ear. Her fingers were burning on his hip.

'I'm going to enjoy it,' he said.

'And mine?' She kneeled up for him to inspect her. Olivia's breasts might have weighed a few ounces more than her sister's. Her hips were a fraction shapelier, her navel a little deeper and her mound a smidgeon more pronounced, but otherwise they were identical.

Cole reached up behind her, wrapped his fist in her long flowing hair and pulled her face down to his. As his tongue explored one sister's mouth, his free hand tried the other's breasts for resilience. Portia, who seemed the more submissive of the two, lay spread out, giving him free rein. She twitched when his fingers nipped a nipple, shuddered as they trailed down her belly and gasped when one slid between the lips of her sex, seeking her clitoris. Otherwise, she didn't move. He found the little nub and wobbled on it. Portia's first motion was to spread her thighs further apart.

Cole rolled, dragging Olivia over his hip, so he could kiss her sister. Between sucks on Portia's lower lip, he told Olivia, 'Stroke her pussy.' He took her hand and placed it where he wanted it. 'Diddle your sister, Olivia. Put your fingers inside her.'

'Yes, Cole.'

He returned to kissing Portia and caressing both sisters. His hands stroked up raspy nylon to sleek thighs, smooth flat bellies and tender little breasts. His cock grew and ached. Its head brushed the satin of Portia's hip. It would have been so easy to mount either sister, thrust into her and pound out his lust, but he had half a day and two of them to satisfy. He promised himself he'd try not to come until he'd sampled both mouths, both pussies and both bottoms – and not until each sister had climaxed twice.

He felt down to Portia's pubes again. So far, he'd only toyed with her clit. He was curious about a pussy that had only ever known a child-sized cock. His finger slid in, passing Olivia's. She was just dabbling between her sister's outer lips. Portia's passage was hot and wet but very narrow, though he couldn't imagine why. He didn't think that pussies shrank from lack of stretching. Maybe it was genetic, like her brother's cock. Fucking Portia would be like buggering any other woman. He'd have to take it slowly. It'd be easier on her if she was desperate with lust. A woman in heat can take just about anything.

He left her mouth and trailed his tongue down her body, pulling Olivia's head with him. It was nice, them both being so small and light. He manhandled Margaret, but with her he had to fake that it was easy. With these two, it really was.

Holding Olivia's face close, he spread Portia's plump lips and pulled them up to expose her clit. 'Like this,' he told Olivia. His mouth went down. His tongue flickered on Portia's button. It, at least, was a normal size, as well as he understood 'normal'.

'Got it?'

Olivia nodded.

'Hold on a minute.' He rolled Portia onto her side, facing her sister, and climbed over her. A hand under her knee lifted her leg so that her toes pointed at the ceiling. Cole bent and squirmed his face between the cheeks of her taut little bottom. His eyes met Olivia's, peering at him between her sister's thighs. Both used their tongues: Cole's worming into Portia's anus; Olivia lapping her clit.

Portia's hips moved backwards and forwards, just an inch, as if she didn't know which tongue she wanted more of. The slight rocking accelerated and tightened. She began to moan. When Cole judged she was getting close to the brink, he pulled back and pushed Olivia's head away.

Portia writhed, moaning, 'No, no, please, don't stop.'

Cole pushed Olivia flat on her back, lifted Portia bodily and set her down with her knees astride her sister's face and looking down on her sex. 'Tongue each other,' he commanded.

Olivia's head lifted to Portia's pussy. Cole knelt up behind her, brushed his cock over Olivia's face and put its head to Portia's diminutive entrance. Olivia goggled up at him, past his cock. Perhaps she'd never watched her sister get fucked from so intimate a vantage point before. His cock squished against the entrance of Portia's sex. Cole took hold of her hips and eased her back towards him. His cockhead pressed into her, then felt the tightness. He pushed, gently, then with more firmness. A woman's sex is a miraculously elastic thing, as he'd learnt from fisting Kate. He felt Portia's flesh stretch to accommodate him. With a deep breath, he pressed deeper. The tightness surrendered. Slowly but inexorably, he forced his way into her.

Portia made little 'ah, ah, ah' sounds.

Cole held still for a moment, savouring the sensations: the constriction around his cock; the warmth of Olivia's face beneath his balls. He looked down at the tawny pucker of Portia's anus, spread by the pressure of his hands on her kittenish hips. When he felt the girl had adjusted to being dilated more than she'd ever been before, he allowed himself to rock, slowly, doing multiplication tables in his head to control his cock's demands. Cole had got almost to the end of the eleven-times table when Portia stiffened, totally rigid. He wasn't sure if it signalled her climax until she went limp and collapsed forwards on her sister.

His cock tugged free. Olivia gawked up at it, disbelievingly. Cole leant forwards and thumbed his shaft down towards the older sister's mouth. Remembering Melinda's liking for being verbally abused, he commanded, 'Suck your slutty sister's juice off my cock, you perverted little bitch.'

Her lips stretched wide. The head of his cock slid between them and butted against the flat of her tongue. Cole thought, 'Eleven elevens are a hundred and thirty-two. Twelve . . .'

When his tables jumbled in his mind, he backed away. A hand on Portia's leg pulled her to the edge of the bed, off Olivia. He tossed her onto her back and wrapped his fist around two delicate ankles. 'Olivia, fetch me a cane.'

Olivia's head bobbed. 'Yes, Cole.'

He raised Portia's feet up over her head, lifting her bum high off the bed. Olivia handed him a yard of supple rattan. He'd have to be careful. It was whip thin. When he brought it down across Portia's upturned buttocks, he jerked back up at the precise moment of impact so that only the cane's springiness actually struck her resilient flesh. Even so, it drew a thin white line, edged with red, horizontally across the cleft of her bottom.

Both sisters drew sucking breaths, as if Olivia had felt Portia's pain. Cole laid his implement aside and stroked a finger along her welt. It was ridged and burning.

He told her, 'I'm proud of you, Portia,' and struck again. The rattan was flexible enough that it wrapped her bottom, marking the side of her hip. Cole shortened his grip and moved back a little. His target was the padded flesh of her bum, not the thinner tissues over her hip. He gave her six in all, from the backs of her thighs, just above where her stockings reached, to the fullest part of her bottom. When he was done, both sisters had tears in their eyes and were biting their lower lips.

He rolled Portia away and dragged Olivia closer, on her face. 'Portia, lie across your sister's calves. I don't want her to kick.'

With the younger sister pinning the elder's feet, he took the rattan to Olivia, six swipes, none of which wrapped. Cole was honing his skills.

He had to keep track. His cock had been in Olivia's mouth and Portia's pussy. Four orifices to go. Cole's hands took Olivia by her hips and turned her to kneel beside the bed, resting on it from her waist up. 'Portia, fetch lube.'

'Pardon, Cole?'

'KY jelly?'

She looked blank.

'Bring me some . . . Do you have extra-virgin olive

oil?' It was Cole's warped sense of humour that specified 'extra-virgin'.

The tiny woman scurried away and returned cuddling a two-quart spouted container. Cole chuckled. Two quarts would be ample.

'Sit astride your sister's back, facing me.'

He pushed his thumbs deep into the cleft of Olivia's bum and spread her cheeks with his palms. The balls of his thumbs prised her anus open. The pit that is exposed when a woman's clamping ring is forced to open is so internal, so much a portal to the forbidden, that it makes her seem incredibly vulnerable. Just looking into it is a violation of her ultimate privacy. Peering into her, with the knowledge that her body was his to desecrate, filled Cole with evil glee, like a vandal who was about to defile a holy shrine.

'Pour the oil,' he said. 'Let it trickle down her crease.'

Portia tilted the container, dribbling it into the dimple just below her sister's tailbone. Cole tilted Olivia a fraction. Golden liquid trickled down the valley to pool in the parted pucker.

'Enough!' He took the oil from Portia with one hand and dragged her face down by her hair with the other. 'Make spit, lots of it.'

Her mouth worked. His rigid cock bobbed against her lips. They parted wide enough to let his cock in. 'Wet it,' he told her. Cole let his cockhead bathe in her spittle for a moment before pulling back. 'More. Spit on it.'

Her first attempt landed on the top of his shaft. The second was a direct hit, on the bald purple plum.

'Now guide it.'

Portia's small hand wrapped his cock and pushed it lower. Concentration furrowed her forehead as she aimed with delicate precision. 'It'll never fit,' she told him.

'Yes, it will.'

'It'll hurt.'

'Very likely. You want it to hurt, don't you, Olivia?'

Olivia grunted what might have been an affirmative.

Cole pushed. Olivia's anus and rectum were tight, but no tighter than Portia's sex had been. A dozen short hard jerks buried his cock to its hilt. He drew back slowly and then eased forwards. The oil had only penetrated to half the depth his cock had distended her. Dry constriction dragged his foreskin back almost painfully at first, but either his pumping worked the oil deeper or the intense stimulation made her lubricate because, after a while, her passage resisted his thrusts less. Cole pumped slowly, taking care not to let his lust overtake him.

Olivia was suffering the restraint and humiliation of being pinned under her sister's bum. Cole's cock was degrading her. She'd been reduced to the status of a living sheath.

That was her taken care of. Cole turned his attention to Portia.

He took her hips in his hands and dragged her closer. Her eyes were yearning. Her lips trembled with need. Cole felt her hunger suck at him. A benevolent sadist is helpless to resist a submissive masochist's cravings. He took her nyloned calves and wrapped them about his own hips. Portia clutched her hands behind his neck to keep her balance. His teeth took her trembling lower lip and crushed it, hard enough that it'd be bruised but not hard enough to draw blood. His fingers found the tiny hard tips of her childish breasts and twisted them viciously. Portia sobbed into his mouth. Her hips humped at him, desperate to find the friction her clit longed for.

Cole released her nipples. His hands delved between her pubes and his. The crease of Olivia's bottom still ran with oil. He smeared it over his fingers. One hand stayed in the cramped space. His other arm stretched round Portia, reaching low. Its hand found the cleft of her bum and followed it down to the tight knot of her anus.

Front and back, his index fingers probed. One screwed into Portia's ass; the other hooked up into her, searching for her G-spot. The base of the same finger squashed her clit against her pubic bone. Doubly impaled, the younger sister swayed to and fro. She became frantic. Her lip jerked from the grip of Cole's teeth. Mouth wide and wet, drooling with desire, Portia slobbered over Cole's face, sucking his chin, slavering on his cheeks, all the while babbling incoherently. Her tongue lashed into his mouth then darted to his neck. He felt tiny teeth indent the muscle between his neck and shoulder. She snatched her head back and glared into his eyes.

'Cole, do it! Do me! Finger me hard, fuck you! Make it hurt!' Her cheeks were wet with tears. Saliva dribbled down her chin.

Cole heaved her straight up for long enough to get two fingers into her in places where one had been a tight fit. Her anus was a strangling elastic sleeve. Her sex was a constricting wet compress. Portia bounced, impaling herself. The sinews in her neck stood out. She rose up by her knees' grip on his hips, sliding her perspiration-slick skin up his chest until her left breast was level with his mouth.

'Bite me, fuck you!'

His teeth sank into her tender flesh. Portia slammed herself down, tugging her nipple from his grip, shuddered and went rigid.

His palms, one pressed to her pubes, one clutching her bottom, held her until she relaxed, limp. Portia toppled backwards, wrenching herself from his grip.

That was Portia's second climax, Cole reminded himself. Olivia hadn't come at all, yet. Nor had he but the thought didn't even cross his mind. He withdrew his cock from Olivia's ass and considered what he'd do to the horny bitches next.

To give his imagination time to work, he told Olivia, 'Fetch me a Scotch.'

# Seventeen

Olivia returned with a triangle of what looked like smoke caught in a cobweb knotted low about her hips. Cole took his drink. 'Did I tell you to put that on?'

'I thought . . .'

'That we were done? I'll tell you when we are.' He plucked the gauzy fabric from her and tossed her onto the bed. Leather cuffs, on chains, secured her ankles to the corners. Her legs were strained so far apart that the hollows at their tops deepened and a taut sinew stood out along the inside of each thigh.

'Fetch a mirror,' he told Portia. His hands indicated the size he wanted. Cole went to the bathroom, ran hot water into Daniel's shaving mug and returned with it and a towel, plus his wicked-looking razor and strop.

He had Portia rest the mirror on the bed, adjusted so that Olivia could see her pubes in it. She shivered as he slathered hot lather over her mound, down both outer lips and dabbed more below, on her perineum. Cole made a production out of stropping the razor. Portia watched every hissing stroke with wrapt fascination.

When he put the sharp edge to the highest point of Olivia's mound, she raised her head and blurted, 'Cole, please, be careful.'

'If you don't trust me, I'll stop.'

Her head sank back. 'I trust you.'

Cole scraped, gently. The fuzz came away with ease. His fingers, hooked just inside her, pressing up, stretched first one lip then the other to meet the razor's threatening caresses. The trickiest part was beneath her slit, between it and her anus. Luckily, she had virtually no fuzz there, so it was more a matter of making a show of shaving her than actually doing it.

He dabbed the last traces of lather away and stroked Olivia's newly bald skin. 'Smooth as satin,' he said. 'Portia, you may touch your sister.'

Portia's fingers smoothed over her sister's pubes.

'Try it against your cheek.'

Portia crouched low and rubbed her face over Olivia's mound.

'Good enough to eat?'

Portia nodded.

'Then use your tongue.' Cole snuggled down and rested his cheek low on Olivia's belly, eye to eye with Portia as her tongue wandered over her sister's smooth skin. 'Shaving has made her very sensitive,' he said.

In confirmation, Olivia shivered.

'Lower,' Cole encouraged.

Portia's tongue probed, pressing on her sister where the delicate lips joined.

'Inside. Find her clit.'

Portia's tongue moved from side to side, parting Olivia. Cole squirmed down with his own tongue extended. With his face pressed against Portia's, their tongues met. Two of Cole's fingers spread Olivia's lips. Together, their tongues entered, slithering over the smooth taut skin that covered Olivia's pubic bone, curling up to find the tiny nub of her clitoris.

Cole paused for long enough to tell Olivia, 'Tell us what we're doing to you, Olivia.'

'You – you're licking me, you and my sister, both at once. Your tongues are in my pussy, on my clit. It's so sinful, what you two are doing to me. Now I can feel a finger working into me – no – two fingers, one from each side. One's pushing down, pressing on the floor of my sex. The other one is moving up, but deep. It's on that place where being touched makes me wetter. It's incest, isn't it, Cole, even though you aren't Daniel? Portia's still my sister. Oh, I love my sister. Oh! There's a finger working into my bum. The finger in the bottom of my sex and the one in my ass – they're rubbing on each other, through me. Your tongues – they're driving me crazy. Finger my ass deeper, please? I love it that what you're doing is so obscene.'

Cole swung round to kneel astride Olivia's face. His cock wagged above her lips.

She craned up to suck its knob. Between slurps, she babbled, 'Love it. It's so good. Your tongues are touching, aren't they? My sister and my Master are kissing, inside me.' She gobbled for a moment. 'I want it all, please? Stretch my fucking pussy. Stretch my bumhole. Make it hurt good! Oh, my clit!'

Cole grabbed Portia's hand and pressed his and her forefingers together. Side by side, they worked back into Olivia's bottom. Both of their free hands delved into Olivia's tight little pussy. Two tongues, working as one, slavered her clit.

Olivia trembled and clenched. Mumbling around Cole's cock, she babbled, 'Yes! Yes!' She convulsed into a wracking orgasm.

While she was still jerking, Cole spun, nudging Portia aside with his hip. He rose up and plunged down, impaling Olivia. 'Get two fingers up her ass,' he commanded Portia. Feel my cock as I fuck her.'

Olivia's spasms didn't stop. She writhed beneath him with soft urgency as he pumped into her, his cockshaft feeling the pressure of Portia's fingers through the thin muscular membrane that divided Olivia's vagina from her rectum. Olivia's wriggling became frantic again. She went rigid three times; each time followed by a moment's relaxation and then renewed squirming. He watched her face, savouring its ecstatic contortions. From time to time, he glanced at Portia, who was frigging herself frantically with the fingers that weren't fucking her sister's bumhole. When Portia froze into her silent climax, he decided he'd achieved his goal. With a deep squirming thrust, he let his jism flood Olivia.

There was one last degradation he'd planned to inflict on the sisters. He dragged Portia's face to her sister's drooling sex. 'Lick my come out of her,' he commanded.

# Eighteen

On his way to the Tiara, Cole dropped by the Lakeshore building to see how Del Barker's renovations were coming on. Del was grimy, in his shirtsleeves, drinking coffee at an old card table that was covered in grit and dust. Behind him, someone was tearing holes in the ceiling. To his left, a man in overalls was using a jack hammer on the floor.

Del took Cole's arm and pulled him outside.

'On schedule, Del?' Cole asked.

Del made a sour face. 'Inside, yes. It's the fucking parking lot that's giving me headaches.'

'What's the problem?'

'City-fucking-Hall. They rubber-stamped the renovations but so far they've rejected three different layouts for the parking lot. I've got asphalt arriving next week and can't tell them where to pour it.'

'Who at City Hall, Del? Give me a name.'

'You can help?'

Cole shrugged. 'No promises, but I'll do what I can. It might cost you.'

'Within reason, OK. Thanks, Cole.'

Cole rode the Silvetti sisters down in their private elevator, crossed the lobby and took them up to Melinda's floor in a public one. He couldn't help envying Melinda their company. His clients, his temporary slave-sluts, were in matching dove-grey knitted jersey skinny-fit dresses that were just long enough to cover the top two inches of their thighs. Their mourning was over, it seemed. Perhaps he'd fucked them out of it. It occurred to Cole that if Kate had dressed sexily for him once in a while, instead of going either naked or in just her kimono, he might have tried harder to preserve their relationship. No he wouldn't have. Whatever, she was a drunk who craved violence, not controlled sadism. There wasn't an erotic outfit made that could compensate for that.

Melinda greeted them wearing a green net cover-up over a matching minute bikini. The sisters eyed her. She looked at them. All three women licked their lips.

'Don't get carried away yet,' Cole told them. 'Melinda, you know what to do, and when?'

She showed him a little bag that matched her raffia wedges. 'My note's already written, in case I don't have time.'

'Good. Show me.'

It read, 'Clarisse, apartment 1911. Come see me.'

'Who's in 1911?' he asked.

'Clarisse Steinbold, in her nineties. She's moving out to a nursing home on Friday.'

'Good girl. Well, ladies, enjoy, but not too much till after, right?'

The 'Pig' had insisted that he and Willow drive to the Tiara. Cole waited in the lobby. When a black stretch limousine pulled up, ten minutes late, he pushed 'send' on his cell. 'Arriving now.'

'On my way,' Melinda told him.

The 'Pig' was swarthy and stocky but not repulsive, except for an excess of ostentatious jewellery. Willow was tall and thin, with prominent cheekbones, big blue eyes and fluffy hair the colour of spun honey. Cole liked her feral, almost predatory looks. Her suit would have been demure except that its straight tight skirt was almost ankle length. In his opinion, very long was as sexy, if not sexier, than very short.

He showed them the lobby, trying to keep the Pig's back to the elevators. Cole made sure to use the words, 'opulent', 'secure' and 'prestigious', watching the Pig's eyes for reactions.

Melinda came out of an elevator. Cole only recognised her by her bikini. She was wearing an enormous floppy hat and sunglasses that covered half her face. Cole ushered the Pig and Willow towards her. She pressed the button and was inside the elevator just before Cole's party. The Pig – whose name was Vincent, Cole learnt – got in first. Cole pushed '25'. 'Which floor?' he asked Melinda.

'Nineteen, please.'

In the mirror, Cole watched Vincent eye Melinda.

Melinda asked, 'New residents?'

Vincent said, 'Just looking.'

'Shame,' she responded, pulling her sunglasses down just far enough for her eyes to flirt with Vincent over their tops. 'There's a shortage of attractive men in this building.'

Vincent preened. Melinda turned so that Vincent could glimpse what she was doing but Willow and Cole wouldn't have been able to if it hadn't been for the mirror. She dug a pencil and her note from her bag. She faked scribbling quickly and slipped her note into Vincent's pocket as she swayed out at nineteen.

'I thought the penthouse had a private elevator,' Vincent said.

'It does. I'm taking you to twenty-five first, to see the party rooms and guest suites.'

'Fuck that. This penthouse of yours better be big enough for us to entertain in or I'm not interested.'

Cole took them down again and up by the private elevator. As they travelled, he used his key words again, once each. He added, 'Thanks for driving, Vincent. I have to hang around for the next showing, movie people, so not very reliable. You've made it easier for me.'

Willow asked, 'Movie people?'

'Some director. Forgive me if I don't mention his name. The Tiara is very private. It's an unwritten rule. Residents don't name-drop.'

Willow loved the penthouse's furniture and decorations. Cole told them that the owners were moving to the West Coast so maybe a deal could be made. Vincent's eyes lit up in the Great Room.

Cole told him, 'Forty by thirty, ceiling two floors high. It's the only room like it in the building.'

'Except for in the next building.'

'No. It was an optional extra. The people in the next building took a second roof garden instead.' Cole pushed a remote. Wall-to-wall drapes swished apart to reveal four sets of sliding glass doors. 'In the summer, your parties could spill over outside. It's paved with slate, imported from a tiny quarry in Wales. The floor in here is antique random black pine. It's the same in the dining room and drawing room but the bedrooms are broadloomed, Axminster.'

They took over an hour to go through, which was encouraging. Cole took them down and then went back up to Melinda's. She opened the door still in her net wrap but without the bikini. Her lipstick was smeared.

She put a finger to her lips. 'You like to watch, Cole?'

'You? Anytime.'

'How about me and the sisters?'

'Sounds like fun.'

Melinda tugged him inside. As she shut the door behind him she called out, 'Thanks, Cole. Call me later.'

Tiptoeing across the room, Cole had a mental flash of some cubbyhole behind the bedroom mirror, which would prove to be one-way glass, or behind peepholes cut through a portrait he hadn't noticed before. Before he could dismiss the fanciful image, Melinda ushered him into another bedroom, which was dominated by a big-screen TV.

She punched a remote to turn it on. 'I like to record, sometimes.'

The screen lit up with split images of her crimson bedroom, obviously fed by two cameras, one hidden on each side of the room.

Cole asked, 'Did you? Us? When we . . .?'

'On a DVD,' she told him. 'For my own private use. Want a copy?'

'Please.' He should have been offended that she'd secretly recorded every lewd thing he'd done to her but he was flattered and intrigued. He'd replayed their obscene scene mentally. Melinda might have watched it over and over on TV, perhaps while masturbating. He wondered if there had been much of it that she'd fast-forwarded and decided that it had been so intense she wouldn't have skipped a moment.

'Make yourself comfortable,' she said, pointedly. 'I might invite you to join us, later. Check the features on the remote.'

Cole watched the screen as he stripped. The sisters were still wearing those sexy little dresses but hiked up now. The hemlines crossed their tummies. The pictures were clear enough for him to see that Portia's pubes had been shaved to match her sister's. It seemed that his arrival had interrupted their lesson in what real, full-sized vibrators were like. The foot of the bed was littered with them: nine-inch ribbed plastic 'classics', jellies in several colours, shapes and sizes, one that was plugged into a wall socket, big as a baby's arm with a giant sphere at the business end, and, most interesting, two strap-ons, with harnesses and a double-ended one that looked to be a yard long.

The sisters were seated facing each other, Olivia on the edge of the bed, Portia on the big bench. Both had their legs spread and thrust out straight, each with a pastel jelly in her fist, pushing it between the top folds of her sex, not into their depths but pressing the buzzing heads on their clits. The sound was clear enough that he could hear muted humming. Cole'd always been curious about sapphic sex, girls doing girls when there were no men present. Now he was watching two who didn't know they were being watched. Somehow, he thought it'd be purer, emotionally, just distilled lust.

Melinda joined the sisters with a split of champagne in one hand and three flutes in the other. She announced, 'Cole had things to do. He might join us later.'

Cole hoped they'd express disappointment but their faces showed rapt concentration. They didn't say a word.

Melinda poured three flutes and sipped one, looking at a camera over the rim of her glass. She winked at Cole and set her glass down. Her fingers poked through the array of stimulators. She chose one and held it up. Cole glanced down at the remote and found the zoom. Up close, he saw that the toy she'd picked was about life sized but with an exaggerated head. The smoothly sculpted dome took up half its length, like a flared cone with a rounded tip. When she twisted its base it not only vibrated but another twist made its head wag in slow circles. At its thickest, it was twice the diameter of his cock. Obviously, he thought, she intended to use it on herself. The sisters had been stretched to their limits when he'd fucked them.

Melinda's hand eased Olivia back onto the bed. She didn't seem to notice that her position had been changed. She was focused on the things the other vibrator was doing to her clit. Melinda moved Olivia's thighs further apart and stooped for a better view. She ran the mushroom head of her vibrator from just above Olivia's knee to the hollow of her groin. Olivia lifted one heel up onto the bed, giving Melinda easier access. The vibrator buzzed on the lips of Olivia's sex, just below where the pink jelly tantalised her clit. It moved from side to side, parting her lips.

Cole's hand dropped to his cock. He hadn't masturbated solo since he'd left Janet and he certainly didn't want to waste his jism before he joined the sylphs he was spying on, but a little gentle stroking up the silky underside of his shaft wouldn't hurt.

The head of Melinda's vibe nudged Olivia's lips apart. There was room between those soft outer folds for the tip. It wouldn't have to penetrate her to feel good. Then Melinda pushed.

Cole took a deep breath and zoomed in as close as the lens would take him. The vibe's end was tapered so that a couple of inches wouldn't ... Melinda pushed. Olivia gasped and arched. Fucking hell! The thing was in her deep enough that it was as thick as his cock inside the tighter channel beyond her lips, and it was still moving. Slowly but inexorably, the vibe sank into Olivia's delicate flesh. He, a man, wouldn't have been so insistent but Melinda, being a woman, knew that Olivia could take more. The dildo sank in until the elongated head passed the lips of Olivia's sex. They closed behind it. Melinda started to draw it out, just as slowly. After a long minute, the glistening head was just touching Olivia's gaping slit. Melinda pushed it back in, faster this time, and tugged it out, and rammed it in, fucking Olivia with a cock that was twice as thick as Cole's.

He was some sadist! Where he'd been gentle, Melinda was being brutal.

Olivia sawed her jelly on her clit. Her head came up off the bed with her teeth clenched. Her entire body curled so that she could stare down, wide eyed, at the obscenities Melinda was inflicting on her. She froze, sighed and flopped back.

Melinda tugged the vibe from Olivia and took it to Portia, who'd been watching while diddling herself.

Portia suckled on her sister's spending until the phallic probe was clean. Perhaps Melinda intended to give Portia the same tormenting treat as her sister but at that moment she too stiffened into a silent orgasm.

Giggling, Portia and Melinda threw themselves on the bed to either side of Olivia. Cole was interested to see how long it'd take before their play resumed. He knew it would. None of the three would be sated after one climax, and Melinda hadn't had one yet, unless it'd been before his arrival.

Olivia turned her face to tongue her sister's mouth, then to the other side to lap into Melinda's. As one, they sat up, the sisters to wriggle their dresses over their heads, Melinda to shrug out of her wrap. They flopped back. Olivia reached to either side, one hand to each of the others' mounds. Their fingers met on hers. They toyed idly, with no urgency. Fingers flickered from side to side, flipping distended lips. Pubes were cupped and compressed. Fingertips tested the wetness at the mouths of parted slits.

Cole stroked his aching erection. He'd just about decided it was time he joined them when Melinda sat up. She leant over the sisters, mouth to Olivia's breast, fingers finding Portia's tiny nipple. Olivia's squirming hand was trapped between her thighs. Melinda nibbled and tweaked. The sisters fingered each other with gentle curiosity, as if for the first time.

Melinda nipped and plucked. The sisters humped each other's hands. At Olivia's urging, Melinda fell back. Olivia and Portia swarmed over her with playful joy. Four fingers, two of each sister's, thrust up into Melinda and tugged her wide open. Portia crouched to peer into Melinda's soft pink labyrinth. Olivia bridged Melinda, who took advantage by stretching up to lave the sweet plane of her belly with the flat of her tongue. Olivia swooped to take Melinda's clitoral jewel in her teeth and tug it up with deliberate cruelty. Portia worked a finger into Melinda's anus.

The three rolled and writhed, limbs entangled. Tongues lapped into groins. Teeth nipped sleek bottoms. Thighs were humped. Nipples were stretched out to points. They didn't hold a position for more than a minute before one or another was tempted by a crevice or mound that required a slither or a squirm to reach. They became a sandwich: Portia on the bottom, grinding her pubes up at Melinda's; Olivia straddling Melinda's nape, humping it, while her hands parted Melinda's cheeks for her probing tongue.

Cole's fist strangled his cock.

'I can't get there,' Portia said with a sob.

'Can we use your vibes, Melinda?' Olivia asked. 'I need to be stuffed.'

Melinda hitched sideways from between the sisters. 'I've got exactly what we need.'

Cole hoped she was going to signal him to join them but the athletic bitch grabbed the double-ended dildo, a strap-on and a bottle of lube.

'Get off your sister a minute,' she told Olivia. Crouching, she squirted lube into the younger sister.

Cole knew what she intended but couldn't believe it. That delicate slot had been tight for his cock. Now Melinda was forcing the bulbous end of a yard of flexible plastic into it. One thing was sure, the sisters wouldn't be in awe of his equipment the next time he fucked them.

Inch by inch, the dildo dilated Olivia, fed into her by Melinda's insistent hands.

Olivia bucked and cried, 'Enough!'

Melinda oiled the other end. 'Portia, mount your lovely sister.'

Portia knelt up astride Olivia. Melinda bent the dong till it pointed straight up and held it in her fist. 'Lower yourself, Portia.'

The girl's bottom descended. Melinda took careful aim. The dome butted Portia's sex.

'Show me how much you can take,' Melinda encouraged.

Portia sank down, rotating her hips. She seemed to have no problem accommodating the first six inches. Her descent paused. She bit her lip. There was strain on her face but she jerked and gyrated until she'd impaled herself on a full nine inches. 'That's it.' She sighed, sounding disappointed.

'That's plenty,' Melinda congratulated her. The older woman's fist wrapped the eighteen inches of bent plastic that joined the sisters. Gripping tightly, she worked it up and down, into Olivia and out of Portia, then into Portia and out of Olivia.

Cole zoomed in as close as he could. Each outstroke dragged their fleshy lips with it. Each in-stroke inverted those engorged petals until they disappeared from sight.

The sisters glared lust into each other's eyes. Olivia snarled, 'It's me, your sister, your own flesh and blood you're fucking, you perverted bitch!'

In response, Portia spat down on Olivia's face, splattering her cheek with saliva.

'More!' Olivia demanded. 'I deserve it.' Her mouth gaped wide.

Portia spat again, directly between her sister's lips.

Melinda barked, 'You're both depraved fucking sluts, doing each other, doing your brother. What sort of incestuous whores are you? Filthy bitches like you deserve to be whipped.'

Portia moaned, 'We do. We're *evil*. Punish us for our sins, Melinda.'

Still pumping, Melinda lifted her head and called, 'Cole?'

He rolled off the bed and slammed through the two doors that separated him from the action. The trunk with the sisters' toys was open. He snatched a length of bamboo from it. Cole's hand shoved down on Portia's neck. 'Move aside,' he told Melinda. His cane whistled and cracked six times, striping Portia's slender buttocks.

Melinda timed her pistoning so that as each blow landed, she was stabbing up into Portia. Portia climaxed at the fourth blow but was still spasming when the last one seared into her flesh.

Without pausing, Cole dropped the cane, shoved both arms under Olivia and flipped the sisters over, still joined. Olivia lasted through her entire beating but three more of Melinda's vicious thrusts took her over the edge.

The sisters tumbled apart. Melinda worked the dildo from their dripping pussies. 'Nice work,' she told Cole. 'Our turn?'

Cole stroked Portia's burning ridges. 'I think we've earned it. Try this on.' He handed Melinda a strap-on that was equipped with a cock close in size to his own. As Melinda buckled in, he positioned the limp sisters, kneeling on the edge of the bed, bums high, heads down. Melinda poured oil over her mock-cock and passed the bottle to him. When he was anointed, they pressed their knobs between the sisters' cheeks, in unison.

'Ready?' he asked.

Melinda nodded.

'Then on three, one, two, three.'

Both thrust.

# Nineteen

Gordon Mayer, in the City's planning department, had rejected Del Barker's layout for his parking lot three times, each time for vague reasons.

Cole put a thick envelope on the narrow-shouldered man's desk. 'Mr Barker's architect can't seem to get it right,' he said. 'It looks like he's good with interiors but an idiot when it comes to landscaping. I was wondering if you'd be good enough to recommend someone who could draw up some plans that made better sense.'

'I do a bit of private work, sometimes,' Mayer said, eyeing Cole's envelope.

'If you'd draw up the plans, that'd be perfect. The problem is, he needs them fast, like tomorrow. There'd be no time for paperwork. Would it be OK by you if he paid cash?'

'How much?'

'If I could have them in the morning, a grand? I've got five hundred here. I can give you the rest when I pick them up, stamped, of course.'

Cole already had some experience with petty officials. He had a deal with a clerk at the County Court. When a separation agreement or petition for divorce was filed and the wife was the 'aggrieved party', Cole got a call. It wasn't illegal. Those were matters of public record. The calls just saved Cole time. Most newly divorced or separated women who hadn't dumped their husbands to

147

be with boyfriends were eager to be bedded. Cole told himself he was performing a public service. Just like a tossed equestrian, a woman who's been thrown off one man should climb onto another before she loses her confidence.

A surprising number of them were looking for something kinky – to act out the fantasies they'd been suppressing while married. Ironically, Cole was sure that their ex-spouses harboured similar dreams.

The widows that he found through the obituary columns were more varied. Often, all they needed was a man who'd assure them that they were still women and a shoulder to cry on. Others just craved cock. Once in a while, Cole came across a widow who fell between those extremes.

The Widow Sims was a Rubenesque fifty. The day he met her, she was red eyed and in dowdy black. She wasn't ready to sign a listing straight away and asked him to return a week later. When he did, she was still in black – a button-through skirt and a top with a widely scooped neckline that was just short of off the shoulder.

Cole stood behind her as she went through the listing agreement. Once she'd signed, she asked him, 'Are you looking at my titties?'

'It'd be hard for a man not to. They're quite spectacular, Mrs Sims.'

She tugged her top an inch lower. 'Better view?'

'Yes, but not as good as ...' He eased her top over her plump shoulders and halfway down to her elbows. Only her nipples held the top up.

'I'm not going to let you kiss me or fuck me,' she stated firmly, 'but you can play with my titties, if you like.'

His hands smoothed down their voluptuous upper slopes. Before he could lift them, she told him, 'You have to close your eyes.'

'I understand,' he lied.

'Closed?'

'Yes,' he lied again.

He scooped her bountiful mounds up over her neckline.

'No peeking!'

'OK.' Cole cupped and jiggled and bounced. His kneading fingers sank into opulent masses. His thumbs rubbed the flat tips of turret-shaped startlingly crimson nipples.

Mrs Sims's head lolled back. She undid one button of her skirt and slipped a hand inside. Cole tweaked and tugged. Her fingers moved under her skirt. Her thighs spread and stiffened. Cole pinched gently, compressing rubbery peaks. Mrs Sims panted. The movements under her skirt became frantic. It only took a few minutes for her to grunt under her breath, sigh, pull her hand out and do her button up.

'Don't think you'll get to do that again,' she warned him as she adjusted her breasts back into her top.

'I won't,' he promised.

# Twenty

Cole didn't phone Vincent. He had Willow to rely on. It was three nerve-wracking days after the penthouse showing that the stocky man finally summoned Cole to his tawdry office.

'They want two point nine mil. What'll they take?'

Cole had told the Silvetti sisters that they'd accept anything over two point four. He said, 'Two point six, if the deal is put together right.'

Vincent squinted, making him look more like the sobriquet his wife used. 'In what way, "right"?'

Willow had told Cole, through Melinda, that her husband had money that the tax man didn't know about. Cole explained, 'If the documents showed one price but there was cash involved that wasn't in writing, it'd save the vendors taxes. It'd also work to the purchaser's advantage. There's no tax on the sale of a principal residence. If the purchaser was to sell it, later, at perhaps three million or more, it'd all be nice clean perfectly legal money, tax exempt.'

'How about two mil on paper, half a mil in cash?'

'How about two mil on paper, point six in cash?'

Vincent thought. 'If it came to a total of two point five-five, there'd be a bonus in it for you.'

Cole loved it. Offer a crook a bent deal and he'll screw himself. 'How much would it be, my cash bonus?'

'Ten grand?'

'I think I can talk them into two point five-five; five hundred and fifty thousand in cash, two mil by cheque.'

Vincent leant forwards. 'How do we work it? You don't think I'm going to hand over all that paper and let you waltz off with it.'

'Reverse offer. I'll have them sign the deal and I'll deliver it to you. You give me the cheque and their cash, plus my ten, at the same time as you sign.'

The sisters were ecstatic. They were getting a hundred and fifty thousand over the value plus cheating the tax man out of about a quarter million. Olivia decided that the bonus Cole was getting from Vincent wasn't compensation enough for the commission he'd lose because of the cash, so awarded him another ten thousand.

They had a party when Cole delivered a suitcase full of bills after dropping the cheque and agreement off at their lawyer's. The twisted sisters were great fun, but exhausting and time consuming. He shipped their trunk of toys and arranged for movers to pack their furniture. At the airport there were tight hugs, wet kisses and flooding tears, and a sense of relief for Cole. There simply wasn't enough time in a day. He was still looking after Willy and Bill out of loyalty. What he made off them seemed trivial now. He had his widows and divorcees to service, not only in bed but selling their homes, and he couldn't neglect Nurse Margaret.

The day after the sisters left he called their cousin Robert's number to check they'd arrived safely.

Robert said, 'Thanks for taking such good care of my cousins. I'll take care of them now but I promise you that your kindness won't be forgotten. If I can put any business your way, I will.'

Cole shrugged. Robert was three thousand miles away, in the import–export business. It didn't seem likely he'd know of any real estate opportunities in Ontario.

Vincent and Willow moved into the penthouse. A

month later, Vincent took off for an extended tour of South-east Asia.

Melinda called Cole. 'The Pig left two days ago. Willow and I got together yesterday. We had fun but two pussies and a cock beats two pussies with no cock, right?'

'Not forgetting four breasts, two bums, etcetera. What sort of scene did you have in mind, Melinda? "This girl", times two?'

' "This girl" misses you Cole, but I told you, Willow's different.'

'Better explain how.'

'Willow likes a man to be masterful.'

'As does "this girl".'

'But "this girl" is obedient. Willow won't do anything unless she's forced to but when she's forced, she loves it.'

Cole's spine tingled a warning. 'She's not into being brutalised, is she?'

'No, nothing like that. She just – you'll see. I have confidence in you, Cole.'

'When?'

'Tomorrow night? Come for supper?'

'Your place or hers?'

'Mine. I have the toys, right? Just remember, no matter how she protests or struggles, make her do whatever you fancy, nothing yucky, but, short of that, subdue her and use her hard.'

Ever cautious, Cole said, 'I know your safe-word, Melinda. What's hers?'

'She can use mine.'

'But she understands what it's for?'

'I'll explain it to her.'

'Be sure you do. If not, I won't touch her.'

'This girl understands.'

Melinda greeted him bare foot and bare legged, in something that reminded Cole of the dancing nymphs on a Grecian urn. It was a simple white crossover wrap, not see-through but fine enough to be translucent, which came three inches down her slender muscular thighs. It veed to the gold satin cord that circled her three times, from just beneath her high hard breasts, to her lean waist. When she moved, the wrap opened at one side to her hip.

Willow was a total contrast. Skeins of honeyed locks were pinned high on her head. She was immaculately made-up, with touches of frost on her eyelids and lips. An inch of black velvet circled her elegant throat. Her shoulders were bare. Her gown was plain, also black velvet. It had a turned-up vertical cuff that barely concealed her nipples. From there, it was tight to low on her hips where it flared into folds that brushed the floor. Her breasts seemed larger than Cole had thought when he'd first met her but that might have been because of the way her fitted bodice lifted them.

Melinda bobbed Cole a little curtsy. 'This girl has prepared sirloin tips and Portobello mushrooms in a burgundy sauce, if it pleases Sir.'

Cole nodded. Willow extended a heavily ringed hand, high, as if expecting him to kiss it. Her expression was arrogant. If Cole hadn't been warned that she would play aloof, challenging him to defile her, he'd have dismissed her as a stuck-up bitch.

He brushed past her, commenting, 'Your friend has nice tits.'

Melinda padded beside him. 'This girl is happy that you think so, Sir.'

Willow overtook them. Cole grinned. Her gown was backless; cut so low she showed three inches of cleavage between the cheeks of her bottom. From the front she was icily sexy. From the rear, she was a whore.

How the hell did the front stay up? Double-sided tape?

The dining table was set with snowy linen and heavy silver. Silver candlesticks flanked a shallow porcelain dish in which white orchid blossoms floated.

153

Cole helped Willow sit. Looking down from above and behind, he could see coral tips that were concealed from in front. Her haughtiness was an act, a deliberate façade that was meant to challenge him. Cole's fingers flexed in anticipation.

Melinda poured Merlot into crystal goblets. While she was fetching their food, Cole asked Willow, 'She's talked to you about safe-words?'

Her, 'Yes,' was hesitant. The topic wasn't in keeping with her cool pose.

'And yours is?' he insisted.

'The same as hers.'

'Which is?'

'*Ça suffit.*'

'Is it, ever, for you?'

'Ever what?'

'Enough?'

Willow was saved from answering by Melinda's return, with a steaming tureen.

The beef was succulent but the sauce was a little too winey for Cole's taste. There was white asparagus on the side, with individual dishes of hollandaise. Melinda's freshly baked rolls melted on the tongue. Cole restricted himself to one. He didn't want to be too full when the fun started.

The women played the flirtation games that asparagus is made for. They licked and sucked the pale stems slowly and lasciviously, Melinda making bedroom eyes at both of her guests. Willow aimed her more modest but still erotic slurps at only Melinda. It must have been a hard act for her – showing her slut side to her sapphic lover while being prim towards the man whom she expected was going to defile her aristocratic body later.

Cole decided to make it harder for her. 'Melinda – your left breast – bare it.'

'This girl obeys.' She pulled her wrap off her left shoulder and down.

154

Cole looked from Melinda's pierced nipple to Willow. 'Are you pierced?' he asked.

'Just my ears.'

'Not your nipples?'

She blushed and glanced down into her cleavage. 'No.'

'I like Melinda's jewels, don't you?'

Willow croaked, 'Yes.'

'Do you wonder what it feels like for her, with that little ball bumping her clit with every step she takes?'

'I . . . um . . .'

Melinda rescued her friend. 'May this girl fetch dessert?'

Cole nodded. Melinda scurried to the kitchen and returned with bowls of lime sorbet.

Cole asked her, 'When you put ice on the metal that impales your nipple, does the chill sink into your flesh?'

'Some, Sir.'

'Show us. No hands, mind.'

Melinda put her hands behind her back and leant forwards over her bowl to dip the pendant U and the tip of her nipple into freezing ice. As the cold bit, her face contorted.

'Poor girl,' Cole said. 'Bring it here and I'll warm it.'

Willow bent low over her sorbet but her eyes were peeking sideways. Melinda stood, keeping her hands demurely behind her, and went to Cole. She stooped to present her nipple to his mouth. Cole sucked. His tongue toyed with her icy pendant. His cheeks hollowed. Willow paused with a spoon almost to her lips.

'This girl thanks Sir.'

Cole pulled his head back, elongating her breast to a pear shape before releasing it. 'Give me your cord.'

She untied the knot. Her wrap parted. It was already off one shoulder. Now it just dangled, wide open, loosely draped to partly cover her right breast. Cole brushed it back. He put a finger to the ornament at her navel then briefly touched the rod that pierced her

155

below her clit's ridge. Eating her nakedness with his eyes, he coiled the cord and set it beside his place.

'You may finish your dessert.'

'This girl thanks Sir.'

Both women eyed the coil surreptitiously while they finished their sorbets. Cole let them wonder what he had in mind for it.

'Coffee, Sir?' Melinda asked. 'Liqueur?'

'Later, perhaps.'

Willow started, 'I'd like coffee –'

'I said *later*,' Cole interrupted. It was time to exert his dominance. 'Clear the table, Melinda.' While she did, he stood and took up the coil of cord.

Willow tried to watch him without betraying her interest but he went behind her. His hands took her bare arms and drew them back.

'What?' she asked.

Cole ignored her as he made figure eights from her elbows to her wrists and tied the cord off, leaving dangling ends.

'I didn't say you could . . .'

His fingers flipped down the cuff that cupped her breasts. Now that she was more exposed, the mystery of her self-supporting bodice was revealed. Two lyre-shaped springs had been sewn to the fabric. Each nipped a nipple, holding her gown in place. Just as the jewel at Melinda's pubes stimulated her clit with each step she took, every movement of Willow's lithe body had to tug on her cruelly compressed nipples. Their bases were pinched and their tips swollen, transforming them into the shapes of chess pawns. They'd been that way throughout the meal and for some minutes, at least, before. How they had to ache for release.

Curious, Cole tried a tip with his finger. It felt hard and glossy.

Willow blurted, 'Don't touch me!'

'I'll touch you wherever and however I wish,' he told her. His fingers burrowed into her immaculate coiffure. Pins showered to the floor and across the table. Her locks tumbled. Cole's fist closed, straining the roots of her hair. The sinews in her neck stood out as she fought his backwards pressure but she was helpless to resist. Willow's head was bent back. She glared up at him. Her lips parted to protest. He covered them with his. Cole's tongue slavered into her mouth, forcing her tongue aside to access the sweet saliva pooled beneath it. He palpitated her nipple gently.

Willow groaned. Her mouth surrendered. Her lips softened. His tongue moved hers. When he sucked, her tongue was drawn into his mouth. A prod sent it back, limp, waiting for his to follow. As he commandeered her mouth, his fingers tormented the tight hard ball that the tip of her nipple had become.

He drew back an inch to tell Melinda, 'Go fetch.'

They'd prearranged what she was to bring: a doggy bowl with sauce from their sirloin tips, a dish of condensed milk and a leash – eighteen inches of heavy plaited leather with a six-inch loop at one end.

Cole's hand deserted Willow's nipple to jerk her chair from under her. She didn't tumble. His hand in her hair lowered her to kneel on the floor. Melinda set the doggy bowl down six feet away.

'What do you think you're doing?' Willow demanded.

'Treating you like what you are,' he told her. 'You're nothing but a bitch in heat. You're a pussy, an ass and a mouth, for me to use if I feel like it. You've been walking on two legs but you haven't earned that privilege. I'm going to teach you to crawl like the nasty little animal you are. When you've learnt to grovel properly, I might just allow you to stand up.'

'Grovel?' she said, savouring the word. Then she added a defiant, 'You think I'm going to let you humiliate me?'

'Humiliate, defile, debauch. All of those, and more.'

'Never!'

'No?' Holding Willow by her hair and her wrists, he propelled her towards the doggy bowl. She had no choice but to walk on her knees, head arched back. Her dress was trapped under her knees. The first movement of one leg past the other yanked it down. The clips were jerked off her nipples. Sparkling fire flooded them, replacing numbness with eruptions of agony.

Cole lifted her wrists painfully higher and kept pushing. Willow was forced to crawl, dragging her dress off her hips and emerging naked but for her heels, hose and choker. He pushed her face down to the bowl. 'Eat!'

'No!'

Cole took the leash from Melinda's hand. 'Each refusal earns you five of these,' he said, coolly. He slashed her rump diagonally, from the top of her right thigh to the fullness of her left cheek. 'Now eat.'

With a soft whimper, Willow dipped her tongue into the sauce and lapped, flicking the rich mixture into her mouth.

'There's a good little bitch,' he congratulated her. 'Lick it clean.' When her tongue had polished the inside of the bowl he twisted her head towards himself. 'Melinda told you about my special champagne cocktail?'

She nodded as best she could.

Melinda volunteered, 'That was the most demeaning thing anyone has ever made this girl do, drink cold jism.'

He told Willow, 'If you're very good, I might allow you a similar treat.' To Melinda, he said, 'Bum on the table, girl.'

Melinda perched, bottom on the edge, legs stretched straight and apart, with just her toes touching the floor. Cole propelled Willow to Melinda's feet. 'This girl' held out the dish of condensed milk. He dipped a finger in and smeared it between Melinda's right big toe and the next.

'You know what to do,' he told Willow.

Melinda lifted her foot to her friend's mouth. Willow's long pink tongue slithered between Melinda's toes.

'Good bitch.' He wiped more milk on the inside of Melinda's thigh, just above her knee, and made a sticky trail of it to the crease of her groin.

Willow's tongue followed that line, then the one Cole painted up Melinda's other thigh. The next smear coated the slightly parted crinkled lips of Melinda's sex. Willow's delicate but lingering little laps cleansed every trace away.

'And now,' Cole announced. He planted the tiniest dab on the very head of Melinda's exposed clit. As fast as Willow tongued it away, he dabbed again, and again. Melinda began to squirm. Cole coated an entire finger with the sweet substance and showed it to Willow. 'You know where I'm going to put this?'

'Inside her?' she whispered.

'Inside her, where?'

'Her sex?'

'Wrong. Turn over, Melinda.'

She turned, lying flat across the table from her hips up, and reached back to pull the cheeks of her ass wide apart. Cole put his fingertip to the muscular iris and pushed. His finger rotated inside her, wiping condensed milk on the inner walls of her rectum before tugging out.

Cole wiped his still-sticky finger on Willow's extended tongue. 'Now show me how long and strong your tongue is.'

Willow nuzzled between her friend's cheeks. Cole couldn't see if her tongue penetrated as far as his finger had, but judging by Melinda's pleased moans and little twitches, Willow was performing her demeaning task to the best of her ability.

159

He drew her face back and turned it to his cock. 'Open.' Her lips parted. He plunged into the warm wet softness of her mouth, not allowing her to felate him, just fucking her face. After a dozen shallow thrusts, he pulled out. With one hand in her hair and the other wagging his cock to beat its wet head on her lips, he told her, 'You want more? Beg for it.'

Melinda turned to watch.

Defiance flashed into Willow's eyes but vanished as quickly. In a voice that was husky with lust, she asked, 'Please, Cole, may I taste your cock? I adore your cock, Cole. I worship it. My slutty mouth craves your come.' Her eyes looked up into his, pleading. 'Beat me, bugger me, fuck me, do anything you like to me, but I beg you, just one taste?'

Pleading abjectly came so easily to Willow that Cole wondered how many men before him had cracked her frigid act and 'reduced' her to the craving slut she hid in her day-to-day life. He had no illusions that it was his dominance that'd transformed her. There are submissives who seduce by their meek obedience. Others challenge any man they sense has dominance in him and trust that by defying him, they'll evoke his darker desires. Then there were women like Melinda, to whom submission was a game, fun, but not vital to their happiness. The meek submissives and the 'fun' ones were both honest. A man had no doubts about where he stood with them. Willow's type had split personalities. He suspected that she believed each of her 'selves' were really her, depending on which one she was wearing at the time. He decided to be careful with her.

'Just one taste?' he said. 'Very well.' He pumped his cock, milking it. A drop of crystal clear pre-come welled up in its eye. 'Tongue.' She extended hers. A strong squeeze on his shaft spilt his dew. It descended, dangling on a thin strand. Cole shook it free, to plop onto the flat of Willow's tongue.

She sucked it in and extended her tongue again, ready for more. Instead of granting it, Cole pulled Melinda's head down, folding her, and put his cock to her mouth. Willow watched with envious eyes as her friend laved the head of Cole's cock with her tongue and then took it between her lips to mumble on and lap. The sensations were so exquisite that his sphincter contracted and his balls tightened. It was too soon. With two lovely women at his disposal he'd likely be able to come two or three times but not yet, not yet.

He straightened Melinda and told Willow, 'On your hind legs, bitch.'

She stood and waited for his next command. It was his first chance to inspect her sex. Her pelt was fair and fine, trimmed close. The top of her slit was divided by a ridge. He parted her sex's lips. The root of her clit emerged from high between her lips. Its shaft was long, with a loose wrinkled sheath that still covered its head. He pushed her hood back to expose a glossy pink seed pearl. As he gently masturbated Willow, the fingers of his other hand toyed with the jewel at Melinda's clit. When both delicate morsels were engorged, he drew the women together by his grips on their shafts. Clit head touched clit head. Both women stiffened at the contact. With one thumb and finger working both polyps together, rubbing clit on clit, he tugged Melinda's nipple to Willow's. With those also pressed together, he rubbed his thumbs on his fingers, rolling clit on clit and nipple against nipple.

'Tongues,' he ordered them.

Each extended her tongue to slither and play with the other's. Their eyes blazed lust. Cole's fingers worked harder and faster. The sense of power was exhilarating. He was frigging two lovely women at the same time. He was in total control. He could stop at any moment and leave both quivering with need, or he could roll their flesh harder and faster and grant them completion. He decided to be merciful. Which would climax first? Willow was the more repressed, less comfortable with her sexuality, but that might spur her. Perhaps ...

Melinda jerked, tilting her pelvis. Three of his fingers, curled below his forefinger and thumb, felt the hot wet splatter of her juices. Cole tugged Melinda higher and pushed down on Willow. Melinda squirted over Willow's clit.

Willow gurgled, 'Oh no!' and thrust her pussy at Melinda's to take the full flood between her gaping lips.

Before her spasms finished, Cole spun Melinda and laid her on the table. He heaved Willow up and dumped her on Melinda, face to pussy. 'Enjoy,' he told them, and wandered off to search through Melinda's toy drawer.

He returned with a butt plug, a six-inch plastic spindle that had an imitation horse tail attached, and a bottle of lube. When Melinda, looking up at him past Willow's bum, saw what he had, she nodded vigorously. Cole lubed the plug and squirted more oil into the crease between Willow's lean cheeks.

Her head lifted. 'What?'

Cole pushed her face back down into Melinda's saturated sex. At its tip, the spindle was as narrow as two of his fingers put together. From there it flared into a bulb the size of a tangerine before tapering again to its tail. Willow jerked as Cole forced the tip into her anus. She stiffened when the bulb distended her sphincter. By the time she was dilated around the thickest part she was rigid and panting. It took only the gentlest push to sink it the rest of the way in. The powerful muscles of her sphincter were clamping on it. Their pressure drove it into her rectum.

Cole toyed, pushing and pulling gently; while he let the women's tongues play with each other's clits. This time, Willow climaxed first. Perhaps it was the added stimulation of her anus's invader. Cole waited for the women to stir from their sated slump.

Willow lifted her head. Her lipstick was gone. Her face glistened with juices from Melinda's sex. Cole slid his hand between the two women's bodies. Willow's nipple was trapped between his knuckles. He crushed it, and her breast, as he lifted her off Melinda and set her, on all fours, on the floor.

'Wag your tail.'

Willow's bum twitched from side to side. He took her hair in one hand again and the cord around her wrists in the other. Moving fast enough to make it hard for her to keep up with him, walking on her knees, with her back arched painfully, he marched her to Melinda's red bedroom. Melinda followed with the leash.

Cole sat on the padded bench and took the length of plaited leather from 'this girl'. He told Willow, 'Still on your knees, run circles round me. Melinda, down between my legs. Amuse me with your mouth.'

Melinda snuggled down, happily, and took Cole's cock between her lips. Willow shuffled round the bench. Each time she passed him, Cole took a diagonal swipe at her bottom, on alternate sides of her wagging tail. 'Faster, bitch! You can move faster than that.'

Willow had made six circuits with a welt across her behind added at each one before she stumbled and fell flat on her face. Cole rose, plucking his cock from Melinda's sucking mouth. He put a foot on Willow's back and nudged her bound arms higher. His leash rose and fell six more times before Willow sobbed, 'No more!'

He said, 'Your safe-word?'

She choked out, '*Ça suffice!*'

Cole tossed the leash aside. 'Melinda, I'm going to fuck you.'

'This girl thanks Sir.'

'On the bed, on your back, spread wide, knees up.'

Melinda lay back holding her knees high and wide. Cole scooped Willow up and tossed her across the foot of the bed.

As he stripped, he said, 'Willow, you will assist. As your hands are bound, you'll have to use your mouth.' He knelt between Melinda's legs with his hips raised, resting on his hands beside her head. His cock wagged as he lowered it to Melinda's pubes. 'Willow!'

The cringing creature Cole had reduced an imperious woman to squirmed across the bed to get her come-smeared face between Melinda's raised thighs. Mouth wide, she turned her head to reach up to Cole's cock. Soft lips closed around his shaft, between its head and his balls. Not letting her teeth touch his skin, Willow manoeuvred his cock until its head touched Melinda's flaccid engorged lips.

Cole pushed in just far enough to hold his cock in place. 'I want to feel your tongue inside her, alongside my cock. You understand?'

'Mm.' She snuggled her cheek down onto the bed as low as she could and poked her tongue out. It tickled the underside of Cole's cock. Its tip touched Melinda where her lips met at the bottom and wormed into that narrow opening.

Cole slid, very slowly, into Melinda's humid depths. His balls dragged across Willow's cheek. He withdrew, just as slowly, until the tongue that his cock shared Melinda's sex with was pressing on the knot on the underside of his glans. Back in, a little faster. The upward pressure of Willow's cheek, on the underside of his cock, pressed his shaft high enough that it dragged over the exposed head of Melinda's clit. On his out-strokes, Willow's ear brushed the short hairs on his balls. Her panting was a warm breeze on his shaft. The air she breathed, with her face trapped in that narrow space, was redolent with his and Melinda's musk. Cole pumped, faster and faster.

Melinda gazed up into his eyes adoringly. 'Will you make her drink our come, Sir?' she asked.

'Every drop.'

'This girl . . . this girl is going to squirt, Sir.'

'Then squirt.'

Melinda's face contorted. Hot juices spurted from between Cole's cock and the lips of Melinda's pussy. Willow gobbled and slurped, sucking up every aromatic drop. Cole let his body take over. His hips thrust hard and fast. His balls tightened. The incredible sensation, like a knotted string of liquid being drawn out of him, coursed up through the core of his cock. As he felt it emerge, he let it start to flow into Melinda before tugging back to flood from him, across and between Willow's lips. When the aftershocks died down, he told Willow, 'Now suck it out of her, bitch.'

# Twenty-one

Cole decided not to ask Del Barker for the thousand he'd used to bribe Gordon Mayer, the planning officer. It'd be worth more as a favour owed and, anyway, Del would likely bitch about the amount.

Debbie brought a parcel to his desk. It was a Rolex Oyster, with no note, but it was engraved, 'Only you know who I really am.'

He called Melinda and told her, 'I'll give it to you to give back to Willow. You know this means I can't see her again, right?'

'Silly bitch,' Melinda agreed. 'She understood, before-hand, that it'd just be for fun. I blame you, Cole.'

'You do?'

'She told me, after you left, that she'd never been so humiliated before. Your "performance" was just too much for her, it seems. It's sad when people confuse lust and love.'

'But not you, right?'

Melinda chuckled. 'Cole, "this girl" adores you. "Melinda" thinks you're great fun when she's in the right mood. That's all.'

'Thank goodness for that.'

'If it reassures you, Cole, tomorrow I have a date with a couple of incredibly beautiful young men. I'll watch while they take turns sodomising each other. They like to show off in front of women, but not to be touched by them.'

'Infinite variety, eh, Melinda? So you're OK with me not seeing Willow again?'

'Of course.'

'Call me, then, when "this girl" raises her pretty head.'

'I will.'

It was a day of relationships ending. Nurse Margaret called him at eleven. In a hesitant voice she told him that her husband had started taking more notice of her. They'd even been intimate. 'I think, maybe . . . You and me . . .'

He told her, 'All good things come to an end. We've had fun, Margaret. I'll always remember our times together. Good luck with your husband.' He thought about adding something about her calling him if things didn't work out but decided against it. A clean break was best.

Cole had just decided to call it a day and was putting his jacket on when Robert, the Silvettis' cousin, called.

'Do you do commercial work?' he asked.

Cole's only non-residential deals so far had been the building on Lakeshore and Margaret's lease, but he said, 'It's my preference.'

'You don't happen to speak Mandarin by any chance, do you?'

'Sorry.'

'No matter. I'm sure you'll manage.'

'Manage what?'

'I've recommended you to a client of mine, a Chinese company. They want to invest over here and Vancouver is being flooded with Chinese money, so they think they'll do better further east.'

'Hong Kong money?'

'No, Beijing.'

'What sort of investment?'

'Big. Capitalism is in, in China, right now. They're thinking of some sort of mall, close to Toronto but not too close. Could you find them a site?'

167

'Yes.' Cole's blood bubbled like champagne. The commissions on assembling a parcel that size could set him up for life.

'I'll fax you everything I know. You'll be dealing with a senior executive, a Madam Soo Li-Sung. I haven't met her yet but I'm told she's a brilliant businesswoman and very tough, so handle her with kid gloves. I'll give you her flight details when I have them but it'll be on or about the third, so you should keep your diary clear.'

'The third?'

'Of next month.'

Cole crossed mental fingers and said, 'I'll be ready. Thanks, Robert. How are your cousins settling in?'

'Fine. We're just one big happy family, now.'

In one big happy bed, Cole guessed.

The third was only ten days away. Cole took his jacket off. It'd be the first of many long late nights. For fourteen hours a day, seven days a week, Cole scanned surveys and checked proposed new developments and studied incredibly complex zoning regulations. He set two half-hours a day aside to phone past, present and potential clients. He picked up breakfast-in-a-bun on his way to the office each morning. His lunch was delivered to his desk. When he wasn't too tired to eat, he zapped his supper in a microwave. The longest break he had was a three-hour lunch with Gordon Mayer. After half a bottle of wine, two glasses of Cointreau and three Martinis, his new buddy assured him that certain exceptions to zoning laws could be arranged, under the right conditions. The 'right conditions' weren't named but Gordon rubbed his finger and thumb together and leered.

The Ho-Fat Corporation hoped to build a two-hundred-and-fifty unit mall. The West Edmonton Mall was something like eight-hundred units; Square One, in Mississauga, about thirty miles from Toronto, had over four hundred. Ho-Fat's couldn't be compared to either, though. The plans called for seventy 'big-box' stores that would serve as giant outlets for Chinese exports, plus cinemas, a theatre, a bowling alley and just about every sort of entertainment facility Cole had ever heard of. With parking, it'd need between eighty and a hundred acres.

Anywhere near a highway, that sort of land went for between one and two million dollars an acre. Cole dreamt of sleek Aston Martins, aromatic truffles, twenty-year-old Scotch and submissive sylphs.

Several Orientals came through Arrivals but there was only one pair of women with no men. One was tall and slender, about forty, wearing an expensive business suit. The other was no more than five feet in her high heels, weighed a hundred pounds, maximum, and wore a traditional cheongsam of scarlet silk embroidered with golden dragons. Cole reminded himself that 'cheongsam' translates as 'long dress' but hers wasn't. It came to just below her knees, with slits to just above them.

He called out, 'Ho-Fat?'

As they came closer, Cole saw that distance hadn't deceived him. The tall one, Madam Soo Li-Sung, he guessed, was a handsome woman with intelligence sparkling in her almond eyes. The other, her assistant maybe, was exquisite though her eyes were modestly averted.

'Cole, real estate man?' the taller asked him in a melodic accent.

Cole made a bow, low enough to be polite, not so low as to appear obsequious.

'It is very tiring, flying,' he was told. 'We wish only to be driven to our hotel, today. Business, tomorrow. Is OK?'

Cole agreed. He directed the skycap with their luggage to his car, which he'd parked illegally with the hood up and flashers on. The two women sat in the back and chattered, in Mandarin probably, ignoring him for the most part, though when they were waiting for lights to change and he glanced in the rear-view mirror, he caught the little one eyeing him speculatively. Their eyes met. She looked down into her lap, perhaps blushing. Cole reminded himself that business took precedence over pleasure.

When he arrived at the lobby of their hotel the next morning, the tall one was waiting. 'Madam Soo come soon,' she said.

Oops! So the cute one was his client and the other the translator/assistant. It was a good job he hadn't made a pass at either of them.

Partly to make conversation, he asked, 'Is Mister Li-Sung also in Canada?'

She said, 'No Mister. Madam is widow.'

'I'm sorry, but I don't know your name?'

'Is Betty. Not real name. Real name, you can't say right.'

Arrogant bitch! Still, it was interesting to know that his client was a widow. Dealing with bereaved women was his speciality. He dared not use his usual tactics, though. The deal was too big to risk and, anyway, Betty was in the way.

Madam Soo's cheongsam was emerald green that day, with silver chrysanthemums. It was shorter by a few inches, just brushing her knees and slit to mid-thigh. Did that mean she fancied him?

He drove them to two adjoining parcels just north of Toronto, not the land he really wanted them to buy but as part of his 'set-up'. As the zoning was already perfect, the price was higher than the one he intended to sell them and then bribe Gordon Mayer to rezone.

Neither showed any reaction. His mild flirtations, through Betty, also drew blank looks. He bought them lunch at a steak house, figuring it'd be exotic to them. Both raided the salad bar and refused steaks. Perhaps he'd made a mistake?

They remained inscrutable when he showed them the lots he really wanted them to buy. Maybe that was just their way.

On the way back to their hotel, he said, 'I've booked a restaurant and a box at the theatre for this evening, if you'd like.'

Betty and Madam Soo conferred in Mandarin. Betty told him, 'Kind man. Which show?'

'*The Phantom of the Opera*?' He held his breath. The tickets had been the devil to get and very expensive.

Betty translated. Madam Soo smiled and nodded. Cole breathed again.

When he picked them up both were in evening dress. Cole wished he'd rented a tux. Madam Soo's cheongsam was black and gold, ankle length, slit to mid-thigh. Betty's dress was Western, also long, green silk, with a high neck, long sleeves and no slit, but clinging.

Both chose the four-star restaurant's blackened cod. Cole ordered the same. After their second glass of champagne, both women brushed their knees against his under the table. For the first time in a long while, Cole was confused. Were they making approaches individually, each not knowing what the other was doing? Was he expected to bed them both at once? Maybe they were just flirting for the fun of it, not meaning it to go further. He thought about dropping a hand to each knee to test the waters but there was too much riding on the potential deal for him to risk it.

Madam Soo bumped her hip against his thigh on the way back to his car. It might have been an accident. When they got to it and he'd helped Madam Soo into the back, Betty went to the front passenger door. Even though she rode beside him, it was with her head twisted back for a non-stop conversation with Madam Soo. He couldn't make anything out of their tones of voice. To his uneducated ear, everything in Mandarin sounded like quarrelling.

There were three upright chairs in the box. They left him the middle one. They crossed their legs towards him. When a woman crosses towards a man it usually indicates interest but, in this case, towards him also meant towards each other.

Maybe they were gay?

Madam Soo's nyloned leg was exposed to the lacy top of her stocking by her dress's slit. Her high-heeled pump dangled from her dainty little toes. When Cole passed a box of Godiva chocolates from one lovely woman to the other, each bit their selections in two with tiny perfect teeth. Cole picked out a truffle and held it to Madam Soo's lips with a, 'This is a nice one,' that she wouldn't understand. She bit it without taking it from his fingers, which was a good sign, but then said something in Mandarin. Betty reached over to steer his hand to her mouth and take the rest of the delicacy.

Cole decided to ignore the mixed signals they were sending until they sent some clear ones.

He had no idea if they liked or even understood the performance. Perhaps it was too Western for their Oriental tastes. Back in the car, he said, 'That second parcel of land we looked at today . . .'

Betty told him, 'No business, please.'

Her hand was on the armrest between them. When he turned corners, his elbow brushed it. She didn't move her fingers away. She didn't move them closer, either.

Cole escorted them into their hotel's lobby. 'Good-night, ladies.. I hope you enjoyed your evening.' He turned to leave.

Betty touched his arm. 'We talk private, OK?'

They saw Madam Soo to the elevator. The hotel's main bar had secluded booths. Cole sat opposite Betty, in case this was to be a business conference. She ordered Martinis for both of them, charged to her room, so whatever this was about, it seemed it was neither business nor a 'date'.

'You our friend?' she asked.

He hedged with, 'I like you both.'

'We can be confidential?' Her tongue stumbled through 'confidential'.

'Whatever you have to say, I won't repeat it, to anyone,' he promised.

'I 'splain. Madam Soo brought up ver' strict. Her family old guard, know Chairman Mao. No television, no books that weren't serious. She smart lady but – innocent?'

'About sex, you mean? But she was married.'

'Her husband – old man – ninety-two.'

'When he died?'

'When she marry him.'

'How old was he when he died, then?'

'Ninety-two.'

That made sense to Cole. How long could a man that age last, married to a hot little thing like Madam Soo?

'Now she soon will marry again,' Betty continued.

'Congratulations to her.'

'Western man, very rich, good business, Calgary, oil.'

'And how old is Madam Soo's fiancé?'

'Forty. Big man.' She looked Cole in the eye. 'You see problem?'

'No,' he said, though he had suspicions.

'Western men have, how you say, "mis-con-ceptions" about Chinese women.'

'Some do, I guess.'

'All the same other way around.' She paused, flustered. 'Chinese women think all Western men – big.' She held her hands up a foot apart.

'Not *that* big, most of us.'

'Western men want wives to do things, things in bed.'

'The same things Chinese men want, I'd think.'

'Maybe so. Problem is, Madam Soo not know about those things.'

'You're a mature woman, Betty. Can't you tell her what she needs to know?'

173

'Betty thinks maybe she doesn't know so much.' Her embarrassment was affecting her command of English.

'So you want me to tell you about the things Madam Soo's new husband might expect from her? Why me?'

'Mister Robert say you pillow-master.' She looked into her lap. 'His cousins tell him.'

That was flattering. Cole couldn't help but ask, 'What did they say about me?'

'They say you number-one perverted fucking bastard. Is good thing?' There was a twinkle in her eye.

'That depends. So, what do you want to know?'

'You tell Madam Soo.'

'I don't speak Mandarin.'

'You tell through me.'

Cole swallowed. He'd have been happy to give Madame Soo an education in Western sexual practices, if it had been a practical one. Doing it verbally, through a translator, wouldn't be as much fun. Still, it could be an interesting exercise in flirtation.

'When?' he asked.

'Now?'

Madam Soo had changed into a long peacock-blue brocaded kimono. Perhaps the stiff fabric was supposed to defend her from him, in case he got carried away. Betty excused herself, leaving Cole to smile and make awkward gestures at Madam Soo. When the handsome secretary returned she too was in a kimono, but red satin and mid-thigh long. Cole suppressed a grin. Maybe there'd be practical as well as oral lessons.

Betty poured drinks and the three sat, Madam Soo on a love set, Cole and Betty facing each other in armchairs.

Cole asked, 'So, what would Madam like to ask me?'

'How big are Western men?'

'The average, I understand, is about six and a half inches.' He held his hands that far apart. 'Some are bigger; some smaller.'

Madam Soo let loose a stream of Mandarin. Betty spat a few words back. Madam released another torrent, with chopping motions.

Cole asked, 'What was that all about?'

Betty looked at the floor. 'It's hard for me to tell you.'

'But we're friends. You can tell me anything.'

Her fingers knitted together. 'Madam Soo tell me to ask you, please, to show how big.'

'She wants to look at my cock?'

'For research.'

'Of course.' So much for him delivering a lecture. It was all a game. That was fine by Cole. He slumped back in this chair, hips pushed forwards, legs spread. 'In the spirit of pure research, you may help yourself.'

Betty put her hands to her mouth. 'You want *me* . . .?'

'Or Madam Soo. Either of you. Lesson one – Western men don't take their own cocks out when there are pretty women around to do it for them.'

'Oh.' There was another exchange of Mandarin, following which Betty dropped to her knees between Cole's feet. Her fingers shook uncontrollably as she tugged Cole's zipper down. A trembling hand slid into the slit. It fumbled around, exploring, found the elastic of Cole's bikini briefs, tugged it down, and froze.

Betty was wide eyed as Cole's fevered cock unfolded to fill her palm.

Madam leant forwards and said something commanding. Betty parted Cole's fly with one hand as the other manoeuvred left and right to tug his rigid length into the open.

'Ah!' Madam Soo said.

Suddenly bold, Betty delved back into Cole's slacks and drew his balls out.

'Ah!' Madam Soo repeated, followed by some Mandarin.

'What's she say?' Cole asked.

'Madam says your cock is much bigger than her

husband's was but your spheres are e-norm-ous. You will make many sons.'

'Thank Madam for me. Now, she has some questions?'

Betty was still holding his cock in one hand and cradling his balls in the other but Cole wasn't about to remind her.

As Madam Soo spoke, Betty gave a running translation. 'We watch three-X TV last night. Men even more bigger than you. Is normal?'

Cole explained how male porn stars were selected.

'Is normal for men to like lick ladies in private places? If so, why?'

'You mean their pussies? Pussies taste very good. When a woman has her pussy licked, it gives her pleasure. Men like to please women.'

'You do this?' Betty's hand squeezed his shaft a little harder.

'Often. Whenever I get the chance.'

'How? Push tongue in and out?'

Cole closed his fist over the fingers that wrapped his cock. Looking straight into Betty's eyes, he pumped slowly and said, 'It's hard to explain but I'd be happy to demonstrate.'

More Mandarin flew between the women, rising in cadence until Betty released Cole's cock, stood up, moved back and perched on the arm of a chair with her legs spread wide. 'Please to show?'

Without putting his cock away, Cole knelt between Betty's thighs. It was time he took control. He brushed her kimono open, lifted her with a hand under each thigh, moved her sideways and dumped her on the seat. Deftly, Cole dragged her bottom to the edge and draped her knees over the arms. That was better. Betty was nicely exposed and accessible. He ran the flat of his tongue from inside her left knee to her groin, squirmed it into that sensitive crease, drew back and parted her lips with his thumbs. Ducking low, he ran his tongue from beneath her, up between its lips, over the smoothness of her pubic bone and to the tiny button of her clit.

Madam Soo rustled over in her brocade kimono to stare down at what Cole was doing. Some clits like direct licking from the start. Others find that too intense until they're close to climax. Cole was cautious. He lapped between Betty's clit and the lip of her sex so that the side of his tongue moved on her sheath rather than her clit head.

That seemed to work. Betty made 'uh-uh' noises. When her employer asked questions, she found it hard to answer coherently. Cole worked two fingers into her and sought out her G-spot. When Betty responded to Madam Soo, it was in squeaky bursts.

The older woman started panting. Her belly heaved. Her head flopped from side to side. Cole sucked her clit, drawing it between pursed lips, and flickered his tongue directly on its exposed head. Her bottom lifted. She trembled, suspended between the chair's arms, then slammed down, yanking her clit from Cole and letting out a thin high-pitched yodelling sound.

Madam Soo made demanding noises. Betty just lay back, gasping.

When she seemed to have recovered some, Cole asked her, 'Did Madam Soo have any other questions?'

Betty gave him a weary smile. 'Movie we watch – *Backdoor Bimbos*. Is true? Do men?'

'Bugger women? Yes, and other men, but I'm not into that – men, I mean – I didn't mean that I don't like to bugger women. I do.'

'Big Western cock can fit in tiny Chinese bum?'

Cole grinned. 'I know how we can find out.'

The women conferred. This time Cole was sure that they really were arguing and it wasn't just the unfamiliarity of the language fooling him.

After a while, he interrupted. 'Betty, if Madam wants

me to bugger you but you don't want it, there's no way I'm going to.'

Betty gave him a 'men-are-such-idiots' look. 'Other way round. She say no need 'cause it obvious not possible. I say maybe so possible. I say we try.'

'We'll need a lubricant.'

'Huh?'

'Slippery stuff?'

The women conferred again. Madam Soo fetched a pot of face cream. Cole turned Betty over to kneel on the seat. Madam held the pot out. Cole pointed from it to his wagging cock. 'Betty, tell her she has to grease me.'

Betty translated. Madam shook her head. Betty said something more. Madam looked at Cole's cock, then at the jar. With an exaggerated shrug, she scooped cream out on her fingers and plopped it onto the head of Cole's cock. It struck cold on his fever-hot flesh.

'She has to smooth it all over, from root to head.'

There was another argument but when Madam finally capitulated, her hand was slow and curious.

'And she has to work some into your bum.'

'She never will.'

'Tell her.'

Betty was wrong. Madam Soo showed no reluctance at all. Her thin elegant fingers smoothed cream around the puckered entrance to Betty's core and then worked as much into her secretary as she could without forcing her fingers inside.

Cole took hold of Betty's left thigh and steered the dome of his cock into position. 'Ready?'

She nodded.

Gripping her narrow hips with both hands, he pushed. To his surprise, once he'd overcome her ring's resistance, his full length slid into her with ease. Cole crouched over her back to whisper in her ear. 'You're a bad girl, Betty. You've been deceiving me. You've had

cocks up your bum before, haven't you?' He ground his
pubes on her tailbone for emphasis.

'No tell Madam Soo?'

'Your secret's safe with me. Anyway, I don't speak
Mandarin.'

Betty said something long and involved to Madam.

'What was that about?'

'I was telling her that it hurt a bit when you went in but
now that you're moving deep inside me it feels very good.'

'The truth, at last.'

'Cole?'

'Yes?'

'When you come, pull out, please? Madam wants to
see how much cream you give.'

'How about her lessons in giving head?'

'Next time? Now, please to bugger me hard, huh?'

Cole obliged, drawing back until his cockhead was in
danger of emerging, then thrusting back hard enough
that the fronts of his thighs slapped the backs of hers
and his balls swung up to kiss her pussy. For some
reason, although he wasn't holding back, it was a long
time before he felt his jism rise. Perhaps it was because
he felt absolutely no emotional connection to either the
woman whose ass he was fucking or the woman who
was watching, expressionlessly. Even with his widows
and divorcees, he felt protective. With these two, both
lovely, both exotic, he felt absolutely nothing, not even
a sense of fun. When the surge began he had no problem
pulling his cock free of Betty's clinging rectum and
letting himself jet across her back.

It was then that he understood his emotional detach-
ment. Neither woman needed him. They had the money,
the power. For once, he was in the subordinate position.

With that realisation, Cole's cock shrank. He·tucked
it away quickly and made his goodbyes.

The next day, when he drove them to the airport,
Betty sat in front again, and again spent the entire drive

talking over her shoulder, in Mandarin. As he saw them into the terminal, Cole asked Betty what her real name was. She told him. She'd been right. There was no way he'd ever be able to pronounce it.

Cole waited two days before calling the number for Ho-Fat. He got a machine that he thought introduced him to a telephone tree but it didn't offer the option of using English. Four days after that he called Robert.

'I'm sorry, Cole. They've made an offer on a parcel in Calgary, where her fiancé lives.'

'That's OK,' Cole lied. 'Thanks for giving me a shot at it.'

When he hung up, Cole swallowed hard to keep from vomiting. His wonderful dreams had crumbled into a steaming pile of crud. He shook himself. Other real estate agents' 'impossible deals' sometimes cost them years of work before they evaporated. His had cost him two weeks and maybe a thousand bucks. He'd got off lightly.

He was still determined to make it big, but the old-fashioned way, one deal at a time.

# Twenty-two

Ronald Rumm, owner of Park Realty, asked Cole, 'You still aren't interested in taking your broker's exam?'

'Get a headache licence? No thanks.'

'Shame. Anyway, I'm giving you another point on your split.'

'Thanks.'

'You don't exactly sound overjoyed.'

'It's great, thanks.' The improved deal saved Cole the trouble of changing offices. New agents usually split their commissions 50/50 with the firms they work for. When agents become successful, real estate brokerages compete for them by offering them 60/40, maybe 70/30 or in a case like Cole's, 80/20. If Ron hadn't offered it, some other broker would have.

Ron said, 'I want a little favour, in return.'

'A very little one, I hope.'

'Cole, you're very busy. You could do with help – paperwork, research, that sort of thing.'

'You're offering me a private secretary?'

'You need someone with a licence. I'm offering you the chance to mentor a new agent.'

'No, thanks.'

'Just for a month? All she'd expect is to follow you around, watching you work. She could save you a lot of time. How much of your day is wasted delivering documents?'

'No, thanks, Ron, really.'

Ron shrugged. 'OK. It's up to you. You can tell her yourself. Her name's Lana. She's been waiting in your office for almost an hour now.'

'You're a manipulative bastard, Ron.'

'That's why I pay myself the big bucks.'

Cole paused outside the glass door to his office. Lana was standing beside his desk, back straight, hands behind herself. Had she been there for an hour, just standing and waiting? There were his leather swivel and two comfortable guest chairs for her to choose from. What sort of woman stands for an hour simply because no one has invited her to sit?

Cole knew two answers to that question. Either Lana was stupid, or she was a submissive who got a kick out of not doing anything she hadn't been told to do. No one had told her she might sit, so, by standing, she was obeying an unspoken command. Melinda, for all her 'this girl' games, would have taken a seat. Melinda *played* 'sub'. Only the real thing would endure discomfort, unobserved, because it was her nature. Cole had read about 'submissive-to-the-bone' women. He'd never met one. Neither Kate nor Melinda qualified.

Damn! It'd been a month since the Madam Soo fiasco; a month with Melinda and Willow playing house; with Margaret back with her husband; with no widows or divorcees. After thirty days of celibacy, Cole was more than ready for a new woman. The problem was, he was supposed to mentor Lana, which gave him authority over her. In the complex ethics of D/s, you don't dominate anyone sexually if you have economic power over them. You can provide for your 'sub', but not until after she's submitted to you.

And the hardest thing to resist, to Cole, was a woman's submission.

Maybe she was ugly. Just because she looked good

from behind, it didn't mean she didn't have the face of a horse, with acne.

Cole marched into his office. He strode past Lana without a word, sat behind his desk and appraised her. She didn't move or speak. Her hair was a platinum pelt, cut short and close to her shapely skull. Her forehead was clear and high. Cole couldn't tell what colour her downcast eyes were but they looked big and sad. Her mouth was full, with temptingly plump lips. The figure under her severe business suit was very feminine, busty, but proportionately so. Her waist looked naturally trim. It didn't seem as if she starved herself or sweated at a gym. Lana's hips and thighs were shapely. Her calves, from below her skirt down, tapered nicely into slender ankles.

And she *radiated* submission. It'd be *very* easy to drift into a dangerously emotional relationship with her. The place where he kept his guilt was still overflowing from the way he'd treated Janet and Kate. Cole didn't need to hurt a third woman.

In a neutral tone, he asked, 'So you want to learn how to sell real estate?'

She murmured, 'Yes, please.'

He cleared his throat. 'Well, we'll start with the basics, the paperwork.' Cole got up and moved a visitor's chair to behind the desk, next to his. 'There. Sit down.'

For the rest of the morning he taught Lana things that the real estate course doesn't teach about offers to purchase. She caught on to the differences between 'condition precedent' and 'condition subsequent' immediately, which meant she was very bright. There were agents who'd been in the business for twenty years without understanding the subtleties of those clauses. Cole explained that most people wouldn't notice if you added the word 'business' to a conditional clause, even though 'thirty days' is just over four weeks but 'thirty business days' is almost six.

Lana called him 'sir' until he told her to use his name. She sat demurely, ankles crossed and tucked to the side, not making a show of her legs, although they were worth showing off. When he made a point of staring into her cleavage, she didn't react. Lovely as she was, Lana seemed totally unaware of her own beauty.

For lunch, he ordered bento boxes from the Yum-Yum Palace. She was better with chopsticks than he was. Her eyes were mossy green. When her tongue lapped out for a morsel of pickled ginger, it was narrower and longer than any tongue Cole'd seen before. Her teeth were very small and very white.

After they'd eaten, Lana asked Cole if she might be excused for a moment. Cole could tell that her request wasn't just a polite formality. He felt that if he'd told her, 'No,' she'd have accepted that and sat without complaining, even if she'd *really* needed to go to the ladies' room. She returned with her make-up refreshed. Cole inhaled. Her perfume was Chanel No. 5, he was almost certain.

'We'll go take a look at a new listing of mine,' he told her, 'and I'll teach you about "tell twenty".'

Lana waited by the passenger door of Cole's Lexus until he opened it and helped her in. When he leant over her to adjust and fasten her seat belt, she accepted it with a soft, 'Thank you, Cole.'

Her mouth was close enough to his that he could taste the sweetness of her breath. Lana was incredibly tempting. As he drove to Melvin Street, he thought about giving her a small command, something innocent but loaded. He resisted the urge.

When they arrived, he unbuckled her and helped her out. The property at 2117 Melvin was a Willy and Bill renovation, just finished. Cole pointed out how neutral the décor was and that the bathtub was new, as was some of the plumbing and most of the wiring. When Lana had absorbed the selling points, he took her to call on next door.

'Hi! I'm Cole. This is my friend, Lana. We're with Park Realty. We've just listed next door and thought you might like to know about it before we put the sign up.'

They were invited in for execrable coffee and pumped for information for twenty minutes before Cole made polite goodbyes.

Outside, Cole explained, 'We do this twenty times: five houses each side, ten opposite. Our line is, "We thought you might want to choose your new neighbour." Half the time, you get asked in. People are nosey, particularly about the price of a house on their street. One time in forty, on average, someone's Uncle Joe is interested in buying in the area, so you get a good sales lead. More often, someone knows someone who's thinking of selling, so you get a listing lead. This is a good way for a new agent to start. All you need is that one listing to get the ball rolling.'

'But this is your listing.'

'You can work it for me. Come on.'

They'd knocked on seventeen doors and had been invited in nine times when a woman told them that a friend at work was thinking of selling. Cole persuaded the woman to call her friend and tell her that Cole and Lana were on their way. By seven o'clock that evening, they had a new listing with both their names on it.

'You make it look so easy,' Lana said.

Cole looked her straight in the eye. 'It's not. It's a tough game. Sometimes you break your back for people and they hate you for it. Deals that look solid fall apart. Sometimes deals close but the agent still doesn't get paid. Eighty per cent of new agents give up in their first year. The average agent makes less selling real estate than he could make flipping burgers. If you're good, and tough, you can make a good living. If not, forget it.'

'I can learn from you though, right, Cole?'

'I can teach you to be good. I don't know about "tough".'

He took her to the Delhi Deli for supper. It had a buffet of thirty different curries but he ordered from the kosher-style deli section – hot corned beef on rye, extra mustard, slaw and a pickle on the side. He didn't ask Lana what she'd like. She didn't object to his ordering for her.

Before she bit into her steaming sandwich, Lana asked, 'May I ask a question, please, Cole?'

'Yes.'

'Why are you doing all this for me?'

'You'll be running errands, that sort of thing, for me.'

'Not enough to repay how kind you're being.'

'I'm not "kind". Don't ever accuse me of that.'

'Sorry. Then why?'

'If you're worried that I'm being nice to you to get into your panties, don't.'

She blinked. 'I'm sorry you don't think I'm attractive.'

'I do, very, and you know it. Don't be coy with me, Lana.'

Her eyes dropped. She mumbled, 'Sorry.'

'Look at me, Lana.' He waited until her shy eyes met his. 'You know what I am. I know what you are. Correct?'

'Yes, Cole.'

'You're not owned, at the moment. If you were, you'd be hiding your nature from me. I don't own anyone, nor do I want to. I enjoy playing, and that's all. I'm not going to play with you, though, even though you attract me.'

Her eyes looked sad. She bit her lip.

'You want to ask me why?'

She nodded.

'We have an apprentice/master relationship. That puts you off-limits. That's why.'

She nodded again.

'Any questions?'

186

Lana braced herself. 'We – we'll be working together. Each of us, knowing what the other is, it'll be very hard for me, to act normal, I mean.'

Cole reached across the table and lifted her chin on the tip of his finger. 'D/s couples fake being straight all the time, when they're with straight people. You can manage that, I'm sure. Your problem is when we are alone together, right?'

'Yes, Cole.'

'When no one else is around, you may be true to your nature. I won't be your owner but you will show your respect for me as a dominant male and I will guide and protect you, as a submissive female. It'll be our little private game. Can you handle that: a professional relationship in public, a playful one in private, but no commitment and sex?'

Her eyes crinkled at the corners. 'Is flirting allowed?'

'Sure.' Cole felt himself grin. 'I like you, Lana. You're bright and you have a sense of humour. Just don't get emotional, OK?'

'I'll do my best. Cole?'

'Yes?'

'If I may mention it, you have mustard on your lip.'

The little tease was wasting no time. Two could play at that game. 'Then you'd better do something about it.'

She reached across the table to touch the corner of his mouth. Her finger went into her own mouth for a long slow suck.

'You're good,' he said.

'Thank you, Cole.'

When he put her into her car, he pulled the strap of her seat belt tight enough that it'd feel like bondage. Leaning so close, his nostrils were filled with her scent. 'I like the way you smell, Lana.'

'It's Chanel.'

'I wasn't talking about your perfume.' He closed the door before she could respond.

The next morning, as he drove them back to Melvin to complete their 'tell twenty', Lana adjusted the hem of her skirt to just above her knees. Out of the corner of his eye, Cole saw her watching him from under her lashes. When he didn't show any reaction to two inches of her thighs being on show, she readjusted her skirt to show four.

'Stockings or pantyhose?' he asked.

'Stockings.'

'Good. In that case, you may raise your skirt a little higher.' She tugged her skirt up slowly, until the lace tops of her stockings showed and he told her, 'That's enough.' It was deliberate self-denial on his part. The whole point of a woman wearing stockings is the promise of naked thighs. Skin that is displayed above the top of a stocking is far sexier than the same skin exposed by shorts or a swimsuit or even by a short skirt when her legs are bare.

Cole wanted to see Lana's thighs. He knew he would see them, eventually. Meanwhile, he had the pleasure of anticipation, intensified by the knowledge that it was only his own willpower that was making him wait. A man has no power unless he has self-control.

Who got the most pleasure from a pair of pretty legs: the man who looked at them or the woman whose legs were admired? Cole decided that the question made no sense. 'Looking at' and 'being looked at' were like 'penetrating' and 'being penetrated' or 'commanding' and 'obeying'. Each was essential to the other. Together, they created pleasure for the participants to share.

Cole let Lana do the last of the 'tell twenty' solo, with him parked ready to assist or rescue. Submissives are more vulnerable than other women.

He reminded himself of that, often.

# Twenty-three

They divided the 'tell twenty' for their new joint listing, ten each. Lana picked up a lead. With Cole guiding, she made her first sale. At his insistence, they split the listing half of the commission but she was credited with the entire selling end.

'My first deal,' Lana said. 'I couldn't have done it without you, Cole.'

'You haven't done it yet. There are a dozen things that could go wrong. When you've banked Ron Rumm's cheque, *and* it's cleared, *then* you have a deal. That won't happen, if it happens, for almost three months. Divide your commission by twelve weeks. Can you live on that much a week?'

Lana admitted she couldn't.

'Then we'd better get working on your next deal. Lana, do you have any other income?'

'A little, sometimes.'

'How much?'

'I made thirty-eight hundred last year.'

'From?'

'Writing. That's what I really do, write. I'm selling real estate to keep myself until I can sell a novel.'

Cole shook his head. 'Well, that confirms it.'

'Confirms what?'

'That you're crazy. You're in one business that's extremely chancy and takes a lot of work and long

189

hours. To support that, you get into another line that's just as chancy and takes even more hours.'

Lana bit her lip. Her eyes filled.

Cole hastened to assure her. 'We can make it work, Lana. If we work as partners some of the time, you won't be on call 24/7. What if you devoted two days a week to just your writing? Would that work?'

'Are you offering to carry me, Cole?'

'No, I'm not. You'll earn every penny. Five days a week, I'll expect you to be in the office by eight, checking the new listings. I'll teach you what to look for. Any likely ones, you'll do "drive pasts". Whatever looks good, you'll make appointments for me to see them. When we list, you'll split the "tell twenty". I'll work you like a *slave*, Lana.'

She smiled at his emphasis on the word 'slave'. 'Cole – I don't know what to say.'

'Just so it isn't "thank you".'

'But . . . May I ask a question?'

'Yes.'

'About what we are – you – me.' She looked at him for help but didn't get any. 'You being the way you are. Me being the way I am. I thought – hoped – I *do* understand that nothing can happen between us, not while I'm sort of working for you. Does this mean that I'll always be . . .?'

'Off-limits to me?'

'Yes.'

Cole took a moment to consider his own motives. Lana was dangerous. He acknowledged that. If, back before he'd sworn off emotions, he'd been given the chance to design his ideal mate, he'd have designed Lana. She was the most submissive woman he could imagine and yet she still sparkled with personality. She could surrender and tease, simultaneously. Lana was a sub who could laugh at her own submissiveness.

Their working relationship protected him from her. While he was her 'boss', he couldn't touch her. Was he, under the guise of 'kindness', prolonging the tutor/pupil relationship out of cowardice?

He didn't know, so he procrastinated. 'Lana, you are still my apprentice. You will be until you are financially independent. The day you tell me that you've got enough in the bank to survive on for six months without any help from me, I'll consider you a free agent, my colleague, not my protégée.'

She looked up at him through the bars of her eyelashes and purred, 'And then, Cole?'

'And then we shall see. Who knows, between now and then you might meet someone – your ideal master.'

'I've already met –'

'Don't say it!'

'No, Cole. But I can think it, can't I?'

Lana didn't need to be told that when they were in the office or with clients she had to act and dress in a businesslike way. The same went for Cole. In public, he didn't give her orders or snap his fingers when he wanted a pen.

His Lexus was their playground. When Cole buckled Lana's seat belt he drew it tight, to simulate bondage. He instructed her how she should sit and how much leg to show. If he wanted anything from his briefcase, he simply named it and held his hand out.

She had the advantage in their teasing games. Submissives always do. When they were alone and Cole helped her in or out of the car, Lana turned it into intense foreplay. When he made a rule that while they drove her skirt's hem should always bisect the lacy tops of her stockings, she found ways to disobey the spirit while obeying the letter. She had a knee-length straight skirt with three-inch slits. With its hem at the prescribed height, the slits bared tantalising triangles of white thigh. Lana bought a wraparound skirt that didn't have much overlap but was kept decent by press studs, which somehow always came undone when she was in the car. The hem was at mid-thigh. The slit opened all the way to where her thong's tantalising bow showed at her hip.

A bell-shaped skirt was perfectly decent until she adjusted it as ordered, with her feet tucked in and her knees high, showing the undersides of her thighs.

Perhaps Lana's most powerful ploy was to hold her wrists behind herself as Cole strapped her in. The diagonal strap crossed between her breasts, emphasising them, while her being 'restrained' with her hands trapped behind her made her exquisitely vulnerable.

Cole enjoyed Lana's games. Teasing and being teased were fun. He sometimes wondered if it was *too* much fun. The cynic in him warned him about 'bait and switch'. Janet had promised she'd be less puritanical once they were wed. She'd broken her word. Kate had sucked him in with her deep depravity and her need to be protected from its excesses, but she'd lied about wanting to be saved.

Lana *seemed* to want playful perversion within the limits of safety and sanity. Cole's weaknesses were his need to protect and cherish. Without words, Lana asked for those. She was bright, beautiful, vulnerable and submissive – the perfect woman.

That was scary.

The day Cole had walked out on Kate, he'd sworn off caring. If he broke that vow for Lana and she betrayed him, it'd be bad. Just thinking about the possibility made Cole feel as if he had his back to the edge of a bottomless pit and the ground under his heels was crumbling.

Flirtation that went no further was best. He resolved to have innocent fun with Lana and work his lust off with other women.

The problem was, since he'd met Lana, other women didn't appeal to him any more.

Lana stood close enough to his office chair that his arm could feel heat radiating from her thigh.

'Stand with your feet exactly twelve inches apart,' he told her.

'Yes, Cole.' She took a ruler from his desk, squatted, measured and adjusted her feet, stood and replaced the ruler.

'Good girl.'

'Thank you, Cole.' She leant as if to look closer at the document he was working on but actually to quickly whisper, 'I'm not wearing any panties today.'

'Teasing bitch!'

'Thank you, Cole. If you wanted to check under my skirt, you know I wouldn't stop you.'

'Of course you wouldn't. Lana, I want you to pick up a release from Carlew and Drew. Do you know where their office is?'

'Sorry, no.'

'I'll draw you a map.' Cole sketched streets and turnings but his mind was on Lana's pussy. He'd never seen it or touched it. It was six inches from his shoulder, naked under her skirt. He'd been invited to explore it. He could have. No one in the outer office would have seen his hand slide up Lana's leg, under her skirt. He could have kept a straight face and so could she, while his fingers toyed with those lips, parted them, penetrated . . . But he wasn't going to do any of that. If he did – one overtly sexual touch, one kiss – there'd be no turning back.

Cole's briefs were keeping his cock uncomfortably bent. He could have adjusted it but doing so would have acknowledged Lana's power.

'There,' he said, giving her his rough map. 'Take the Lexus. We'll get lunch when you get back.'

It took her two hours to run a forty-minute errand. 'What happened, Lana?'

'The roads are wrong, Cole. They don't go the way your map shows.'

'Show me.' He looked at the map and saw his error immediately. 'The roads were wrong? Not my map?'

'You drew it, Cole, so it has to be right.' She spoke with such sincerity that although she was obviously mocking herself, knowing her words were absurd, on some level she seemed to believe them.

Cole turned his back to her in case his feelings showed. There was a lump in his throat. His insides were melting. If he hadn't known that it was impossible for him to love, he might have mistaken the strange sensations for that treacherous emotion.

One evening, when everyone had left the office but them, Lana handed Cole a printout of a listing. 'What's this for?' he asked.

'You've said that when you're ready, you'd like to buy a condo like the Tiara. That listing's for a one-bedroom at The Palisades. I know that's not the Tiara, but it's close.'

Cole read the listing. A one bedroom, on the first floor, it was about as cheap a unit as you could find in that level of luxury condos. 'Valerie Carp is the listing agent,' he observed.

'Do you know her?'

'I know of her. She's a part-timer – one of those women who doesn't need to work but takes listings from friends and relatives, doing real agents out of their commissions. She lists about two a year and never works them.' He frowned. 'You know, Lana, you might be right. I could be interested in this one but I'd never buy it through Mrs Carp.'

'But she has the listing.'

'For now. It expires in six weeks. I think she should lose it.'

'Are you going to list it, Cole?'

'No. You are. Lana, do you have any girlfriends, really good ones?'

Lana put her hand to her mouth in mock shock. 'Cole! Are you suggesting a threesome?'

194

'Not right now, I'm not. I want you to show apartment One-hundred-and-ten, The Palisades. I want you to show it about once every ten days, from now until the listing expires. Can you find four friends who'd pretend to be interested buyers?'

'That's sneaky, Cole. If I show the place more often than the listing agent does, the vendor will think I'm doing more for her than Mrs Carp is, so she might give me the listing.'

'That's the idea. Lana, I'd really like to move out of my ratty motel and into somewhere I could feel comfortable and maybe entertain a guest once in a while.'

'Entertain a guest?' She perched on the corner of his desk and crossed her legs. 'It's interesting you should say that, Cole.' One finger made little circles on her nylon-sheathed knee. 'If I listed that apartment, and sold it, my commission would make me financially secure for a good six months.' She shimmied along his desk. Her shoe fell off. Lana lifted her stocking foot and set it down on his thigh.

Cole took her ankle in his hand and moved it aside. 'You know the rules, Lana. When we're alone, flirtation is allowed. Touching isn't.'

Her eyes dropped. 'I'm sorry, Cole. I guess I got carried away. The thought of ... of ... you know, us being free to ...'

'The first rule of freedom is discipline. You broke my rules, Lana. If you were mine, you'd be punished for that.'

She got off the desk and stood with her head bowed and her hands behind her back. 'I'd accept your punishment, Cole, no matter what.'

He'd never let their games go this far before. When a submissive woman offers herself to a dominant man for discipline, it's the ultimate temptation. If he'd had an ounce of sense, Cole would have backed away, instantly.

Perversely, he felt compelled to take the scene just as far as he could without actually violating the rules he'd imposed. It was like being on the brink of an orgasm and holding off for as long as he could, except that, in this case, there'd be no climax – no touching.

'You accept my discipline, no matter what?'

'Yes, Cole.'

'Wait.'

Cole checked the outer office and the other agents' areas. They were alone. He locked the front door and returned to his office, where Lana waited, trembling with anticipation.

'Do you expect me to spank you?' he asked.

'Oh!' Her hips wiggled. 'Whatever you decide, Cole.'

'But we have a "no touching" rule. In any case, for you, a spanking would be a reward, wouldn't it?'

'Yes, Cole.'

'So your punishment is to be thirty minutes of corner time.'

'Cole?'

'Go stand in the corner. Naughty girls have to learn that no matter how lovely they are, they can't tempt a man like me to let them break the rules. You will lift your skirt at the back, all the way up to your waist, and stand facing the corner. Half an hour of standing with your bum exposed and ignored will teach you a lesson in humility and obedience, I trust.'

Lana went to the corner and stood with her feet a foot apart. She lifted her skirt slowly so that the pale skin above the tops of her stocking was revealed a tempting inch at a time, then the sweet curves of her deliciously rounded, deeply cleft bottom. The little tease wasn't wearing panties once again. No doubt she'd had some plan or another to let him know that before the day was done. Lana was working hard at testing his resolve.

Cole pretended to be doing a crossword while he secretly watched Lana's bottom, and lusted after it.

From time to time, she raised her heels, flexing her calves. The long muscles in the backs of her thighs tightened and relaxed. Her left bottom cheek clenched, then the right. After twenty minutes or so, her bum trembled. It might have been from the strain. More likely, it was deliberate. She leant forwards a little at her hips and pushed her bottom back. If the light had been better, the action would have silhouetted her pubes. She wasn't to know how deep the shadows were between her legs.

At exactly thirty minutes, Cole adjusted his cock so it wouldn't be so obviously erect when he stood up, and said, 'That's your half-hour. You may lower your skirt, Lana. I'll see you down to your car.'

When she turned and looked at his crotch, she grinned but didn't say anything. Some erections, like some emotions, are hard to hide.

# Twenty-four

Cole's plan wouldn't have worked if Valerie Carp hadn't co-operated. A few days before her Palisades listing expired, she took off for three weeks in Cancun. Lana explained to the vendor that someone ought to take care of her property, 'just until Valerie gets back' and got a two-week listing signed. Cole made his offer, complete with all the extra documentation an agent has to go through to protect vendors. It was ten past three in the morning when Lana called to tell him his offer had been accepted. Cole liked that – the time. He'd told Lana that if you can keep negotiations going until three, often the vendor would sign just to get some sleep.

'Take tomorrow off,' he said. 'Sleep in. I'll pick you up at one for a late lunch to celebrate.'

'Not a working lunch?'

'No – social. We have things to talk about, Lana, personal things.'

'Yes, Cole. I understand.'

When Lana came down from her apartment she was wearing a little pillbox hat with a wisp of veil, a boxy hound's tooth jacket, a black mid-calf pencil skirt, hose with seams and wing-tip shoes with Cuban heels. In honour of her 1940s look, Cole took her to LaVerne's, an upscale burger joint that was decorated in pastel plastic, chrome and pink neon. In a secluded Naugahyde booth, he ordered eight-ounce burgers and chocolate shakes for them both. The booth had a miniature jukebox. Cole fed it change and punched up three Glen Miller numbers.

When 'String of Pearls' started, Lana beamed. 'I *knew* you'd get it.'

'You like to play "dress-up", don't you?'

She nodded.

'Good. I'll enjoy that.'

'When – will you tell me how I'm to dress, Cole?'

'Sometimes. Sometimes you'll surprise me.'

'What if I get it wrong?'

'I doubt you will. If you do, I'll tell you.'

'Thank you.'

Their waitress delivered enormous platters, stacked with 'build-your-own' burger fixings and enough French fries to feed ten.

When she left, Cole said, 'Lana, we have to have a serious talk.'

'Did I do something wrong?'

'No, silly. We have to talk about us. You'll be solvent once you get paid for The Palisades. That changes our relationship.'

Almost bouncing with glee, Lana agreed, 'Yes, it does, doesn't it, Cole?'

'So we have to define the rules.'

Lana put on a sober expression. 'I understand.' Her fingers toyed with the top of her jacket's three oversized buttons.

'Number one, I'm sure we'll get emotional as well as physical enjoyment but what we will do is "play". No commitment. The "L" word is forbidden. Either of us can call an end, anytime, no recriminations. Agreed?'

'Cole, I'll try not to love you but I can't promise that. I can promise not to say it, though.'

'Very well. Next, I don't do "harm". If that's what you need, tell me now. I will give you discipline and pain and pleasure. I'll guard and guide and control you. I will

199

be your strict Master, but I *won't* damage you. There'll be no blood, no scars, nothing that won't heal in a week.'

'Thank you, Cole.' Her top button came undone. Her fingers moved to the next one.

'Your safeword?'

'Mayday.'

'And you will use it, without hesitation?'

'I'll try.'

'You'd better explain that.'

Lana studied a French fry. 'I . . . um . . . disassociate, sometimes, if the pain is very good. When I do, speaking can be hard. It's like I'm somewhere else, in a wonderful place, but I'm disconnected.'

'That could be dangerous.'

She bit the end off her fry. 'I know.' Her second button came undone.

'When you find it hard to talk, can you still move?'

'Yes.' Lana fiddled with the button that was hidden below the table.

'Then two quick taps, anything, hand or foot, counts as a "mayday". Could you manage that?'

'I'm pretty sure I could.' Her jacket fell open. Lana's cleavage, three inches wide, ran straight down between her opulent breasts to below the table. He wondered if she planned to take the tease further by 'accidentally' twisting her body or brushing her jacket open wider. If she *did* flash her bare breasts, he couldn't claim it was a breach of his rules. It was a day off for Lana, so she didn't have to dress suitably for business. 'Flashing' wasn't touching.

Cole smiled. 'What'll you do when the waitress comes back?'

Lana folded her arms, drawing her jacket closed.

'That'll do. Third thing. If you meet another man and decide to go to bed with him, tell me. We'll be finished. For my part, I'll flirt with other women but that's all, unless it's a threesome, with you, with your agreement.'

'Thank you, Cole.'

'How about you? Any questions?'

'Just one, Cole.'

'Go ahead.'

'When?'

'When am I going to take you for the first time?'

'Yes. Can it be soon, please?'

'The sale closes on the fourteenth of next month. I'll have furniture delivered on the fifteenth. On the sixteenth, at ten in the morning, you will come to me, ready to submit.'

'That's another three weeks!'

'Are you complaining?'

Her eyes dropped. Her lush lips formed a delicious pout. 'No, Cole. It'll be hard but I can wait, if I have to.'

'You have to.'

'Cole?'

'Yes?'

'I have a powerful hormonal cycle. I can't help it. At the lowest part, I like sex just fine but I'm not . . .'

'Desperate?'

'Right. Then I get hornier and hornier until I peak and I really suffer. When I'm like that I play with myself four or five times a day but it's never enough. That's when I really need . . .' She bit her lip.

'Pain?'

'Yes. I need to be sent to that special place.'

'And where are you in your cycle, right now?'

'At a low part.'

'Where will you be in three weeks?'

'Cole, on the sixteenth, I'll be at my absolute peak.'

'Then we'll have fun, won't we? Lana, make a note in your daybook. From the twelfth onwards, no masturbation.'

Her eyes grew in alarm. 'But, Cole! I'll go crazy!'

He sat back and grinned. 'Yes, you will, won't you?'

* * *

Cole couldn't take Lana with him when he shopped for his furniture. That would have been intimate in an inappropriate way. Even so, he found himself discussing everything he considered buying with her, in his head. That was OK, provided she didn't know. It'd have been cruel if he gave her the impression he was building a nest for two. Even though his *affaire* with Lana hadn't actually started, he had to plan for when it, inevitably, ended. He'd learnt that much from his relationships with Janet and Kate – which were both supposed to have been 'forever'.

He kept reminding himself that although Lana seemed like his ideal woman, sooner or later he'd discover exactly how she was deceiving him about who she really was and what she really wanted.

Decomania, a store he'd only window-shopped at before, had a sale on 22-inch leather cubes. The Lana in his mind giggled and blushed at his thoughts on how he might pose her on them, so he bought six, all the black ones they had. Most of the furniture he picked was slabby blackened pine, though the bed was a sturdy wrought-iron four-poster. Cole knew his selection was overly macho but he could soften the effect later by adding splashes of brilliant colour, scarlets and yellows. Those'd have to wait until his bank account recovered from the deposit on his apartment.

Cole splurged in the sex shops, dropping a few hundred at Stag, about the same at Northern Leather and a little less at Linda Lovelace. When the sixteenth came, he wanted to have everything a hot little submissive could possibly desire, close to hand. Lana was the most submissive woman he'd ever met. She'd warned him she'd be 'in heat'. Satisfying her would present two challenges. Emotionally, she was expecting to be subjugated, so his domination would have to be carefully orchestrated. Physically, she'd be ravenous. Men can't match women, orgasm for orgasm. He'd have to hold his climaxes back and rely on all the electronic help he could get if he was going to leave her limp and drained by the time they were done. He'd count anything less as failure.

The erotic tension between them grew as the sixteenth approached. Each morning, when Cole entered his office, knowing Lana would be waiting, his cock was stiff and his mouth was dry. The delicious little bitch did her best to make it harder for him. One day he found her on her hands and knees behind his desk, 'picking up spilled paper clips'. It certainly wasn't by accident that she was crawling about with her bum towards him and her short skirt hiked above it. Another time, he found her standing on his desk, 'changing a light bulb'. Reaching high, lifted her skirt above the tops of her stockings. Cole repaid her by holding her ankles, 'to steady her' and making sure his breath warmed the backs of her thighs.

She wore jackets over gauzy blouses, buttoned at the office, open in the car. Sometimes her breasts were supported by half- or quarter-cup bras; other times they swayed freely. Her nipples, dusty-pink cones, made his palms itch but he never surrendered to the urge to simply reach out sideways, and . . .

The sale closed on the fourteenth, without a hitch. By then, Lana seemed to find it impossible to look directly at him. If his hand touched her arm, her knees buckled. When he deliberately breathed on the back of her neck, she almost convulsed. When they left the office that night, Cole told her to take the fifteenth off. 'You know what you mustn't do?'

'Yes, Cole, I know.'

'The day after tomorrow – ten o'clock. You'll wear heels, stockings, a full skirt and a peasant blouse, off-the-shoulder.'

'Yes, Cole.'

He wanted to say something more, but there was

nothing left to say. The next time he saw her, she'd surrender and he'd take her. Everything between them would change. Cole didn't know whether to be glad or sad.

# Twenty-five

Cole forced himself to stay in bed until eight. His preparations were done. All that was left was breakfast and grooming. He made poached eggs on toast and had them with juice, no coffee. Cole brushed his teeth, shaved, showered, brushed again and shaved again.

This was ridiculous! He'd fucked maybe fifty women so far in his life. He'd dominated, to a greater or lesser degree, about a dozen. What was the big deal with Lana?

At nine-forty he put on black silk pyjama pants and a matching robe. Just a spritz more of cologne? Why not? All the percussion toys were neatly organised in their cabinet. The big vibrator with the orange-sized head was plugged into the wall and hidden under a towel. The other vibes and dildos were arranged by size and function in two drawers, along with a variety of lubes and lotions. He didn't plan to restrain Lana this time but, if he changed his mind, he had straps, cords, cuffs and chains hanging in a closet. He had finger foods ready to zap in the microwave for whenever he decided to break for lunch.

At ten, exactly, Cole opened the front door of his apartment. Lana had a purse in one hand and her coat over the other arm. Her platinum pelt was burnished. Her make-up was lavish, with layers of iridescent mascara and succulent crimson lips. Her peasant blouse was translucent and perilously low on her breasts.

'Lovely!' Cole sighed and drew her inside. Once he'd taken her coat and purse, he led her to his living room. He sat in his big black leather recliner chair with her standing before him and fixed her with his gaze. 'Do you surrender to me, Lana?'

'Yes, Cole.'

'Then I accept your submission. You've nothing on under your skirt?'

She drew its hem up to prove her obedience. Lana's mound was pleasingly plump. A few silky wisps, very fair but not platinum, complemented rather than veiled the pleated pillow of her sex.

'Good girl.' He pointed to the oversized black satin cushion beside his chair. 'Sit.' She sank with natural grace. On a whim, Cole reached down to tug her neckline down with one finger, just enough that her left nipple peeked out. The sweet slut had lipsticked it to match her mouth.

He handed her a manicure set. 'My fingers are going to be inside you soon,' he said. 'Make sure my nails are short and smooth.'

Lana clipped and filed and buffed, frowning prettily with concentration. When she'd finished his right hand and looked up to request his left, her eyes were misted, just slightly out of focus. Cole understood the mindset she'd entered. No matter how consumed by lust she'd been in anticipation of this tryst, now she'd given herself into his control, *she* was serene. Her need hadn't disappeared. It had been surrendered to him, to turn on or off at his will. For now, he'd given her a task to perform. She'd perform it patiently. If his words or caresses told her he expected lust, she'd respond in whatever measure he allowed. For Lana, it was the ultimate freedom. Until Cole released her from the spell she'd cast on herself, she had no will, zero responsibility.

Surrender frees a submissive from failure. If anything, physical or emotional, goes wrong in a D/s relationship, only the dominant is to blame. Mastery means responsibility. Slavery is freedom.

Cole inspected his nails. Lana awaited his verdict with puppy-dog intensity.

'You did a good job, Lana. I'm pleased.'

She bobbed where she sat, as if unable to control her delight at his approval.

'Stand up,' he said. Cole tugged the bow of her blouse loose. The sheer fabric fell to her waist. 'Hands up high.' She stretched. He plucked her blouse from her waistband and lifted it up over her head. She looked so delicious, topless, that Cole promised himself days when she'd come to his apartment early and spend hours bare breasted, perhaps working on her writing while he read a book. Her breasts would just *be* there, available, caressed by his eyes, tempting his hands, for half a day or more, until the whim took him and he'd take those lush globes in his hands and . . .

But this wasn't the time to fantasise. Today, for the first time, he'd do all the things he'd been dreaming of doing to Lana.

He unbuttoned and unzipped her skirt. It fell to her ankles. Her stockings were white and came halfway up her shapely thighs. Apart from those, she might have been a Greek statue, a more voluptuous Aphrodite, posing with her hands raised high. Without the stockings, she'd have seemed as chaste as marble, untouchably perfect.

And Cole was about to deface the purity of Lana's skin. He was going to take her sweetness and debauch it. Whatever there was in her that was pure, he was going to defile it. Within the hour, he planned to transform her into a drooling lust-consumed mindless animal. His glee at that prospect was so powerful he felt his chest would burst from it.

The power of his role as dominant surged through Cole, seeming to thicken his muscles. He scooped his eager victim up without her weight registering. Her shoes fell to the floor. Lana didn't react to being lifted. She didn't cling or wriggle but just accepted it, as if she were an inanimate object, even when he flipped her over to set her down on four of his leather cubes, knees on two, hands on the other two. The cubes were placed so that Lana's limbs were slightly splayed. There is no position more flattering to the female form than being on all fours. If a woman's breasts are pendulous, there's no sag when they hang straight down from a horizontal torso. If her breasts are small, gravity is the perfect uplift. Lana's breasts were, in Cole's opinion, quite magnificent. Even so, dangling enhanced them.

Cole circled Lana, inspecting her from a short distance. It didn't seem to disturb her one bit. She posed, perfectly still, her face serene. His fingers touched the lacy top of her left stocking. 'You did right, wearing stockings,' he told her. 'I like your legs in them. Today, though, I'm going to study my new toy. I want your body to be covered by nothing but skin.'

He rolled the stocking down, lifted her knee, rolled it to her ankle and tugged it off. Once the second stocking was gone, he pulled a cube closer and sat on it, behind her. The view from that level was intoxicating. Her thighs were parted at forty-five degrees. Lana's sex was a bow between them. Looking along her torso, from underneath, her breasts hung, sweet and succulent, tipped with arrowhead nipples.

Cole turned his attention to her feet. His fingers massaged every pretty toe, one at a time, tugging as if milking them. He kneaded the soles of her feet, complimenting her high arches, the soaring curves of her insteps and the intricate meshing of the small bones. His fingers stroked the delicate structures of her ankles. Cole's touch traced the tautness of her sinews to where the muscles of her calves were rooted then followed their

208

subtle swelling and tapering until his fingertips grazed the sensitive skin behind her knees.

Lana reacted for the first time. The tendon that ran inside her left thigh twitched.

Cole moved to her hands. 'Let your fingernails grow a quarter-inch longer.'

'Yes, Cole.'

He lifted her right palm to his mouth and tasted it. His tongue worked between her fingers. He nibbled on the heel of her hand then mumbled and licked up her wrist. His fingers followed his lips and tongue, probing, defining bones, massaging muscles. Cole learnt and memorised. In his mind he was drawing a three-dimensional map of the underlying structures of Lana's limbs. Eventually, he'd know her entire body from her bones out, every muscle and every nerve, every organ and gland.

A man can't own what he doesn't understand.

Cole's spread fingers slid though Lana's hair, close to her scalp. 'Your hair looks silky but it's very coarse,' he told her. 'It's like the pelt of some jungle cat. I like that. It betrays the animal inside you, Lana, and it's easy to grip.' His hand closed and twisted to tilt her face up.

'Thank you, Cole.'

He experimented, turning her head from side to side. There was no resistance. Lana just let her head be moved. Cole could have pushed her face down, down to his cock, and fucked her mouth. She'd have accepted that. She'd have been pleased to be used for his pleasure.

But then he'd have come, and he could only come so often in a day, and it wasn't even time for lunch yet.

He kneaded the bones in her face, the helmet of her brow, the fragility of her temples, the drama of her cheekbones and the narrow strength of her jaw. His thumb hooked between her lips and pulled them apart. Cole inspected the inside of her mouth visually for several minutes before thrusting two, then three, fingers inside. The lining of her cheek felt much like the inside of a pussy. Her teeth were hard and smooth. Lana's tongue quivered when he stroked it, absorbing the subtle wet textures before lifting it to probe the more intimate structures beneath it.

Her mouth was wet. Cole let her suck on his fingers and explore their tips with the sinuousness of her tongue.

Cole's mouth watered for the taste of Lana's. He denied it that pleasure. She had to feel that his inspection was coldly impersonal. If their tongues were to touch, his would betray his lust.

He stroked both sides of her neck with just enough pressure that she'd be aware of the strength of his fingers. A submissive needs to know that it is within her Master's power to break her. At the same time she must be totally confident that he won't. A she-wolf offers her throat to the wolf she favours. A vixen won't lift her tail and present her vulva until she feels a fox's teeth in her scruff. Animal bitches will only copulate when they know they are at their dogs' mercy. So it is with the most sexual of human bitches – the women who acknowledge their submissive natures.

Cole's fingers drifted down the slopes of Lana's breasts with a touch as light as a sprinkling of talcum powder. He let their tips glide across the glossy skin of her undercurves. His palms rotated beneath her breasts, barely touching the tips of her nipples. His hands lifted, trying the divine heft of their weight. Spider-delicate touches became caresses; caresses became manipulation; manipulation became torment. The granular glands deep inside Lana's delicate flesh moved between Cole's clutching fingers. As he squeezed, he watched her eyes. Her pupils dilated and lost focus. It was as if she was watching something wonderful, a million miles away. His fingers sank into her flesh, distorting it. Dewy tears filled her eyes.

'Mayday?' he asked.

Lana blinked. Awareness returned to her eyes for long enough that she could shake her head before it disappeared again.

Cole milked, mercilessly. His pumping fingers engorged her nipples and darkened them. His grip shifted to take a nipple between each thumb and forefinger. He plucked and squeezed and twisted, compressing rubbery flesh into unnatural shapes that had to be agonising but although Lana gasped she endured the torture without protest.

When Cole's fingers had done everything they could do to Lana's breasts without damaging them, he moved on. One hand's fingers traced the line of her spine. The other's stroked the arched cage of her ribs. As he caressed the curve of her hip, above, he fondled the subtle swell of her tummy, below.

He said, 'One.' Cole's hand cupped Lana's mound and compressed it, gently, then relaxed. On 'Two,' he squeezed harder and released. With 'Three,' his fingers crushed until her legs quivered before they relented. Cole repeated, 'One.' After a dozen repetitions, his 'Threes' wrung nectar from her as if her sex was a saturated sponge. Her lips parted. Still massaging with one hand, Cole let his other drift down Lana's bottom, fingers trailing its valley, crossing her pucker without pausing, to the sensitive skin of her perineum – the delicate place between anus and pussy. He palpitated on it, matching the rhythm he was using to compact her pubes.

Lana mewed and arched. It was the closest she'd come to asking for more.

Cole moved to his cube, the seat that put his face a foot from Lana's sex. His thumbs hooked into her and spread her wide.

'I'm looking inside you,' he told her. 'You're mainly a very pale pink, like an oyster shell, but there's a mottling of rose and in some places you're almost crimson. You're wet, my pretty one, and very complex. I can see convexities and concavities.'

One thumb moved to press down on the inside of her pubic bone. Lana's G-spot covered an area as big as a dollar coin and was thicker, spongier, than any Cole had felt before. He rotated on it, gently at first, savouring its texture, then pressing harder, gripping her bone between his thumb inside her and his fingers, which crushed her clit. He spat onto two fingers, put them to her anus and twisted them into her. That thumb joined his other, inside her. One hand held her pubic bone captive; the other gripped the thin muscular membrane that separated her vagina from her rectum.

Cole pushed and pulled and twisted, pretending savage indifference to her suffering but actually acutely aware of every nuance of his manipulation of her internal organs. There is no humiliation, no helplessness, as intense as having another's hands move your insides. Lana was being subjected to the deepest degradation while simultaneously being masturbated, both her G-spot and her clitoris. Her sex twitched in Cole's grip. It seeped, then flowed. The lemon-vanilla essence of her ran between Cole's fingers and palms. He sucked in the sweet scent and abused her flesh with greater strength, more urgency.

Her head tossed. Lana made little, 'uh, uh,' noises. Her thighs flexed. Ripples ran across her belly. The muscles inside her flinched in Cole's grip and she ducked her head then lifted it, arched back and let out a strangled moan of agonised ecstasy before going completely limp.

As he felt her convulse and relax, Cole snatched his hands from inside her and thrust them under her body in time to catch her before she could tumble to the floor.

Cole carried Lana to his armchair and cradled her in his lap. 'You're lovely, little one,' he crooned to her.

'I've seen your body, all of it, inside and out, and you're beautiful. Not only are you gorgeous, but you are very brave. I inflicted things on you that most women couldn't have endured. I'm so proud of you.'

She snuggled closer and gazed up at him with misty distant eyes.

'Can you speak?' he asked.

There was a long pause while she absorbed the meaning of his words before shaking her head.

He stroked her cheek. 'Then you must nod for yes, sweet baby. You deserve a reward for your courage. Would you like me to spank you?'

She nodded.

'Lunch first?'

Her head shook.

'Spank now?'

Nod.

Once more he lifted her, cradled in his arms. Cole sat on a cube and set Lana down across his left thigh, resting on her pubes. His right leg crossed both of hers, just above her knees, holding them captive. 'Hands,' he said.

She reached back and crossed her wrists for him to grip. Her bottom, round and ripe and cleft, was uppermost. Cole stroked her cheeks, marvelling at the slick smoothness of their skin. He cupped and compressed, delighting in their resilience. This beautiful flesh was his. He was about to punish it for the very first time. Once he'd landed the first blow, there would never be another 'first time'. His hand lifted. He paused with his palm raised above the purity of Lana's twin, unmarked globes. The moment stretched. She was holding her breath. Cole waited. As she exhaled, his hand cracked down.

Lana jerked. Cole waited for the mark on her right cheek to slowly blossom into a ruddy handprint before he slapped her left. Much as he would have enjoyed watching each blow's bruise develop before delivering the next, she needed a steady rhythm to maintain her bliss. She'd also want to be proud of her endurance, so he kept his blows to light, clipping slaps, alternating cheeks. As he spanked, he counted. By forty, her entire bottom was glowing and rosy. At fifty, her wrists tugged against his grip and her feet came up. By the time he got to seventy she was rigid and panting.

Cole redirected his slaps, concentrating on the tops of her thighs so that his fingertips flicked her engorged lips every time they landed. Her entire body fought his control, arms trying to pull free, legs straining against him. Her head lifted. Little wet sobbing sounds babbled from her mouth. A keening started from deep inside her, growing louder and higher until once more, she convulsed and screamed before going limp.

Lana was still twitching as Cole stood with her in his arms and set her down, kneeling, on a cube. His hand in her hair lowered her head until it rested on her arms, on the floor. Her lovely body was angled down steeper than 45 degrees. Cole gripped a cheek of her bottom in each hand and squeezed, parting them, exposing a pucker that hadn't yet completely recovered from his penetrating fingers. His drooling cock jutted from the fly in his silk pants. He pulled Lana back onto it, not pausing, just one long smooth thrust into the depths of her ass. The way her body was angled down, the head of his cock was forced against the rear wall of her rectum. The lubricious friction was an almost unbearable delight.

Cole became blind and deaf. Nothing existed except the sensations: the head of his cock, her bum, one violating, one welcoming the violation. He had no idea how long he pounded Lana's bottom but pressure built inside him, in his shaft and in his balls and in his chest, growing and insisting on release and becoming uncontainable and finally erupting in a stream of liquid ecstasy that spurted from his cock and in the joy that exploded in a triumphant bellow from his throat.

When sanity returned, Cole found himself on his back, on the floor, with his limp cock lolling from the fly of his pyjama pants. Lana's cheek was resting on his thigh. Her eyes were on his cock and she was licking her lips.

'Cole? Please, may I taste, now? I'd really like to suck your cock.'

He ruffled her hair. 'Of course, you may, little one, but not until after lunch.'

# Twenty-six

Cole lent Lana one of his dress shirts so that the D/s tension would be relaxed a little while they ate. If she'd been naked and him dressed in his silk robe and pyjama pants, the differential would have rendered her inarticulate. Being partly covered enabled her to flirt, which empowered her.

Cole served hot and cold hors d'oeuvres and fed Lana by hand. Her eyes betrayed her distaste for *escargot en brioche* and smoked mussels and her delight with the crab cakes and pastry-wrapped jumbo shrimp. Like the sweet subbie she was, Lana licked the crumbs and sucked the juices from Cole's fingers, looking into his eyes, sending him her lust. 'If I were your pet mouse, I could live off your crumbs.'

'And make a home in my pocket?'

'Inside your shirt, please, Cole? I'd be a good little mouse. You wouldn't know I was there until you wanted to pet me.'

He smiled. 'I think my Mouse would want a lot of petting, especially at this time of the month. Today *is* the peak of your cycle, isn't it?' he asked.

'Yes, Cole.'

'And you need a dozen climaxes?'

She looked into her lap, blushing.

Cole continued, 'Two climaxes, so far, right?'

'Three.'

'Oh?'

'One when . . . when you were . . .'

'Fucking your ass?'

'Yes, Cole.'

'Show me your bottom.'

Lana's eyes lit up at this chance to show off. She stood, turned, lifted the tail of Cole's shirt and pushed her rump out at him. Her cheeks were mottled with several shades of pink but the blue blotches were fading rapidly.

'I gave you eighty-seven slaps,' he told her. 'You didn't use your word to stop me so I imagine you could have endured more.'

'Yes, Cole.'

'You'd like to have some marks that'll still show tomorrow, wouldn't you?'

'Please, Cole.'

'Then you shall, but first you are going to show me what a horny little Mouse you are. Follow me.'

He led her to his chair and sat her in it. Lana looked up into his eyes then down to his crotch. His orgasm had been cataclysmic but now, an hour later, Cole's cock was thickening again. There'd been something very different about his first climax with Lana. Until then, no matter who he'd fucked or buggered or been sucked by, a part of him had remained an observer, a little aloof. Once in a while the moment of release had brought a grunt to his lips, or a sigh. This time, his glee had exploded from him in a bestial scream of triumph. He had to think about that, but later. For now, in case he'd shown weakness earlier, Cole was going to re-exert his domination over Lana.

His left hand gripped her hair and pushed back, reclining the chair, bringing her face down level with his cock. His right hand pulled his shaft from his pants and wagged it, inches from her sweet longing face. 'You want this?' he demanded.

217

'Please, Cole.'

'In your mouth?'

'Please?'

'Beg for it, then.'

'Please, Cole, please let me suck your cock. Put it in my mouth.' She looked up at him with saucy eyes, letting him know that although her pleas were real, she enjoyed being made to beg. 'Fuck my face or just let me lick it, but I beg you, Cole, I'm desperate to taste your lovely cock.'

'Tongue!'

She poked it out, long and flat, still gazing into his eyes longingly. He slapped his cockhead on her tongue in a rapid tattoo. He couldn't tell how much of the drool was from his cock and how much from her mouth. Lana strained forwards against his grip, mouth working. Cole allowed her to take just his knob between her lips to mumble and slurp on.

The obscenity of that classically lovely face, distorted with animal lust, avidly gobbling his cock, almost overwhelmed Cole. He fought the urge to thrust into her voracious mouth. Self-control was the essence of how he valued himself. Thighs trembling, he reached out for the big round-headed vibrator and thumbed it on. The trembling globe touched the tip of Lana's left nipple before drifting down her breastbone, over her tummy and nestling between her thighs.

'Spread,' he told her. 'Hook your knees up over the arms of the chair.'

Cole teased her sex lips, letting the vibrations blur them. Lana tensed. He moved the globe higher, to her mound, and pressed it against the resistance of her pubic bone. 'Take it,' he said. 'Use it on your clit. I want to watch you come.'

The index finger of Lana's left hand pushed her clit to one side. She pressed the globe into the crease between her clit and her labia. As the vibrations trembled into her, her laving on Cole's cock slowed down. Her face became perfectly serene but the muscles in her thighs were twitching. Her mouth stilled, lips wrapped around his shaft but unmoving. Tiny crinkles of concentration showed at the corners of her eyes. A ripple ran down her belly. Her lips went slack. Cole took his cock from between them, almost absently. Like Lana, he was focused on what the vibrations were doing to her clit.

Her toes curled. Her belly bulged, then relaxed before bulging again. Lana's face twisted as if in agony and she let out a short, sharp yelp.

'Again!' Cole demanded.

'I . . .'

'Do it!' He took her feet, crossed her ankles and lifted them above her head so that she was dragged down to lie with her back on the chair's seat with the cleft roundness of her bottom elevated. Cole reached for his crop.

Lana manoeuvred the vibrator back into place. Cole aimed. His blows, diagonally across the valley of her bottom, were light, almost taps, at first. As Lana's eyes glazed, he brought the crop down a little harder, just enough to sting. Her neck arched. Little shocks trembled her tummy. Her ankles resisted Cole's grip with more strength.

Lana choked back a sob, signalling that her climax was imminent. At that signal, Cole raised his crop high and brought it down hard, once, twice, three times, driving pain into her at the same time as the contractions inside her forced her orgasm out.

He dropped his crop, straddled the base of the chair, loomed up over Lana and thrust his cock down into the convulsing hot pulp of her sex. He pumped and pumped, not holding back, until the eruption began to climb the shaft of his cock. With an intense effort of will, he wrenched it from her.

'Watch!' he barked. A great gout of ivory foam arced from his cock into the air and flopped across Lana's body, splattering her in a line from her navel, between her heaving breasts, up the side of her neck and flecking her sweat-soaked hair.

Cole staggered backwards until his calves felt a leather cube. He sank onto it but sitting was too much effort so he slid sideways to sprawl on his back on the floor. After a while, he felt the soft warmth of her breasts on his chest and her cheek snuggling into his shoulder.

'Cole?' she whispered.

'Hm?'

'If you don't mind, I think I've had enough for now.'

He didn't have the energy to form words, so Cole patted her shoulder in agreement.

# Twenty-seven

Tina Ruggles wore sandals made out of old tyres. Her granny dress was hand stitched from fabric she'd woven herself. She had a dozen bangles on her left wrist. Cole recognised Navaho turquoise, silver hammered into Celtic knots and one made from elephant hair as well as several in dollar-store plastic. She had a laughing Buddha tattooed where her cleavage would have been if she'd had any.

Her companion, Ed Parsons, was in Western boots with half their heels worn away, oily jeans and a torn black muscle shirt. The ankh that hung from a thong around his scrawny neck looked like it weighed about a pound and a half.

Cole asked, 'Big place? Two and a half storeys, clapboard, wraparound porch, lots of gingerbread?'

Tina nodded. 'That's the one.'

'It's been "for sale by owner" for at least three years,' Cole continued.

'Can't do business with that freak, Garner,' Ed contributed.

'You've tried?'

Tina said, 'Last time, he run us off with a shotgun.'

'Loony as a tick,' said Ed, then added, 'Loony-tick,' in case anyone had missed his pun.

Cole asked, 'Did someone recommend me to you?'

'We bin to two other real estate offices so far today. Nobody wanted to talk to us till you. Why'd you reckon that is?'

Cole made his reply, 'Karma,' portentous.

Tina looked at Cole as if he'd said something incredibly wise.

Ed said, 'Right on!' and punched the air.

A familiar feeling came over Cole. He'd said just the right thing, at exactly the right time. Now he had them. Tina and Ed would do as they were told – which meant he was honour-bound to look after them.

'What did you offer?' he asked.

'Half a mil.'

'That sounds about right. It's got ten or fifteen acres?'

'Thirteen and a half, six usable, the rest ravine.'

'It might be hard to mortgage, it being an unusual property.'

Tina told him, 'We don't want no mortgage. There's eleven of us. I weave. Ed carves wooden statues. We're poets and potters – artists and craftspersons. We've pooled our resources and plan on doing our thing, and a bit of farming, raising llamas mainly. We've got the money, cash.'

'Like a commune?'

'Like,' Ed grunted.

'Did you tell Garner what you planned?'

Both nodded.

'And he knows your names?'

More nods.

'Then the offer can't come from you. It'll come from me, "in trust". The deposit will be fifty thousand. I'll have my secretary draw up four offers and a power of attorney that authorises me to act for you in this matter.'

Tina blinked. 'Four offers?'

'Three genuine, one totally bogus.' Cole paused to give them each an intense look, in turn. 'You're in my hands now. I'll take care of you.'

Lana wanted to go to Garner's place with Cole because the old man might be dangerous. He didn't let her for exactly the same reason. At eight o'clock the next morning, Cole rapped on the stained-glass panel of a century-old door with peeling paint. Garner, grizzled, skinny and grimy, opened the door wearing dirty dungarees over dirtier long johns.

'What?'

Cole held up a rolled-up offer. 'I have an offer for your property.'

Garner reached for it. Cole pulled it back.

'Y'have to give it to me. That's the law.'

'Only if your property's listed with the Real Estate Board.'

'I ain't payin' no real-la-tors.'

'The commission comes out of what the purchaser pays.'

Garner squinted at Cole, absorbing, or failing to absorb, his words. 'Y'can come in, I guess.'

They sat in a farm-sized kitchen, at a splintery pine table, Garner with coffee, Cole without. Cole pushed a listing form at the old man.

'This thing expires at midnight tonight. How come?'

'I don't want to be responsible for helping you for a minute longer than I have to.'

Garner scowled. 'There ain't no askin' price on it.'

Cole shrugged. 'Put anything you like down. I don't care.'

'What if I put a million dollars?'

'Go ahead. I've got the offer right here. What you ask won't change it.'

'Hm.' Garner scrawled $800,000, crossed it out and wrote in $750,000. 'See? I come down fifty-thousand dollars already.'

Cole took his time checking and witnessing the listing before handing the offer over. Garner read it, took Cole's pen, crossed out $505,000 and wrote in $575,000 before pushing it back. Without another glance at the form, Cole slowly tore it in half, then in half again.

'Watcha doin'? I know the law. I marked it back. You gotta take it to 'em.'

'No, I don't. I have my instructions. You've rejected the first offer. Now I'll show you the second one.'

'Fuckin' crooks.'

Cole took three offer forms from his briefcase.

'Show me 'em all!' Garner demanded.

'No. Look at this one, and then I'll show you the others.'

Garner stamped and thumped the table when he read the second offer for $500,000. 'This one's for less than the other, you fuckin' idiot!'

'I know. Now you can see the other two.'

Garner's brow creased. 'Y'got it all wrong. This here offer ain't for my property at all. It's for some other place, way over on Fourth Line.'

Cole leant across the table and fixed Garner in a stony glare. 'Listen, Mister Garner. You rejected an offer of five-hundred-and-five-thousand dollars. That means you've thrown away five-thousand dollars, so far. If you don't grab the five-hundred-thousand dollars, I have an offer of four-hundred-and-ninety-five-thousand dollars for you. If you still don't come to your senses, I'll be taking a drive over to Fourth Line and I promise you, you'll never see me or my offers again.'

Cole sat impassive and Garner swore and spluttered and stomped for a good half-hour before he signed.

Later, Lana asked Cole, 'Which property was that other offer on, the one on Fourth Line?'

'A fictitious one, Mouse, totally bogus.'

She grinned. 'You're bad, Cole.'

'And you're naughty. In celebration of our mutual wickedness, and of a quick and easy deal, and as it's midweek and off-season, tomorrow I'm taking you to Niagara for a couple of days of debauchery.'

224

Lana beamed. 'Oh, thank you, Cole. May I have my instructions, please?'

Lana had a switch in her head. Most of the time she was bright, witty and alert but if Cole's firm tone or subtle gesture warned her that it was 'playtime', both her willpower and her ability to reason turned off. He might have mentioned his plans for her a dozen times that day. They still surprised her. In that state she had no expectations. She was totally 'in the moment'. If Cole had lit a firework and told her to watch the fuse burn, she'd have done so, and would have been shocked by the bang.

In submissive mode, she could hear and see and feel but thinking or talking took major effort. That's why, when Cole helped her into the passenger seat of his Lexus and she saw a long thick leather strap hanging from his free hand, her eyes misted and her mouth softened. He fastened her seat belt and then wrapped the strap around her and her seat before pulling it tight and buckling it. The constriction emphasised the vibrant thrust of her full breasts against the black knit jersey of her skinny-fit turtleneck. Her arms were pinned to her sides. If she'd wanted to, she could have tugged them free. That thought didn't occur to her. Cole had confined her, so he wanted her to be restrained. If that was what he wanted, Lana wanted it, too. She sat with her face blank as Cole touched the control and the servo-motor hummed and the back of her seat lowered to horizontal.

Cole got in. He popped the press studs that fastened the flap of her wraparound skirt. When he parted it, he saw that she'd been obedient, not that he'd had any doubts she would. She was wearing a scrap of white lace.

He contented himself with sideways glances, gloating at how lovely she looked and how vulnerable, until he'd crossed the Burlington Skyway Bridge. From there,

Niagara Falls was a straight run, about forty miles. He could take it easy and do it in well under an hour at that time of the day. Cole drove with one hand and let the fingertips of his other glide over the glossiness of Lana's nyloned knee. Coming out of Stony Creek, he let his hand wander up her stocking, to its lacy top, and tucked a finger between the lace and her thigh. Driving past the roadside fruit stands in Vineland, he began making little circles on her taut bare skin, each circle a fraction higher than the one before.

Lana's knees fell apart. She made a little noise deep in her throat. Entering St Catherine's, Cole was teasing the tender hollow just below the crease of her groin. Ten or so minutes before Niagara Falls, Cole rested his fingertips on the lace that was stretched over Lana's mound.

She arched.

Cole scratched the lace, very gently. His scratching travelled, perhaps a quarter of an inch for every mile he drove, moving over the plump curve of her pubes, creeping towards the place her pussy lips bracketed the base of her clit shaft.

By the time he passed the WELCOME TO NIAGARA FALLS sign, the tip of one nail was softly scratching the head of Lana's clit through the lace of her thong. She was seeping. He could taste it when he sucked air in through his mouth. His fingers could feel the dampness.

He turned into a strip plaza and pulled up. A wetted fingertip traced the line of Lana's groin. When it reached the fleshy bulge of her outer lip, it eased under the edge of her thong. It ran there for a while before sliding over to her crinkled crease. She was seeping, almost dribbling liquid lust. Cole lifted a droplet to his tongue, whetting his own appetite, before smoothing the lace back into place. Reluctantly, he fastened her skirt, powered her seat up and unbuckled the heavy strap.

His hand shook her thigh, gently. 'We're almost at the hotel, Mouse. Can you function?'

226

Lana nodded, slowly and solemnly, as she gathered herself together enough that she'd be able to perform simple tasks. After a moment, she lifted Cole's hand to her lips and kissed it. He'd taught her to do that when she was in her submissive role and needed to ask him something.

'Yes, Mouse?'

'I'm horny, Cole, really, really horny.'

'I know.' He put her hand on his erection. 'Me too. You're going to be horny all day. That's the way I have it planned. I want you drooling with lust before I take you.'

There was admiration in her voice as she said, 'You're so cruel, Cole.'

Lana waited demurely behind Cole as he booked them into their hotel. She followed him into the elevator and stood with her eyes downcast, her legs barely trembling at all, as they rose forty floors to their suite. Once they were inside and alone, her playful side emerged. She darted to the wall-to-wall window, with its spectacular view of the Falls. From there, she bounced on the bed and off the other side to gloat over the seven-foot long oval Jacuzzi with two walls and ceiling that were pink mirrors.

Lana fell to her knees and clutched Cole's hand. 'Please, Cole? Please fuck me in the Jacuzzi?'

That was exactly what Cole intended but he gave her a smile and told her, 'If you are good, tonight I'll not only fuck you in it, but I'll bugger you in it as well.'

She showered kisses on his fingers. 'You're so kind to me. I'll be a *very* good girl, I promise.'

A great wave of affection welled up inside Cole. Lana's ability to 'double-think' amazed him. Part of her was almost mindless – lust and adoration incarnate – a too-good-to-be-true sex and pain slut. Another part was wise, witty and playful. Cole suspected that, except for when the pink mist of disassociation took over, wise

Lana observed lust-crazed Mouse with detached amusement, enjoying her excesses thoroughly.

Which made Lana a text-book-perfect woman: an elegant lady partner, a teasing playmate and a ravenous harlot, as required.

Cole gave himself a mental shake. That line of thinking could be dangerous. 'You've got five minutes to freshen up,' he told her. 'We have a busy day ahead of us.'

The Falls were only a hundred yards from the hotel. The woman who sold tickets to the tunnel under the cascade put her paperback romance down for long enough to sell them tickets and direct them to the rack of sou'westers and slickers. The air in the tunnel was clammy. The roar grew until it seemed to be pushing them back. By the time the tunnel's side opened to become a cave behind the torrent, the sound had become a throbbing vibration, almost too low and too loud to be heard.

Lana shrank back from the power of tens of thousands of tons of water cascading a yard from their faces. The wall of water looked so solid, it seemed that if you reached out and touched it, it'd sever your fingertips.

Cole held Lana firmly against the vibrating safety rail. His hands parted her slicker and slid under it. He pulled her skirt up and massaged her mound through her thong. 'Feel the power,' he shouted into her ear.

Cole's hips pressed her forwards, squashing her pubes against the metal bar. Spattered and splattered by stinging bullets of water, deafened by the rumbling, Lana stood, the awesome power of the Falls vibrating though her sex, the might of her beloved Master crushing her from behind.

When Lana's knees trembled and almost gave way, Cole pulled her back, turned her round and took her mouth in a long ravaging kiss. He had to half-carry her back out of the tunnel.

They strolled past garish tourist traps eating foot-long chilli dogs with fried onions. Lana's eyes sent Cole obscene messages as she sucked grease from his fingers. Their next stop was the new casino.

'What's your favourite game?' he asked her.

'Blackjack.'

'Fine.' Cole had played pontoon in the army and had usually come out a few pounds ahead.

The first blackjack game they came to was electronic, built into the counter of a bar. Cole staked them to $100 each. It took him almost an hour to lose his money. By that time, Lana was $700 ahead and ready to cash in.

'You're good,' Cole told her.

'I dealt cards for a living for a while, back in Saskatoon.'

It made Cole realise that Lana'd had a life before him and he only knew snapshots from it. She had a BA; had lived with a musician for a few years; had an affair with a married man who'd uncovered the submissive in her but hadn't cherished her – Cole knew a hundred tiny pieces of Lana's past but he'd never know it all, not if he spent a lifetime . . .

He wrenched his mind off *that* slippery path.

'Next, we go shopping,' he announced.

The salesgirl at Spikes had a snake's body in a tight black skirt and crisp white shirt. She had sooty urchin-cut hair, racoon eyes and thin blood-red lips. Cole bought Lana a pair of black pom-pom mules and a pair of ballet-style kid loafers that were butter-soft and totally flat before he asked to see some high-heeled pumps. Lana couldn't manage five-inch heels so Cole had her try on a pair with ankle straps, on four-inch pencil-slim spikes. The straps buckled with tiny heart-shaped padlocks. When the girl locked them, her fingers lingered on Lana's ankles.

'We'll take those,' Cole said. 'What do you have in Mary-Jane's – schoolgirl style but not clunky?'

When the girl went back into her stacks, Cole said, 'She fancies you, Lana.'

'Do you think so?'

'Definitely. How about you? Is she your type? Would you fuck her?'

Lana flushed and bit her lip. 'If you told me too, I'd like that,' she confessed.

They left Spikes and went straight to Slutz, a store that boasted of being 'Like Frederick's of Hollywood, but trashy'.

Lana hugged Cole's arm. 'Please, Cole, haven't you spent enough on me today?'

He gave her a cold stare. 'Is that something you're entitled to have an opinion about?'

Lana shivered. 'Sorry, Cole. Do I have to do corner time?'

'No, but be warned.'

'Thank you, Cole.'

Cole bought Lana some 'sensitising' bath oil and a clitoral cream that promised to 'Make her cum like Niagara'. He wanted to make some purchases privately so he led her to the Leg Avenue displays. One was of stockings in rainbow colours and scores of designs. The other showed plastic packets of 'dress-up' outfits, Sexy Secretary, Cute Convict, and so on, mainly made from stretchy and translucent fabrics. 'Pick out six pairs of stockings,' he said, 'and five outfits that take your fancy. Here's my Visa. I'll be back in fifteen minutes.'

Lana looked alarmed. She clung to his arm. Of course – he should have thought. As her normal self, Lana was bright and confident. In her submissive state, she was helpless and confused. Being alone in a strange place frightened Mouse.

Cole gave her a hug. 'I don't want to see what you buy, so you'll be able to surprise me. I won't go far. There are the racks. Pick out what you want and take it to that cash register, there. Give the girl the Visa card.

She'll take care of everything. Just sign when she tells you to. Take your bags and sit in that chair, next to that display of slave collars. I'll be back for you in ten minutes. OK?'

She nodded.

Cole shopped quickly. There were some bondage items that smaller stores didn't carry and in the next department they had sexier swimwear than he'd find in a local mall. When he got back to Lana she was hugging two big bright plastic bags and gazing with longing eyes at the display of collars. She seemed to be focused on the most brutal – three inches wide, half an inch thick, solid stainless steel, hinged on one side, padlocked on the other.

Damn!

True submissives want to be collared more than anything else. Accepting a man's collar is the ultimate surrender. Granting a woman a collar is the most powerful commitment a man can make. Divorcing Janet had been hard, dumping Kate had been a wrench, but when a man accepts a woman as his collared slave, he's bound to her for life, only she can sever the relationship.

And Lana craved a collar. Much as he wanted to make her happy, that was one step he wasn't ready to take and didn't think he ever would be.

On their way out of Slutz they paused by a rack of magazines. One, *Rattan*, had a picture of a girl with electric-yellow hair, Goth make-up and a loop of chain from an earring to the ring through her nose. She was wearing a powder-blue latex catsuit that fitted so tightly it divided the lips of her sex. Lana licked her lips so Cole bought a copy.

'We'll eat at the hotel,' he announced.

# Twenty-eight

Cole ordered lobster tails. While they waited to be served, Cole sent Lana to the ladies' room with instructions to return with her thong in her purse. She sat, blushing, while he fed her succulent chunks of white meat with one hand and stroked the insides of her thighs with the other.

'Would you like some dessert?' he asked her, once the waiter had cleared their plates.

Lana wriggled and looked at the ceiling meaningfully. 'Please, Cole? I've been a good girl, haven't I?'

'And now you want me to fuck you?'

She nodded.

'Say it.'

Lana whispered, 'I want you to fuck me, please.'

'Where?' he teased.

'In the Jacuzzi, in my pussy, my mouth, my bum, wherever you want to, but soon, please, Cole.'

While the Jacuzzi filled, Cole sat Lana, both of them naked, in his lap and leafed through the copy of *Rattan*. There was an illustrated article on nipple jewellery that made Lana wriggle.

'Would you like me to have a piercing?' she asked.

'I might get you some clip-ons. I know that piercing is safe but I wouldn't want to take even a million-to-one chance of damaging your lovely nipples. I'm sure I can find something that's painful but safe.'

'Thank you, Cole. Cole?'

'Yes?'

'Sometimes, when I'm at my "peak", I think about *really* bad things.'

'Things you'd like me to do to you?'

'Perhaps. I'm not sure.'

Cole took her by her hair and forced her to look him in the eyes. 'Can you tell me what things you think about?'

'No. I'd be too ashamed.'

'I thought not. So what you're telling me is, when it's that time in your cycle, you want me to take you to the edge – make you use your safe-word.'

'Yes, I think that's what I mean.'

'Have I been too kind to my Mouse?'

Her eyes dropped, avoiding his. 'You will be as kind or as cruel as you wish, Cole. I am yours to use as you decide I should be used.'

He stood, lifting her in his arms. 'Right now, I decide that you should be subjected to the unbearable torments of the Jacuzzi!' With the greatest care, he dropped her, squealing, into the steaming waters.

There was a chrome bar all the way around the tub, just below its rim. It was four feet deep, with a tiled ledge that had recessed adjustable spouts that squirted powerful pulses of bubbling water. Cole got in and sat Lana over a spout.

Her eyes widened. Her hips moved forwards three inches then back two.

'Is it hitting the spot?' Cole asked.

'Oh, yes. Exactly. Oh, Cole, I like this, a *lot*.'

'Relax and enjoy.'

Lana's arms spread so she could grasp the bar to each side. Her eyes closed and her head lolled back. Tiny bubbles streamed up between her thighs. Her lovely breasts floated, nipples half out of the water. There was serenity on her face, interrupted from time to time by a delighted twitch as the masturbating waters caressed her in a particularly thrilling way.

Cole watched her and stroked himself, taking pleasure in her pleasure, until his cock demanded more. He rose up, went to his Mouse, took her coarse hair in his fist and pulled her mouth to his cock. Standing with his thighs spread and rock steady, Cole push-pulled Lana's loving lips on his engorged glans while the finger and thumb of his free hand rolled a resilient nipple with slowly increasing pressure.

Her face distorted. Lana's eyes snapped open in a fury of lust. Cole understood. He'd kept her horny all day and now the water was titillating her, stoking her need, but its throbbing caresses weren't intense enough to take her to climax.

He stepped back, stooped, reached under the water and grabbed Lana's ankles. Lifting, he pulled back to stretch her, floating, on the surface, anchored by her grip on the rail. Cole stepped between her thighs, bent his cock down and thrust into her, hard and fast.

Lana sighed. 'Yes!'

He held her hips and fucked her, angling to stroke her G-spot with the head of his cock. 'Diddle yourself,' he commanded.

Her right hand went to her sex. Cole released her hips and fucked her hands-free, letting his jolts flop her about, slapping the surface of the water. The frigging of her fingers foamed the water and she half-sat up, pressing down on Cole's cock, and yelped her climax.

Without a pause, Cole withdrew, flipped her over, tucked her thighs under to kneel her on the bottom, spread her buttocks with his thumbs underwater and shoved his cock into her bumhole. Hunched over her, arms wrapped around her body, Cole bore down. His weight forced her thighs to spread wide, lowering her pussy to the edge of the ledge. Cole's fingers fumbled with the nearest nozzle until he had its jet pointed at Lana's clit. Two fingers of his right hand spread her lips. His left hand crushed her left breast, mauling pain into her flesh. Slowly and inexorably, Cole drove his rigid shaft deep into his sweet Mouse's rectum, and pulled back, and drove slowly in again. It wasn't until she was mewling and writhing in his arms that Cole released his lust and pounded out his own bellowing climax.

When he woke in the morning he felt emptiness where he expected Lana's warmth. He blinked his eyes open. His Mouse was on the foot of the bed, kneeling in the classic 'submissive waiting to be used' pose. She was naked, sitting back on crossed ankles, knees wide apart, back straight, hands linked behind her neck and elbows pressed back to lift and offer her sweet breasts.

'How may I serve my beloved Master?' she asked, smiling slyly.

'I'll have some of your honey.'

Her brow creased for a second before she dropped a hand to her sex, hooked two fingers up into herself and worked them in tight little circles. In less than a minute, Lana was able to offer Cole her fingertips, dripping with her milky dew. He sucked them clean and told her, 'I'm going to shower. Have the big vibe, that new clit cream and my peppermint oil ready for me.'

He showered, shaved, cleaned his teeth and was back, on his back, in fourteen minutes. 'I want you to make my cock as big and as hard as you can, Mouse. You may use the oil, the vibrator, hands, mouth, whatever.'

'Thank you, Cole. Cole?'

'Yes, Mouse?'

Her eyes twinkled. 'Would you pretty-please roll onto your side?'

Cole rolled. The bed sank behind him. He felt a soft cheek brush his hip, then little kisses, trailing, until a warm wet tongue laved the base of his spine. Tiny teeth nibbled the pad of muscle there. Her hand, running with oil, reached over him and found his shaft. Cole lifted his upper leg. The big ball of the vibrator hummed on the skin behind his scrotum. Lana nuzzled, parting the cheeks of his bottom. Her tongue trailed their crease.

That was a caress Cole had never commanded from any woman. For some reason, no matter how much a woman might want to be ordered to perform, he didn't want her to lick his anus unless it was her idea, totally voluntary. He never so much as hinted he'd like it.

Lana's tongue found his sphincter and rimmed it slowly. He felt her dribble, then the probing of her stiffened tongue as it tried to penetrate him. The feeling was incredible but Cole was more moved by Lana's adoration – her showing him that nothing was forbidden between them – than by the sensations.

She pressed her face deeper, slobbering in her eagerness to perform the obscenity. Her oily fingers smoothed his shaft. Her palm polished its helmet. The vibrator quivered his cock. It felt to Cole that each beat of his heart engorged his cock more, transforming it from a length of bloated flesh into something almost alien, as if a rigid bone had been grafted onto his body.

'Straddle me,' he said.

As Lana mounted him, he rolled onto his back and gripped his cock's base. 'Lower. I want your bum.'

She sank down, moving her hips to and fro until his cockhead nestled between her cheeks and butted against the tightness of her anus.

'Hold still,' he told her. For a long moment, he savoured the exquisite anticipation. He looked up into her adoring eyes. There was hunger in them. She was biting her lower lip. Like Cole, she was enduring the expectation. Unlike Cole, she had no control over how long it would last.

'Impale yourself, Mouse,' he whispered. 'Just the

head. Stretch that tight ring over my cockhead and then hold still.'

She nodded. Her forehead creased in concentration as she bore down, forcing the dilation, taking glee from inflicting pain on herself at her Master's command. Her sphincter was compelled to expand until Cole's plum passed within, then began to contract and grip his cockshaft.

'Enough!' he told her. 'Now use the vibe. Make yourself come.'

Lana pressed the ball sideways against her clit shaft and switched it to 'high'. As her eyes glazed, Cole pulled back slowly, until the iris of her anus almost closed, then pushed in again. Lana stayed totally rigid, letting the vibrations get to her, as Cole, with strict control, buggered her in slow motion.

He could feel the vibrator. He could feel that the walls of her vagina were twitching. Her anus clenched on him. He gazed up at the sweet curves of the undersides of her lovely breasts and their engorged nipples. Her head was thrown back. Lana was panting softly as the delirium of desire rose within her.

Everything conspired to overcome Cole's willpower. The lust in him was a raging beast, almost, almost, *almost*, beyond his control. Cole felt his sinews tighten into steel bands that surely had to burst out through his skin.

Lana's body curled. She looked down at him with blazing eyes. Her free hand made a clenched fist. Her mouth worked, forming words but soundless. Her abdomen rippled.

'*Cole!*' burst from her lips as if the word was torn from deep in her gut.

As she slumped, Cole felt her hot juices flood across his stomach.

Now that his Mouse had climaxed, Cole released the beast he'd been reining in. Holding Lana erect with one

237

hand in her hair and the other gripping her arm, knowing he was hurting her but heedless of her pain, Cole fucked up into her ass, hard and fast and furious and merciless, blind to anything but the insane imperative of his cock's needs.

He climaxed with a massive convulsion that tossed Lana aside to tumble across the bed. She stared with joyful eyes at the massive eruption that jetted from Cole's cock.

Cole lay, drained, and decided to let himself sink into the seductive warmth of sleep.

# Twenty-nine

They didn't talk much on the drive back from the Falls. Cole stole sideways glances at Lana from time to time, enjoying the novelty of being able to look at her and appreciate her without feeling lust. They hadn't left their suite for the last 24 hours of their mini-vacation. They'd napped, made love, eaten room-service snacks, made love, showered, made love, then started over.

*No!*

Cole corrected his thoughts. They'd had sex. No matter how glorious the fucking, no matter how affectionate he felt towards his Mouse, he mustn't start thinking about their sex as 'making love'.

'There were short stories as well as articles and pictures,' Lana said.

'Huh?'

'*Rattan*. That sex magazine.'

'Oh? Short stories? Any good?'

'Not bad.'

'But you could do better.'

'Do you think so?'

'I can't imagine any woman better qualified to write about the pleasures of pain, and that's what *Rattan*'s about, isn't it?'

'Cole, if I wrote sexy stories, you'd be in them. I couldn't help that. Would you mind?'

'Best change my name, but otherwise, no problem.'

'I'd be shy to have you read them.'

'But I would.'

Lana bit her lip and frowned. 'I don't know.'

'I do. Lana, how much writing is a good day's work?'

'A couple of thousand words.'

'Then take the rest of the week off. You've got two days. I expect to see five-thousand words of short stories, suitable for *Rattan*, on Sunday.'

'That's twenty-five-hundred words a day,' Lana protested.

'I know.'

'Cole – Sunday? I'll be at the peak of my cycle.'

Cole put his hand on her knee. 'I know. I plan to be really cruel to my Mouse.'

'Thank you, Cole.'


Lana arrived on Sunday morning wearing her lightweight retro A-line coat over nothing, as Cole'd instructed. He took her folder from her and helped her out of her coat. 'Five-thousand words?'

'Fifty-two hundred and ten.'

'Good girl. Now my Mouse shall have a treat. What's your safeword?'

'Mayday.'

'Good. And you won't hesitate to use it? Lana, I'm going to do something very different to you so I must be sure that if it's too much, you'll use your word.'

She shivered. 'You're scaring me, Cole.'

'Good scare?'

Lana nodded, biting her lip.

He took her into his bedroom. There was a pair of tailor's shears and a double-sized pack of cling-film on the bed. Lana's eyes widened and then misted. Her face went blank. If Cole's understanding of her mental processes was right, she'd started to work out what his plans were but had switched off before full understanding dawned.

240

'Stand straight and still.' Cole fitted a black velvet sleep mask over her eyes.

He knelt at her feet, steadying her with his shoulder, and started wrapping her. The thin clear plastic went around her ankles and lower calves four times before he started working his way up, wrapping her knees, lower thighs, then trapping her hands against her upper thighs. She swayed. Cole braced her as he went round her hips and up to her waist. He lifted her bodily to perch on the edge of the bed, legs extended straight out. Returning to his task, he sealed her lovely breasts under three layers of transparency and moved up to cover her shoulders and neck.

'Do you want to use your word?'

Her head shook slightly.

Cole lifted his brave submissive and laid her tenderly on his bed. She really was quite remarkable. Lana was totally immobilised and unable to see. Almost anyone would find the experience terrifying and be begging for release. All the comfort Lana had was her absolute trust that Cole would never allow harm to come to her.

The depth of her submission was almost scary. When a woman offers her man her unquestioning obedience and mindless adoration, her power is overwhelming. A part of him almost wished that she would show some slight disrespect or make some demand – somehow weaken the bonds her surrender had forged. Until and unless she did, he would keep, guide and cherish his Mouse. The words 'honour bound' were hackneyed, but described his feelings perfectly, damn it!

Cole sat beside Lana and picked up her manuscripts. With his ears alert for any change in her breathing and with glances at her every couple of minutes, Cole read.

Forty minutes later his timer chimed. There are submissives who claim to have endured 24 or even 48 hours of 'mummification'. Cole wasn't going to test his Mouse to those extremes.

241

From what he'd read about sensory deprivation, the first sensations someone experiences after a long period of 'no sensation' are intensified tenfold. The cold sadist in him found that interesting.

He lifted Lana and draped her face down over the edge of the bed, legs extended to the floor. Taking infinite care, he snipped through the cling-film from between the tops of her thighs to the fullest part of her bottom. The tight wrap parted, exposing an oval of Lana, the pout of her vulva and the crease between her buttocks. Her skin glistened with sweat. His actions until then were gentle and slow so as not to bring her mind back to reality. Still using a tender touch, he eased her lips apart and set the head of his cock between them.

He thrust.

She was so hot and wet that for the first couple of inches it felt like he was pushing his cock into thick soup but beyond that her passage was so tightly constricted he had to force his erection into her.

Lana jerked and said, 'Oh.' After a second's pause, she was writhing back at him like a snake convulsing to shed its skin. A stream of 'ohs' flowed from her lips, as if each of his thrusts was a fresh and delightful surprise.

Lana clenched. She yelped. Still fucking, Cole began to tear the wrap from her body. Her skin was slick with sweat. By the time her back was bared, he was slithering on her. He reared back, dragging her up with him till she was half-kneeling on the edge of the bed, shreds of plastic flapping around her, and Cole was pounding into her while standing. Lana's arms came free. She ripped the cling-film from her own head and upper body. With each slap of their bodies, perspiration splattered.

Lana gyrated, slithering in Cole's arms, but when he put a hand down to tear at the wrap that still restricted her thighs she begged, 'Please, not yet.'

She spasmed through another climax, twisting and arching and unbalancing Cole so that they sprawled on the bed, still locked together by his cock inside her. Rolling, they reached the other side and toppled off just as Cole's orgasm gushed from him. They landed, him beneath her, with a mighty thump. Both burst out laughing.

In the shower, Lana asked, 'Were my stories any good, Cole?'

'They made *me* horny. Lana, *Rattan*'s office is in Steeltown. That's where you're going tomorrow morning, to deliver your work.'

# Thirty

Lana bounced with excitement, much to Cole's amusement. Her 'baby' outfit was ideal for bouncing in. The top was a ribbon with a four-inch frill in fine white pleated net. It ran beneath her arms and was tied in a bow between her bobbling breasts. The bottom matched, tied six inches below her cute navel, but had a thong in the same material attached. She had another ribbon around her neck, with an oversized baby's comforter attached.

She stretched both arms out towards Cole, offering him an envelope in her right hand and a flat parcel in her left. 'Please, please, please, Cole,' she begged.

He took the envelope. 'It's addressed to you, Lana, from *Rattan*. Why haven't you opened it?'

'Please, Cole? I don't dare. It's sure to be a rejection.'

'It's pretty thick for a rejection, baby-Mouse.' He ripped the envelope open.

'What's it say, Cole? Please?'

'It's exactly what I expected, Lana. Congratulations. It's from the editor of *Rattan*, Alice Blue. She wants to buy your stories and would like more from you. She's sent you two passes to the Toronto Sex-Hibition next month and hopes to see you at *Rattan*'s stand.'

He gave her a big hug and nuzzled her ear. 'I'm so proud of my Mouse. I knew you'd make it. First this, then more short stories, then novels. Your writing career is launched, my sweet baby. You're going to be famous.'

Lana pulled back and held the parcel out.

'What's this?' he asked.

'A prezzie. Please, Cole. I know I'm not supposed to buy you things but I guessed what might be in the letter so I got this to celebrate. It wasn't expensive, I promise.'

Cole pursed his lips. 'Well, considering it's from the first professional writer I've ever known, thank you.' He tore the paper off and opened the box. 'Thank you, Mouse. A nice big hairbrush with a flat smooth back! I can think of *all sorts* of uses for this.'

Lana turned her back and flounced her bottom at him.

'Oh no,' he teased. 'I might spank a big girl with this but it'd be far too painful for a little baby, like you.'

Lana pouted and swayed her hips. 'Not even if I was *very* naughty?'

'How naughty?'

'This naughty?' She pushed a hand down the front of her panties and rubbed herself.

'You'd have to be naughtier than that to deserve a spanking with this hairbrush.'

Lana cocked her head in thought. 'How about . . .?' She took the comforter from her neck, pushed her panties down to her knees, spread her thighs, and worked the egg-sized sucker inside herself. Masturbating with it, she purred, 'Am I naughty enough yet, Cole?'

'What a wicked little girl!' Cole scolded, grinning. He took her by her hair and led her to his big chair, where he trapped her across his knee. 'I'm going to teach you a severe lesson, miss!'

Lana wriggled her naked bottom at him. 'I was very, very bad, wasn't I, Cole. If I take my punishment like a brave girl, may I suck your lollipop after?'

\* \* \*

245

Cole let Lana wear her coat over her costume from the parking garage and into the exhibition hall. He knew she was nervous about being seen in public in the Leg Avenue 'Sexy Schoolgirl' outfit he'd picked for her. They'd be doing a lot of walking, so he excused her the high heels she'd usually wear when dressed up and allowed her flat loafers. Her socks were plain opaque white, reaching to just above her knees. That left a dramatic length of naked thigh showing beneath a micro-kilt that rose to just two inches above the swell of her mound. Her semi-translucent white shirt tied just below her breasts, leaving her slender midriff bare.

Cole was bursting with pride as he took her coat and exposed his Mouse to the public gaze. He felt like shouting, 'This gorgeous creature is *mine!*'

Lana wrapped both of her arms around one of his and buried her face in his shoulder.

'You're safe, little one,' he assured her. 'Cole will take care of you.'

'People will look at me,' she whispered.

'Yes, they will, and they'll want you but they can't have you – not unless they're cute and you want them too. I'd never give you to anyone you didn't want, Mouse. You know that.'

'I'll try to be brave.'

'Good girl. Look! There are girls here who are showing more skin than you are.' He nodded towards a statuesque pair in glittering thongs, with pasties on the nipples of their naked breasts and nodding plumes on their heads. They were handing out free samples of D-Lay crème.

'They're pretty,' Lana said, huskily.

'Yes, they are. They're pretty but you are beautiful.'

'Thank you, Cole.' She giggled.

'*Now* I'm intimidated!' Cole exclaimed. A tail-coated and top-hatted 'wicked squire' strode by on stilts, twirling his moustache with one hand while cracking a short whip in the other. His middle leg dangled five feet below his crotch. He was chasing a cowering 'maiden', who wore ragged white muslin that looked as if the whip had slashed it to ribbons.

'Fun, huh?' Cole asked. 'Who said that kinksters have no sense of humour?'

They browsed the displays, picking up free samples and brochures and making the odd purchase. A handsome couple, him in bulging trunks and her with silicon breasts that threatened to burst out of her bikini, tried to sell them a swingers cruise.

Lana shivered as they inspected the offerings of Dungeon Furnishings. Cole made her kneel on the spanking stool and pose against a St Andrew's Cross but he didn't make her try the padded stocks in case it put her too far into a disassociative state.

There were three stage shows scheduled – the Chippendales male strippers, a lingerie fashion show and a demonstration of belly dancing – but those wouldn't start till later. Cole bought Lana an ice cream, two side-by-side spheres of strawberry, each topped by a maraschino cherry. She made a display of licking and sucking the cherries and then sank her perfect little teeth into them, so he knew she wasn't too intimidated to enjoy herself.

Admission was restricted to eighteen and older but apart from there being no youngsters there, the crowd was a wide cross section of the general public. There were people, both male and female, that had to be in their seventies or even eighties. Some wore jeans and a lot were in business suits but there were enough in 'dress-up' that Lana wasn't out of place. Cole exchanged grins with a youngish fellow in a purple 'zoot suit' who looked like a character out of *Lil' Abner* or *Dick Tracy*. Two girls in leather hobble skirts, holding hands, toured the exhibits at geisha-step pace. When they saw Lana, they playfully leered and licked their lips, sending her into happy confusion.

Cole had to explain the display of 'Furries' to Lana. She'd never heard of 'Plush Fetish' and was surprised by the stuffed pandas with cocks and fuzzy bunnies with pussies. 'I don't think I want to try that, please, Cole?' she asked.

'Don't worry. You're the only Mouse I'll ever want.'

*Rattan*'s booth was fronted by a display of past-issue covers blown up to eight feet tall. Most of the models shown were in vinyl or latex domme costumes, though there was one with a 'naughty nurse' and two of bondage: one an Oriental sylph in classic Japanese rope bondage and the other a naked girl posing as Andromeda, chained to a rock.

Lana squealed and clapped her hands. 'Look, Cole! Look!' The blown-up cover of the latest issue promised a short story, 'Looking Up', by Lana's pen name. 'It's me!' she crowed before she realised she was drawing attention.

'I'm so proud of you, Lana,' Cole told her.

The inside of *Rattan*'s booth was decorated like an art gallery with black walls and spotlights on framed artwork from the magazine. There was a girl in a torn slip manacled to a whipping post. The effect was spoiled, somewhat, by the smacking sounds of the gum she was chewing.

Alice Blue, editor and publisher, was sealed in azure Lycra that dimpled at her navel and divided the lips of her sex. Her wrists, ankles and throat were circled by spiked leather bands. Her cobalt hair had been pulled to the crown of her head, where it formed a spray six inches high. Alice's eyes had been painted in three shades of blue into sequin-lined commas that tilted up to her hairline and covered a third of her face. At first glance, Cole thought she was taller than him, but when he mentally subtracted her four-inch platforms and eight-inch heels, he realised she was of middling height, at the most. She was posed by a lectern, selling subscriptions to her magazine. Her restrictive costume would have made it impossible for her to bend over a desk.

He held his hand out. 'Alice, I'm Cole. This is Lana, who you've been buying stories from.'

'Are you a writer, Cole?'

'No.'

Alice cocked her head as if to ask what his relationship to Lana was. After she'd held that pose for a while she turned to Lana. 'I like your work, my dear. Can I rely on two stories a month from you?'

Lana looked a question at Cole. He told her, 'You may answer Alice's questions, Lana.'

Looking at her feet and swaying her tiny skirt, Lana whispered, 'If Cole says I'll write two a month for you, I will.'

Turning to Cole, Alice asked, 'Is she for real?'

'Is she really the sweetest and most obedient submissive you'll ever meet? Yes, she is, and I'm proud to own her.'

Lana snuggled closer to him, glowing with pride at the nice things he was saying about her.

'And you're a real dom?' Alice continued.

'I am what I am, like Popeye.'

'You two *have* to meet Lady Lust.' Alice pointed to the far end of the booth, where a lovely Eurasian was arranging copies of her latest book on a desk. 'She'll get such a kick out of you.'

Lady Lust's hair was liquid midnight, cascading to her waist. She was dressed in a Victorian silk corset in lavender and black candy-stripes, worn with a short skirt of multi-layered pleated black lace, fishnet stockings and short flared boots with four-inch heels. Cole had seen her picture at the top of her advice column in *Rattan* and had assumed it was touched up. He hadn't thought that a woman with such bountiful breasts and flaring hips could have so tiny a waist, even if it were cinched by her corset. In the flesh, not only was she incredibly shapely but her hips swayed in an arc that was wider than they were. She was billed as a dominatrix, offering advice to submissive men and transvestites. It was possible that she was a 'switch' but Cole was sure she wasn't entirely dominant.

As he led Lana towards Lady Lust, he fancied he could taste the exotic woman's sexuality perfuming the air around her.

'Are we too late to buy a copy of your book?' he asked.

Lady Lust turned, looked him up and down, then studied Lana. 'Oh my! Isn't she delicious! Of course I'll sign a book for you, Mr . . .?'

'Cole, but make it "to Lana". She's a fan of yours and also a fellow contributor to *Rattan*.'

'She wrote the new short stories? They're *very* good. I thought, reading them, that the author was a genuine sub. I see that I was right.'

As Lady Lust opened a book to sign, Cole touched the quirt that lay on her desk. It was about thirty tapered inches of plaited rattan. 'That's an interesting toy. May I inspect it?'

'Be my guest.'

Cole picked it up and ran it through his fingers. 'It must make some interesting marks,' he observed.

Lady Lust looked up. 'What? Oh, I imagine it would.'

'You haven't used it?'

'It's just for show. My dear sweet "puppies" cringe at the sight of it.'

Cole had read about her male submissives, her 'puppies', in her column. 'What a shame, to waste such a toy,' he said.

'It's a bit too vicious for real use.'

'You think so?' He handed the quirt to Lana. 'What do you think, Mouse? Too cruel?'

She stroked it lovingly, then held it to her cheek.

'Imagine it, Mouse, on your bare bottom – hard on the backs of your naked thighs.'

Lana's eyes closed. She swayed, lost in reverie.

'You think your little schoolgirl could endure a beating from that?' Lady Lust asked, taunting but eager.

' "Endure"? My Lana doesn't "endure" pain. She immerses herself in it. She surrenders to it. It flows through her, dissolving her ego, rinsing her will away. She becomes nothing but pure sensation. Lana enters a state where she has no responsibility, no thought, no concept of right or wrong. All she knows, then, is that she pleases me. For her, that is ecstasy.'

Lady Lust swallowed, hard. 'That'd be something to see.'

Cole fixed her with his gaze. 'Would you like to?'

'Like to? You mean . . .?'

'I'm offering you the chance to watch as I grant Lana the pain she craves. Further, I'm offering you the chance to participate.'

'Participate? You mean you want me to beat her?'

Cole took the quirt back from Lana and made it whistle through the air. 'Lady Lust,' he said. 'I know what you are and I know what you *really* want. If you are ready to admit your true nature, I will help you.'

'My true . . .?'

'Your secret fantasies. You want to surrender. You need to feel a strong man's foot on your neck. Can you admit that?'

Her hands fluttered. 'I . . . I don't know. I'm not sure what I want.'

'I'm sure. I'm offering to let you watch my Mouse's transformation when I take this quirt to her bare bottom. If you have the courage, I'll show you your own true nature.'

'What? When? I mean . . .'

'You've finished here. How about now?'

'Now?'

'I'm not asking you, Lady Lust. I'm telling you. Come with us, right now, and I will help you accept yourself.'

'And if I don't?'

Cole took Lana's arm and led her away, ignoring Lady Lust. They were almost to the booth's exit when she caught up with them. She hadn't forgotten her quirt.

# Thirty-one

There was no point in denying it, Cole's feelings towards Lana were different from any he'd had towards any other woman he'd been involved in a threesome with. He was pretty sure he'd have no problem with jealousy. If Belinda – as he'd learnt Lady Lust's true name was – gave his Mouse a climax, well, so did a vibrator. His concern was for how Lana might feel, sharing him with the luscious Eurasian. Part of her would enjoy the humiliation. Another part, however, might feel threatened. He didn't want her to feel insecure. He resolved to forge a rapport between the two women before his cock got involved, and he thought he knew exactly how to do that.

Belinda asked, 'Can I get you something to drink?'

Cole tossed his jacket onto *Rattan*'s hospitality suite's credenza. 'No thanks, and you're not to have one, either.' He knocked a pair of cushions to the floor and kicked them into place for the women to kneel on. Discomfort can distract from pain.

'Why can't I drink?' Belinda asked.

'When people have been lovers for some time, a drink before, during or after sex is fine. Not the first time, though. The first fuck should be stone-cold sober. That way, no one can fool themselves, "If it wasn't for the booze, I wouldn't have begged him to come on my tits," or, "I must have been drunk to let him bugger me."

253

There'll be no excuses for what we three do. What we do, we'll do because we want to.'

'But Cole,' Belinda protested, with a sly grin, 'aren't we girls supposed to be helpless slaves to your dominant masculine will?'

'Sure you are. You're slaves who are free to walk away at any time. I have power over you – the power to make you do *what you want to do*. You know as well as I do, Belinda, a dominant's power is given to him by his submissives, of their own free will.'

'I'm confused.'

'No, you're not. You're delaying because you're nervous.' He took Belinda's bare shoulders and turned her to face Lana. His hand steered hers to the loose bow that secured Lana's shirt below and between her breasts. Together, their fingers tugged, slowly unravelling it, until the two sides fell apart, leaving his Mouse's breasts bare.

'Lovely, aren't they,' he whispered into Belinda's ear. She nodded, wordless.

'Now her skirt.' Once more he guided her hand. Lana's zipper hissed. Her skirt fell to her ankles. 'Panties next.'

Belinda's thumbs hooked into the band of Lana's white cotton bikini. At Cole's urging, she crouched, easing the brief garment down Lana's legs, to her ankles. Cole held Belinda by her luxuriant hair, her face inches from the gentle curve of his Mouse's tummy.

'Lick,' he said. 'She loves to have her belly licked.'

Belinda's tongue laved Lana's skin from just below her navel to where the swell of her pubes began.

'Good girl,' Cole told her. 'Now it's your turn.' He raised her up and turned her to face him. 'Lana, unlace our guest.'

Belinda bit her lip as Lana loosened her corset. She was a lovely woman and doubtless knew it but being bared in front of two people who were virtually strangers had to make her nervous. Eventually, the corset slithered down her body, taking her lacy skirt with it. Her high-cut, wide-legged black satin French knickers were fastened by a loop and a button. In his teens, before thongs, they'd been his favourite. French knickers offered exploring fingers zero resistance. The flimsy garment slithered to the floor.

Cole feasted his eyes. Her tightly laced corset had narrowed her waist by about three inches but, even without that restraint, the exotic beauty was remarkably voluptuous. The cruel stays had left vertical creases in her soft skin, marks that called to Cole's fingers to massage them away. Her fishnet stockings were opera length, coming to just an inch below her plump pubes. The slit between those pouting lips was divided by the thickest and longest clitoris Cole had ever seen. Belinda's mound had been shaved, except for a tiny trim arrowhead. Her navel was deep, smooth and soft. Her breasts were cappuccino mounds, tipped by conical espresso nipples.

'Very nice,' he told her.

She looked down and muttered her thanks.

'Lana,' he said, 'on your knees, "ready".' Her instant obedience filled him with pride. She dropped and assumed the position, kneeling erect, ankles crossed behind her, fingers laced at the back of her neck, breasts high. 'Now you,' he told Belinda, 'knee to knee.'

With some hesitation, Belinda obeyed. Cole adjusted their positions until their knees touched; their thighs were pressed against each other, as were their mounds and bellies. From their waists up, they parted a little, leaning back at a slight angle, so that only the tips of their breasts were in contact.

'Belinda,' Cole said, 'I want you to watch Lana's eyes. I want you to see what pain does to her and tell me what you see. Do you understand?'

She nodded.

'When it's your turn,' he continued, 'if you can't stand it, just say "stop", and I will.

'You're going to beat her with my quirt, and then me,' she said, not as a question but confirming, as if to be clear in her own mind.

'Yes.'

Cole took careful aim. The rattan quirt was broader than a cane or a crop and not as whippy, but stiffer than a leather strap. Three plaited strips came together in a lacquered knot the size of a pea. If the quirt 'wrapped around' Lana's hip, the whiplash effect would multiply the force of the impact. His best tactic would be to aim the knot at a spot on her lovely bottom but try to land the body of the quirt simultaneously. However the knot struck, it'd be agonising, but, with skill and care, he should be able to keep it from doing real damage. Belinda was right. In the hands of an amateur, her quirt would be too vicious.

He took his first swing.

Lana jerked against Belinda.

'Her eyes?' Cole asked.

Belinda said, 'She winced. There's pain in her eyes.'

'Keep watching.'

He lowered his aim an inch for the next blow, then another for the third.

'Pain,' Belinda reported. 'No – just a minute – there's something else . . .'

The rattan cracked across Lana's tender flesh for the fourth time.

'She's losing focus. Her eyes are misting over. There's something though . . . If she weren't in pain, I'd call it glee.'

Cole resumed the beating, slow and steady as a metronome. The women, his Lana, the lovely Belinda, writhed together, belly on belly, pubes on pubes. He counted, '. . . nineteen, twenty.' His Mouse's skin was mottled and glowing from the tops of her thighs almost to her tailbone. There was a line of small dark dots that ran vertically up the contour of her right buttock. The distinctive plaited pattern was embossed into every inch of her bottom's sumptuous contours.

Belinda, eyes fierce on Lana's, was humping at her.

'. . . twenty-three . . . and twenty-four.'

He fell to his knees beside the bravest, most delightful, most *important* woman in the world. 'I'm proud of you, Lana. You have incredible courage. There never has been nor ever will be a woman to match you.'

Quickly, before she could come down from her endorphin high, Cole reached between her thighs from behind, stabbed his thumb up into her oozing heat, bracketed her engorged clit between two fingers and masturbated her into three rapid gushing climaxes.

'Cole,' Belinda asked, 'give me what you gave her, please?'

'It isn't mine to give,' he explained. 'The ecstasy comes from within her. All I can do is release it.'

She pouted.

'I think it's in you, Belinda. If you surrender, absolutely, you'll get a taste of it. It won't be as intense, the first time, but it'll get better with practice. Are you ready for pain?'

'Please.'

He took Lana's left hand from behind her neck and wrapped her arm around Belinda's shoulders. He put her right hand between their bodies on Belinda's sex. 'Finger her, Mouse. You two may kiss.'

As lips parted and tongues met, Cole swished the quirt across Belinda's bottom. The first blow was only half as intense as the ones he'd used on Lana but when the lovely Eurasian didn't flinch but just moaned into Lana's mouth, he let his hand come down harder. At ten, Belinda was groaning and writhing. He'd only planned on a dozen for her, but she was taking it so well he determined to go to eighteen unless she begged for mercy.

At twelve, Belinda strained out, 'Oh! Fucking hell, you vicious bastard, you soft lovely girl, you two ...' Her 'two' continued into a strangled screech.

'Frig her,' Cole told Lana. He delivered the last six blows hard and fast on a tightly clenched bottom that was juddering as Belinda's frantic hips pounded against Lana's body.

He tossed the quirt aside. Belinda toppled sideways, leaving Lana kneeling alone.

'You did well, Mouse,' he told her.

'Thanks.' Her eyes focused. 'Bugger her, please, Cole? Her bum's on fire from her beating. She needs it. She needs the humiliation of being *used*!'

'You wicked little bitch!' Cole exclaimed. 'Very well, I will, and you may tell her so.' He started stripping off. Cole realised that Lana had sensed his concern about how she'd feel when he fucked Belinda. The sweet slut was telling him it was OK. She really was quite incredible.

Giggling, Lana scurried across the floor and bent her mouth to Belinda's ear. 'He's going to fuck your ass now. Your poor tight little bum is going to be stretched by his big hard cock, and I'm going to watch.' Almost as an afterthought, she added, 'Do you like to be buggered, Belinda?'

Dazed eyes turned towards Lana. 'I've never ...' Belinda started.

Lana clapped her hands and squealed in glee. 'An anal virgin! Did you hear that, Cole? She's never been fucked up her ass before.'

'Then you'd better prepare her,' he said.

Exaggerating the movements of her hips – showing off her fresh marks – Lana knee-walked to the table where Cole had dropped the bags with his purchases from the exhibition. Belinda, sprawled on her side on the floor, watched Lana's mobile rump. Despite having just been flogged and frigged to orgasm, the fingers of her left hand caressed the bas-relief Cole had left on her bottom and her right palm cupped her own pubes.

Lana returned with a vial of lube and set about arranging Belinda's limbs for Cole's pleasure. 'On all fours, please Belinda. Knees a bit wider apart – that's better – hollow back – no – don't lean forwards. Your bum has to be pushed back and at the right height.' Lana looked back at Cole for approval. He nodded. She told Belinda, 'Just go with his thrusts but not too limp, OK? Now, I'll lube you up well, Belinda, as it's your first time.' She paused before adding, slyly, 'I can take it dry, when he wants, of course, or with just a bit of spit.' She went to pour lube onto her fingers but Cole stopped her.

'Spit first, Mouse. Use your tongue.'

'Sorry, Cole,' she apologised. Pressing Belinda's buttocks apart with her palms, Lana worked her face deep between those voluptuous cheeks.

Belinda's head lifted. 'Oh! Oh my! That's your tongue, isn't it, Lana, not your finger. It feels – oh – oh – I like that, dear girl. Mm – I never thought – a tongue – so deep!'

'Now the lube,' Cole ordered.

As Lana squirted lube and worked it into Belinda's anus with a probing fingertip, Cole took his position, kneeling behind. Lana's head turned. When she saw Cole's cock wagging so close, she parted her lips for it and mumbled her way down his shaft, making spit as she went. When she slurped off, she gave the head of his cock a squirt of lube and steered it to nestle against Belinda's sphincter.

'Anything else, Cole?' she asked.

'Get under her, Mouse. Sixty-nine.'

'Perfect.' She lay on her back and wriggled under Belinda.

Looking down past his shaft, Cole saw his woman's gleeful eyes gazing up at him. He took hold of Belinda's hips. 'Ready?'

Belinda nodded. Slowly, inexorably, he pulled the tight sheath of Belinda's rectum over the rigid rod of his cock. She gasped. She grunted. Her body went rigid. Her head sagged between her supporting arms.

Cole paused to give her time to adjust, as much emotionally as physically. A woman's first experience of anal sex, he imagined, had to be a major event for her. If she didn't embrace the humiliation and degradation, Cole thought the impalement could be traumatic. Perhaps . . .

Belinda ground back at him, rotating her hips.

Perhaps he'd been projecting a masculine viewpoint onto a woman who was *very* feminine, for whom 'impalement' had no negative connotations.

He pulled back slowly, savouring the dragging sensation. Lana wrapped her arms around Belinda's waist and lifted her mouth to the woman's sex. Deliberately making the obscene noises that she knew Cole enjoyed, she slobbered and lapped, burrowing her face into Belinda's soft wetness, then slithered her tongue over the underside of his retreating shaft.

Thighs stiff with erotic tension, Cole slow-buggered their new playmate as she and Lana devoured each other. Lana grinned up at him, her face glistening with Belinda's juices. He was delighted to see her so happy. The dominant/submissive dynamic can be a little solemn during sex, even though they'd shared laughter in the warm aftermath. The introduction of a bright and beautiful 'third' had changed the balance of power, subtly. Lana was no less subservient but having a sister in submission seemed to make it more fun for her.

Belinda lifted her head from between Lana's thighs. 'Cole? May I ask for something?'

'Yes.'

'I'd really like it if you came in my bum? Please? I want to find out what it feels like.'

Cole glanced down at Lana. He'd had it in mind to reserve his climaxes for her, as token of her special place. She looked straight up into his eyes and nodded, as if she understood his concern without his expressing it. Sometimes, he thought she knew his mind better than he did himself.

He let his thrusts accelerate, pushing and pulling at Belinda, swivelling his hips to increase the friction on his cockhead, and let himself pound out lust until the boiling feeling came and he released.

It wasn't until Belinda was slumped on top of Lana, with his jism trickling from between the rounded cheeks of her bottom, that he realised he hadn't bellowed as he climaxed. Before Lana'd entered his life, he'd always come quietly. It had only been with her that he'd become so vocal. Maybe . . .?

He had to stop being so introspective. He had two lovely women to attend to.

When he got back from the bathroom he found they'd moved into one of the suite's two bedrooms. They were standing with their backs towards the mirror doors of a closet, comparing bruised bottoms. The quirt had been brought in and left on the bed, which meant one of them wanted more. He could guess who. Lana wasn't competitive but she did take pride in how much pain she could endure. Belinda had taken eighteen stripes to her twenty-four and Lana wasn't to know that they'd been delivered with less force.

'What pretty bottoms,' he told them.

Both wiggled their bums and beamed at him.

Belinda said, 'You two – your relationship – remarkable.'

'It's based on mutual trust,' Cole told her.

Her eyebrow rose. 'Mutual? I can see how Lana has to trust you, but –'

Cole interrupted. 'I'll show you.' He lifted Lana and deposited her gently on her back on the bed. 'Grip your

261

ankles, Mouse.' Her legs bent up so she could reach. Her knees fell apart. 'This is going to be very painful, little one, and quite scary. I'm going to gag you so you won't be able to use your safeword. Do you accept that?'

Lana frowned. Cole never gagged her. He never prevented her from using her word. She blinked, looked straight at him with *trusting* eyes, and said, 'You will do as you decide, Cole. I know you won't do me any harm.'

'Good girl.' He knelt astride her head. 'Open wide.' His left testicle descended into her open mouth, leaving his right one lolling on her cheek. 'You may grip me, gently, with your teeth.' To Belinda, he said, 'You see? If she clenches her teeth, I lose a ball.' He grinned. 'How's *that* for trust?'

'But why would she?'

'Pass me the quirt and I'll show you.'

'You're not going to . . .?'

'Yes, I am.' He hefted the quirt and took careful aim. If the bead at its tip was to strike the delicate flesh between his pet's thighs, not only would it be agonising but it could very well do real harm. The secret would be to strike the bed beneath her with the tiny knot so that the only impact on her pussy would be from the breadth of plaited rattan. That, descending harshly on her soft puffy lips and the tender polyp of her clitoris, would be devastatingly painful but if he pulled his strike at the last moment, would heal swiftly.

Cole leant forwards, quirt high and extended.

Belinda gasped, 'Don't!'

The quirt came down. Lana convulsed. Her gasp was hot on Cole's scrotum. He raised the quirt again. A slithery tongue laved his testicle – Lana's signal that she was OK. The second blow made her grunt and lift her head. Again, Cole waited. After a long moment, the tip of her tongue moved over his sac.

'Last one,' he announced, and swung. He felt her teeth, shivering with tension, indent his loose skin but she controlled her reflexive bite although she couldn't suppress a long strangled moan.

'I'm *so* proud of you, Lana,' he said. 'Belinda, she'll be incredibly sensitive now. Make spit on her poor clit and use the tip of your tongue on it, just the tip, very gently. It'll be exquisite agony for my little Mouse.'

Two hours later, the women were lying to either side of Cole, their cheeks on his shoulders. Their hands toyed with his limp cock. He fondled Lana's breast with the fingers of his right hand and Belinda's with his left.

Belinda grinned at Lana across the broad expanse of Cole's chest. 'I don't know about you, but I'm not going to be able to move tomorrow. I think I'll need a day in bed – alone.'

Lana smiled back. 'He indulges me. All I'll have to do for him for a day or two is look pretty.'

'You don't have a nine-to-five?'

Cole's Mouse chuckled. 'I have a job, 24/7 – as my Master's sex slave.'

'Lucky you! How about your writing? Do you have any work in progress?'

'A novel, almost done.'

'About?'

Lana's forehead wrinkled. 'I suppose it's a "coming-of-age" novel, based on me. It's about me coming to terms with my true nature as a submissive masochist.'

'Sounds fascinating. May I read it?'

Lana asked, 'Cole?'

'Of course Belinda may read it. She might find it instructive.'

'I'm not coming out of the closet,' Belinda protested.

'Of course not, if you don't want to. Maybe, though, once in a while, my Mouse and I will join you in your closet for a private D/s party, one "D" two "S"s.'

Belinda sighed. 'I'd like that. Cole?'

'Yes?'

'You twitched. You don't think . . .?'

'I doubt it but it's worth a try.' He knotted one hand in Lana's pelt, the other in Belinda's mane and urged both their heads down the bed.

# Thirty-two

Three months later, Cole picked Lana up from her apartment. Inspired by Belinda, she'd become enamoured of tight-lacing. Cole had encouraged the fetish. When her waist was cinched four inches slimmer than was natural, her hips blossomed and her breasts became riper. The unnaturalness of her corset-enhanced figure inspired Cole to treat her as his perfect little sex doll — to be posed, admired, manipulated and possessed.

She was dressed as he'd instructed. Her hobble dress was stretchy black net, high at her throat, with long sleeves and ankle length. It restricted her thighs and tapered to only eighteen inches around the hem. Her waist was confined by a steel-boned black leather waspie. Lana handed him the key to the padlocks of her ankle straps. He picked her up and carried her to his Lexus.

'I know how you feel about surprises, Mouse,' he told her. 'I'm warning you now, there is one waiting at my place. It'll be a nice surprise. No one's going to jump out at you or shout. I'll be with you, protecting you. Can you be brave, for me?'

'I'll try,' she promised. 'You'll remind me?'

'Of course.' He'd warned her but sometimes, with Lana, a warning was soon forgotten. Once the process of disassociation started, a treat that they'd discussed in detail, that he'd prepared her for over and over, would astonish her. She often gave him the same joy that a happy child gives a doting parent at Christmas.

At his door, he turned her to look into his eyes. 'A surprise, remember?'

Her forehead creased then cleared. 'A nice one. You'll hold me?'

'Of course.' With his supporting arm around her, he helped her totter into his living room. His guests were seated well back from the entrance, as he'd instructed.

Belinda, her corset crimson and black velvet, her skirt a red tutu, asked, 'Champagne time?'

Cole nodded. She went to the table to pour Dom Perignon into flutes.

Cole had only met the other two briefly, that same day. Rupert Claxton-Smith was Belinda's, and now Lana's, agent. He was a tubby little man with combed-over hair and wire-rimmed glasses, looking somewhat odd, shirtless, in black leather pants and a dog collar. Citron was a fetish model whose image appeared in *Rattan* often. Her orange Afro was streaked with metallic lemon. She had a vulpine face with enormous sad eyes and a tiny pointed chin. Tall and very thin, her hips were wrapped by a six-inch band of yellow latex, with a three-inch strip around her flat narrow chest.

Cole told Lana, say 'hello' to Citron.

'Hello.'

'I'm your biggest fan,' the girl gushed. 'I've read all your short stories. You are *so* clever.'

Belinda rescued Lana from the outpouring by handing both women brimming flutes. She turned to Rupert and commanded, 'Fetch!'

He scurried to his briefcase and returned grinning, bobbing up and down, looking like he'd have wagged his tail if he'd had one, with a folded document.

Cole told Lana, 'It's for you.'

'What? Please, Cole, could you read it for me?'

'Reading can come later,' he said, 'just look at the cheque for now.'

She took the piece of coloured paper, looked at it, looked again, then a third time, before turning to Cole with her face blank. 'I . . . I don't understand.'

'It's a contract, for your novel. The cheque is an advance on your royalties.'

'But . . .?' She looked at the cheque again. 'It's . . . Cole, this is enough money that I could live on it for maybe three years. It's mine?' She shivered. 'Cole, tell me what it means, please?'

He became solemn. 'It means that your hard work and talent are being recognised. It means that you are now independent. You can support yourself. You don't need my financial help any more.'

She moved into his arms. 'Cole, I'm frightened.'

'Freedom can be scary, I know,' he said. 'I'll keep you safe, Mouse, for as long as you want me to.'

'As long as . . .?'

He held her shoulders and looked into her eyes. 'You have to decide, Lana. You don't need to be guided or controlled any more. You can stand on your own two feet, if you want to. You'll always be special, to me, my Mouse, but if you wanted to be free, no longer my slave, now you can be.'

Lana, tears streaming, pushed past his arms and snuggled to his chest. 'Cole, please, Cole, being your slave *is* my freedom. Don't release me, I beg you.' She lifted her head and blinked. 'If you want to be rid of me, I'll go, of course, but if you will allow me to stay, all I will ever want, for the rest of my life, is to belong to you. Let me worship you, Cole, please?'

He hugged her with his heart bursting. 'In that case, my Mouse . . .' He signalled to Belinda to pass the package from the table. 'Kneel, Lana.'

She fell to her knees before him. Cole unwrapped a collar – the same one she'd craved at Niagara but now

267

gold-plated and silk-lined – and locked it about his true slave's throat.

Cole tilted her head up to look at him. 'Lana,' he confessed, 'my own precious Mouse, I love you. If you would like a matching gold band for your left hand, it would be my privilege to take you as my wife.'

She blinked away her tears, smiled, and touched her collar. 'Master,' she told him, 'I have this. Nothing else counts.'

## nexus

### The leading publisher of fetish and adult fiction

## TELL US WHAT YOU THINK!

Readers' ideas and opinions matter to us. Take a few minutes to fill in the questionnaire below and you'll be entered into a prize draw to win a year's worth of Nexus books (36 titles)

Terms and conditions apply – see end of questionnaire.

**1. Sex:** Are you male ☐ female ☐ a couple ☐?

**2. Age:** Under 21 ☐ 21–30 ☐ 31–40 ☐ 41–50 ☐ 51–60 ☐ over 60 ☐

**3. Where do you buy your Nexus books from?**

☐ A chain book shop. If so, which one(s)?

_____

☐ An independent book shop. If so, which one(s)?

_____

☐ A used book shop/charity shop
☐ Online book store. If so, which one(s)?

_____

**4. How did you find out about Nexus books?**

☐ Browsing in a book shop
☐ A review in a magazine
☐ Online
☐ Recommendation
☐ Other _____

**5. In terms of settings, which do you prefer? (Tick as many as you like)**

☐ Down to earth and as realistic as possible
☐ Historical settings. If so, which period do you prefer?

_____

☐ Fantasy settings – barbarian worlds

- ☐ Completely escapist/surreal fantasy
- ☐ Institutional or secret academy
- ☐ Futuristic/sci fi
- ☐ Escapist but still believable
- ☐ Any settings you dislike?

_____

- ☐ Where would you like to see an adult novel set?

_____

## 6. In terms of storylines, would you prefer:

- ☐ Simple stories that concentrate on adult interests?
- ☐ More plot and character-driven stories with less explicit adult activity?
- ☐ We value your ideas, so give us your opinion of this book:

_____

_____

_____

## 7. In terms of your adult interests, what do you like to read about? (Tick as many as you like)

- ☐ Traditional corporal punishment (CP)
- ☐ Modern corporal punishment
- ☐ Spanking
- ☐ Restraint/bondage
- ☐ Rope bondage
- ☐ Latex/rubber
- ☐ Leather
- ☐ Female domination and male submission
- ☐ Female domination and female submission
- ☐ Male domination and female submission
- ☐ Willing captivity
- ☐ Uniforms
- ☐ Lingerie/underwear/hosiery/footwear (boots and high heels)
- ☐ Sex rituals
- ☐ Vanilla sex
- ☐ Swinging

☐ Cross-dressing/TV
☐ Enforced feminisation
☐ Others – tell us what you don't see enough of in adult fiction:

_____

_____

_____

8. Would you prefer books with a more specialised approach to your interests, i.e. a novel specifically about uniforms? If so, which subject(s) would you like to read a Nexus novel about?

_____

_____

_____

9. Would you like to read true stories in Nexus books? For instance, the true story of a submissive woman, or a male slave? Tell us which true revelations you would most like to read about:

_____

_____

_____

10. What do you like best about Nexus books?

_____

_____

11. What do you like least about Nexus books?

_____

_____

12. Which are your favourite titles?

_____

_____

13. Who are your favourite authors?

_____

_____

## 14. Which covers do you prefer? Those featuring:
(tick as many as you like)

☐ Fetish outfits
☐ More nudity
☐ Two models
☐ Unusual models or settings
☐ Classic erotic photography
☐ More contemporary images and poses
☐ A blank/non-erotic cover
☐ What would your ideal cover look like?

_____

## 15. Describe your ideal Nexus novel in the space provided:

_____

_____

_____

## 16. Which celebrity would feature in one of your Nexus-style fantasies? We'll post the best suggestions on our website – anonymously!

_____

## THANKS FOR YOUR TIME

Now simply write the title of this book in the space below and cut out the questionnaire pages. Post to: Nexus, Marketing Dept., Thames Wharf Studios, Rainville Rd, London W6 9HA

Book title: _____

**NEXUS NEW BOOKS**

*To be published in June 2006*

### UNEARTHLY DESIRES
Ray Gordon

When Alison comes into money, she uses the small fortune to buy a country home. A house unlike any other she has ever experienced. From the discovery of a sinister playroom in the basement, to the strange men who call upon the house and request unusual and bizarre services, Alison begins to wonder about the previous owner. And herself, when she is compelled to oblige the visitors' demands.

Both the mystery, and Alison's alarm, ratchets-up another notch when she realises her country retreat was once a house of ill-repute, run by an elderly madam. And as she and her friend, Sally, sink further and further into committing depraved sexual acts with their guests, she becomes certain that the previous owner is still in control . . .

£6.99   ISBN 0 352 34036 3

### EXPOSE
Laura Bowen

Lisa is a successful book illustrator with a secret that could ruin her reputation. The two sides of her life – the professional and the erotic – have always been strictly separated. Divided until mysterious events begin to act powerfully on her imagination. And when her secret is discovered, she is drawn inexorably into circumstances ruled by her own unrestrained desire in which her fantasies, however extreme, become real.

£6.99   ISBN 0 352 34035 5

## THE DOMINO TATTOO
### Cyrian Amberlake

Into this world comes Josephine Morrow, a young woman beset with a strange restlessness. At Estwych she finds a cruelty and a gentleness she has never known.

A cruelty that will test her body to its limits and a gentleness that will set her heart free. An experience that will change her utterly. An experience granted only to those with the domino tattoo . . .

£6.99   ISBN 0 352 34037 1

If you would like more information about Nexus titles, please visit our website at www.nexus-books.co.uk, or send a large stamped addressed envelope to:
  Nexus, Thames Wharf Studios,
  Rainville Road, London W6 9HA